Forced To Flee

Hazel E. Gott

Forced To Flee

Hazel Goss

Published by Final Chapter Publishing

Fiction Statement
This novel is a work of fiction. Some of the events described really happened but the characters are the product of the author's imagination and do not represent actual persons, living or dead. Any resemblance is purely coincidental.

A CIP catalogue record for this book is available from the British Library.

ISBN 978-0-9955576-0-4

Book layout and cover design by Clare Brayshaw

Cover images   © AC Manley, © Leo Lintang, © Chelovek
                  Dreamstime.com

Prepared and printed by:

York Publishing Services Ltd
64 Hallfield Road
Layerthorpe
York YO31 7ZQ

Tel: 01904 431213

Website: www.yps-publishing.co.uk

To my sister Lesley, my daughter Amanda and friend
Sue for reading my manuscript, and to my husband
John for his patience and support.

Chapter 1

The bombs landed so close the whole building shook. Debris rained down upon us huddled in the basement. The single light bulb swung with each explosion making moving shadows of the old stored furniture and the cold boiler.

'We're all going to die,' cried the old lady. Her husband held her close as if his frail body could shield her. ' Shh, we're safe here; the roof is solid concrete.'

I hoped he was right. I was curled into a tight ball, hugging my knees, head bent, rigid with fear, willing the noise to stop. The last bomb must have exploded right above us. We all screamed as the basement shuddered and the light went out.

I woke up sweating, heart pumping and realised I was safe. As I uncurled myself and stretched out, my limbs felt stiff. My mouth was dry so I crept out of bed and went downstairs for a glass of water. It was too early and too cold to stay up so I went back to the warmth of my bed and tried to think of a place where I had been happy. Closing my eyes, my body relaxing, I thought of the last summer holiday we had with Granddad and Grandma.

I heard Vjolica and Grandma singing as they kneaded bread, on the big oak table in the kitchen. Then I joined them, pretending to want to help but really hoping for

Ëmbëlsië me Kumbulla. I pulled out a stool and sat looking at the stove, the stockpot bubbling and kettle getting ready to sing. Above my head hung herbs, drying for the winter and behind me a dresser with crockery, and a shelf laden with home made jam, bottled fruit and spicy pickles. Eventually my patience was rewarded. Grandma covered the dough, left it to rise and said.

'Go tell Granddad his tea's getting cold Davud.'

I went out knowing she hadn't even made it but Granddad never come in for a drink or a meal until he was ready. Eventually we all sat around the table, now wiped clean of flour. Grandma gave everyone tea, goats' milk for me, and we sank our teeth into the luscious sweet plum cake with the yeasty smell lingering in the air, along with pungent odour of the goats below.

Where we lived, in the town of Pristina nobody made bread or goat's cheese. We bought our food from shops and outdoor markets.

"You're all too skinny and it's that poor food you buy in the town."

It was not true, what Grandma said. We were not all skinny. Mum was round, like her, soft and cuddly. Grandma's hair was streaked with grey and usually tied at the back of her head. Mum's hair hung free and was black but sometimes I heard her asking Vjolica to pull out the grey ones that were appearing.

Every summer we stayed with our grandparents in the country. Their big family home was a Kulla, a cube shaped building, three storeys high with thick, stone walls. Vjolica, my older sister, slept in a room at the top. My tiny room was on the first floor along with the living room, cool and comfortable and the kitchen, hot and steamy. Half of the ground floor was covered in straw for the goats. There was a wooden fence to stop them going into the rest. That was for the log pile and Granddad's workbench with all his tools. There were only small windows but in the summer the doors stood open and the sunshine streamed in making the straw dust visible, dancing in the air.

Granddad used to wear a leather apron when he sharpened knives or tools. He let me turn the big grinding wheel and I had to shut my eyes because sparks came out.

'You have to hold it still Davud; just at the right angle and then it'll slice through anything. See?'

He seemed big to me but when he stood next to Dad he was shorter, but much wider with a wobbly belly that hung over his trouser belt. I loved working with him. He showed me how to use a saw and never minded if, when I tried to hammer in a nail, I hit it all wonky and it bent over. He'd just straighten it up, saying, 'Try again, you'll get the hang of it.'

I liked to help weed the vegetable patch so he made me a special, small fork so I could really help. When I stood up after filling a basket with weeds I would put one hand on my back and groan. My back was fine but that was what Granddad did.

Those summer days were hot and dry. I never remember it raining. One glorious day followed another and if we were not needed to help we could play, running through the meadow thick with wild flowers, climbing trees, or making dens. If an adult came with us, we could paddle or swim in the river. I remember the shock of the cold water and the oozy mud under my feet. It was lovely; we never wanted to go home. But we had to.

In Pristina we lived on the third floor of a ten-storey apartment. We rented it and Mum said we were luckier than most having such a modern, comfortable home. It was close to the hospital where she and Dad worked and not far from my school. There were three bedrooms so Vjolica and I had our own rooms. Our bedrooms were big enough to have a desk where we did our homework. We had no garden but there was a children's playground not far away with swings, a roundabout, a slide and a climbing frame. Beside the playground was a large grassy space where I played football with my friends. If you stood in this space you could just see the Golijak Mountains poking up beyond the concrete apartments. Grandma and Granddad lived between Pristina and those mountains.

Mum was a midwife, at the University Hospital and sometimes had to work at night.

'Babies never time their arrival to suit the midwives,' she'd say.

Dad worked there too but he was a consultant surgeon so he only worked at night in an emergency. He wore a suit to go to work and looked smart, tall and slim, with dark hair that sometimes flopped over his brown eyes. In those days I was proud but also a little scared of my dad.

Our life was good when I was seven years old but changes began to happen at school.

We spoke Albanian but there were lots of children who spoke Serbian so once in school you quickly picked up each other's languages. We also learned English and all the normal subjects like maths, history and geography. I liked going to school until we were told we could no longer have lessons with Serbian children. They would be taught in the mornings and we had to go in the afternoons. It was no longer fun; I never saw my Serbian friends. They also stopped us using the gym so we had to use the playground for all physical exercise lessons. It seemed unfair and I didn't understand why everything had to change.

Vjolica 6th May 1992

Hello Diary. I'm so glad I was given you for my tenth birthday yesterday. Now I have someone that I can talk to, privately, confidentially, totally mine! I was allowed to have Fitore Bardici over for tea. (She's my best friend and we go to school together). Grandma came all the way on the bus and managed to carry gorgeous veal and bean pie, (byrek me mish), my favourite. She also bought a cheese and some bread. It was lovely and Fitore declared it the best she'd had for ages.

I'm looking forward to tonight because the Dhomi family are coming for dinner. I've been helping Mum cook and we'll finish the meal with Grandma's creamy cheese.

I really love little Rita, especially now she can talk and I get out all my old dolls, toys and books for her to play with. Anyway I must stop scribbling and lay the table. They'll be here any minute.

Vjolica and I had been looking forward to seeing Mr and Mrs Dhomi, Alek and Rita. Mr Dhomi worked with Dad, specialising in orthopaedics and Mrs Dhomi stayed at home. Our families had been good friends ever since I could remember. Mr Dhomi had twinkly brown eyes and always made us laugh.

On this occasion the dinner was lovely and they said it was delicious but there was something wrong. Mr Dhomi had not regaled us with silly stories and he and Dad were unusually serious. Then Dad gave a little cough. He was going to speak. I suddenly felt scared. What was he going to say?

'We have something very important to discuss,' he said.

Grandma, Mum, Mrs Dhomi and Vjolica all stood thinking he meant the men wanted to talk alone. I didn't know if I should move or not. Then Dad raised his hand signalling them all to sit down again.

' No, don't go ladies. This will affect us all. Please sit and listen. We've been given a hard choice at the hospital. We've been asked to sign a declaration of loyalty to Serbia. If we refuse to sign then we have to leave our jobs. It's a very big decision to make. If we leave the hospital, we may not get another position anywhere else.'

There was a brief silence and then Alek asked what we were all thinking, 'Why have they done this? Why won't you get another job in another hospital?'

His dad answered him. 'Serbia wants to rule over many parts of Yugoslavia. They want to rule Bosnia, Croatia as well as Kosovo. There are quite a lot of Serbs living here, as you know, but also a lot of Albanian Muslims like us. They want to have more Serbs and fewer Albanians so they are going to make it harder for Albanians to get work, hoping they will leave.'

'Is that why we're being treated differently at school?' asked Vjolica.

Mr Dhomi nodded, 'Yes. Things are being made difficult for all of us. I am going to refuse to sign. I believe Kosovo should be independent of Serbia, not ruled by it. I'm not sure I'll be able to get another job so we might have to move away or even emigrate.'

'Why Dad?' asked Alek. 'Why not sign it and let's all stay here?'

'I've already said what I believe Alek but it 'll be hard to be here, having signed, because we could be ostracised by all Albanians; seen as traitors. Do you want that?'

'No, but I don't want to move away. What about you Mr Kahshoven? Are you going to sign?'

I watched Dad's face as he struggled to reply holding my breath. 'Yes, Alek, I will be needed in the operating theatre even more, I suspect, because of the worsening situation. Ajshe will do the same so our family can stay together.' He looked at Mr Dhomi. 'I will understand if you no longer want to acknowledge us, after tonight, Fadil. It seems impossible that our long, happy family friendship may be broken. It makes me very sad to have to say this.'

At the time I only understood the Dhomi family were moving away. What did ostracise mean? I said nothing but Vjolica started to cry and asked if she could leave the table.

A few weeks later the Dhomi family moved away. They didn't come to say goodbye but wrote to us. Dad read it out.

Dear Donjeta, Ajshe, Vjolica and Davud.

We are leaving Kosovo. I am not sure where we will finally settle but I am thinking of heading for England. I can speak the language a little and doctors are welcome everywhere, except here. When I have a place to stay I will write or ring you with the address and if you should ever decide to leave yourselves you are welcome to join us. Our friendship will remain true, no matter that you signed and I did not. I know you did it for humanitarian reasons. I respect that and hope others of our race do not treat you with contempt.

You are all in our prayers,

Your good friend,

Fadil Dhomi

Vjolica, writing in her diary

Grandma is still with us and it's lovely to have her here but we have noticed when we go shopping that many small businesses like the bakers and the butchers have closed. Albanians ran them so the Serb people wouldn't go in. Many Albanian people have found it too hard, like the Dhomi family, and have gone away. We had another letter from them a few days ago. Mr Dhomi sent it to the hospital because he had heard that not all Albanians were receiving their post. They were in Macedonia staying with a distant relative. He said they were safe and well but there was little room for them. They will have to try to get a boat to England. Macedonia is flooded with Kosovar refugees. Some are in camps especially built and some have nowhere because the camps are full. (I can't imagine having nowhere to stay) He said he would write again. I hope he does. I miss their visits and playing with Rita.

Grandma will be going home soon. I asked why Granddad hadn't come with her and then I wished I hadn't. She said he had stayed to look after the goats and the house because the country isn't so safe anymore. The police had visited some people in the village. She looked grim, saying all the police are now Serbian and scary. Although she tried to hide it, I could see she was worried, not her usual smiley self. I think Mum was worried too because she asked Davud and me to go with Grandma to the bus stop to give her another hug before she got on the bus.

We were happy to do this but Grandma walked slower than normal and then we all had to rush to say goodbye because the bus arrived at the same time as us. We waved and waved until it was out of sight. I felt sad. When would we see her again? It's ages before the long summer holiday.

Chapter 2

Dad had a phone call this morning and then went out of the living room and made another, then another. We all looked at each other, wondering. When he came back he ignored us going straight up to Mum putting his arm around her.

'I'm sorry Ajshe. Your mum phoned with some really bad news. When she got home from the village today she found your Dad, unconscious in the yard. He'd been badly injured in a fight. She was crying begging us to come immediately.'

Mum's face went white. She almost fell onto a chair and tears slipped down her cheeks. I've never seen either of my parents cry before and felt my own eyes pricking.

Dad turned to Vjolica. 'Would you find the medium suitcase and pack some clothes for Mum? I'll add mine later.'

Vjolica went out to Mum's bedroom. I sat still, not sure what to do.

'Davud. I think Mum and I could do with some tea.'

I went into the kitchen, put the kettle on to boil and busied myself getting out cups. Then I heard Mum asking if he had any more details.

'I only know that the fight was with some policemen who came to the house and told your Dad he had to get out. They'd done this to others saying they didn't want 'Albanian trash' in the villages.' Mum gasped.

Dad went on. 'He must have refused, probably said he needed to stay to look after the goats. They shot them all.'

'Oh...no. He really loved them; no wonder he fought back. Where is he now?' Mum's chair scraped as she stood up.

'He's at home. When they heard what had happened friends came and helped get him into bed.'

I came in carrying the tea very carefully. Mum's face looked even more upset at the sight of me. Her eyes opened wide. 'What about the children? We can't leave them.'

Just as she said that Vjolica came in. 'I've packed Mum enough clothes for four days. Will that be enough?'

Dad nodded. 'I'll add mine, then we can go.'

'Don't worry about us Mum,' Vjolica said, 'I rang Mr Bardici and told him our problem. He said Davud and I were to stay with them. He was very kind. Davud go and get your night things and your cuddly rabbit. As soon as we go Mum and Dad can too.'

Vjolica is only three years older than me but at that moment she seemed grown up, someone to lean on. I ran into my room, found my rabbit, pyjamas and toothbrush and put them into my rucksack. When I got back Dad was all packed, Vjolica had her rucksack and we were ready. Outside the door Dad gave Vjolica the key.

'We'll keep in touch, I have Mr Bardici's number.'

We hugged quickly and then they were gone.

I looked at Vjolica. Her shoulders had slumped and tears were brimming over, running down her cheeks. My arms went around her, we didn't move until she felt better, her wailing reduced to sniffing and she pulled away to blow her nose.

'We should go to Fitore's house now,' I said. 'They'll look after us until Mum and Dad come home.'

She nodded and led the way out of the apartment block and along the street to another. It was not as smart as ours and when we arrived I realised they were not rich people. There were three bedrooms, but all the rooms were smaller than ours, the furniture shabby and sparse. Fitore was their only child so I was given the guest bedroom for myself and a mattress for Vjolica had been placed next to Fitore's bed. Once our things were in our rooms we went into the living room where places were laid at the table.

'Please, sit here because the meal is ready. We will talk after we've eaten for everything seems better if you're full.'

Mrs Bardici was smiling and I found I could smile back as we thanked her and took our places. It was a vegetable stew and the bread was not very fresh but there was enough. Vjolica spoke when everyone had finished. 'That was a tasty meal, thank you, and you were right, things don't seem so bleak when you're full. It was all so sudden.......... a terrible shock.'

They looked at her sympathetically but did not interrupt as she went on. 'Tomorrow there's no school so, with your permission, I'd like to go to my house to collect some clothes for us and to empty the fridge. There is milk and a lovely cheese that will go off if we don't eat it.'

'We can't have food going to waste when it's so hard to get. You have my permission, of course. I have to work tomorrow in the hardware shop but the rest of the family can accompany you and help to carry everything,' Mr Bardici said.

Mrs Bardici and the girls cleared the table and stayed in the kitchen to wash the dishes. I was going to help too but Mr Bardici asked me to sit with him and tell him what had happened to Granddad. When I'd finished he was sympathetic, 'I'm so sorry Davud but he couldn't be in better hands with your mum to nurse him and your dad to see to his injuries.'

'Dad said he would ring you to tell us all what's happening. I'm hoping he'll ring tonight.'

When the girls came back in Vjolica had red eyes and I could see she'd been crying again. I stood up to go to her but she signalled me not to. 'I'm fine Davud. I just got upset when I was telling Mrs Bardici and Fitore about Granddad.'

Just at that moment the telephone rang.

Vjolica 3rd June 1992

I have to stay brave and strong for Davud but it's really hard. Dad phoned on our first evening at Fitore's to say that Granddad was very ill, slipping in and out of consciousness. He was having difficulty breathing and Dad thought a broken rib had punctured his lung. He said he was trying to arrange to get him to the hospital, where he works, for an x-ray. If he can arrange this he will be home to see us tomorrow evening but Mum will stay with Grandma. I'm worried but I can't tell Davud. If policemen attacked Granddad what might they do to two women? I've heard terrible stories but I can't write them. Somehow if I voice these awful thoughts I think they'll come true. Must sleep now but I'm scared to shut my eyes and let bad dreams in.

Davud

Dad came home yesterday and said Granddad was more comfortable in a hospital bed, being given oxygen. He took Vjolica and me to the ward and we saw him for a few minutes. He opened his one good eye, saw us and gave a lopsided smile but didn't speak. His face was purple with bruises; one eye closed up with dried blood caked on it and his lips swollen. It hardly looked like him.

Although we were upset at seeing how poorly he was, it did feel good to be able to sleep in our own beds that night, although we knew we would have to return to Fitore's house when Dad went back to fetch Mum and Grandma.

Vjolica June 10th 1992

Dear diary, my friend, I can scarcely write for tears. Granddad died early this morning and we are all so sad. It's too hard. We loved him so much. Grandma seems to have shrunk with grief, unable to eat, just rocking, rocking. It's a nightmare.

People that know us came to support us this afternoon and evening. I had the task of offering them refreshment. It kept me busy and I will do it again tomorrow when we have the funeral. Granddad's body will be brought here in the morning and then in the afternoon we will take him to the cemetery.

Davud

We all stood, silent, as Granddad's body was lowered into the ground. It was covered in a white shroud and Grandma wore a white scarf on her head. Mum had her arm around her as they stood, heads bowed. Prayers were said and Dad recited a passage from the Quran, 'From the earth have We created you, and into it We shall cause you to return and from it shall We bring you forth once more.'

Then we stood without speaking for a while but it was not silent. I could hear traffic going along the road, birds cheeping from the bushes and trees, and then Grandma sobbed. It was hard to believe that Granddad would not be at the Kulla, tending his goats any more. Our holidays there would never happen again. Grandma would now live with us. It was too many changes for me and tears ran down my cheeks too.

For several days after the funeral, Mr and Mrs Bardici and a few other friends, brought food to enable us to be free from worrying about shopping or cooking. We missed having Mr and Mrs Dhomi with us and couldn't even tell them what had happened because we had no address to send a letter. It was likely they were travelling to England and I hoped they were well.

Vjolica and I had to go back to school soon after which helped us to forget for a while. Mum and Dad returned to work. Everyone began to cope with a life without Granddad except Grandma. She had no appetite and no energy. Instead of bustling around she sat listless in an armchair. When Mum came home from work there was no meal ready, no shopping done. It was as if Grandma was not with us. She actually made more work because Mum had to remind her to bathe and wash her clothes. I always look to my parents to know what to do but even they seemed helpless as Grandma grieved.

I was nearly eight years old so it was difficult for me to understand how people we knew, had said hello to in the street, had become our 'enemies'. If we found ourselves in the presence of Serbs, whilst shopping we dared not speak Albanian for fear of ejection or worse. It had happened to Mum when she took Grandma to get some groceries. Grandma saw some bread flour and she asked Mum to buy it. Suddenly the shopkeeper and other shoppers were hissing at them and they were told to get out of the shop. When they hesitated they were shoved roughly towards the door. After that they were very careful and had to shop further away. Grandma was upset and confused, apologising several times for her thoughtlessness.

I asked Dad why all these bad things were happening.

He tried to explain. 'Serbia is ambitious,' he said. 'They want all Albanians to leave so they can make their own republic bigger and more powerful. It's not only in Kosovo this is happening. They are fighting right now to stop Bosnia-Herzegovina becoming independent. Terrible things have been happening there. Sarajevo is under siege, surrounded by the Serbian army and in the villages they are doing the same as here, making non-Serbs leave their homes. Many people have been beaten, like your Granddad. Houses and even whole villages have been burnt to the ground. All these people have become refugees and are asking for shelter in Albania, Croatia and Macedonia. It is a cruel and frightening situation, Davud.'

'But we're all right because you signed the form, aren't we? A war like that with guns and bombs couldn't happen here, could it?'

'Well, I hope not and the United Nations Peace Force have come to help in Sarajevo so that's good. Other countries are watching what's happening and now they're trying to help stop the war. I can't tell you, Davud, that all will be well in Kosovo, but we can pray and hope.'

I prayed and hoped but everything in Bosnia got worse. This persuaded Dad to have a family meeting. 'Yugoslavia is becoming unstable and what's happening in Bosnia could happen here. We need to prepare for an emergency.'

My tummy did a somersault when he said that.

'What about your brother in Albania? Would he give us a home for a while?' asked Mum.

'The last time I spoke to him he said he was sheltering refugees and he had no room for any more. Those refugees may have moved on now so it would be worth contacting him. If he couldn't house us we would have to keep travelling and try to find shelter each night. It could be very rough, perhaps even spending nights in the open We'd need money and I'm not sure our currency would be welcome everywhere.'

Vjolica, who had been listening thoughtfully, now sat up straight. 'I know what you should do Dad, take the money out of the bank and buy gold bars or coins. Gold is valuable everywhere.'

'Now that is a good idea, Vjolica, I had been thinking of dollar traveller's cheques or a European currency like Deutsche Marks but perhaps we should do both. I'm going to ask for my wages and yours Ajshe, to be paid to us in cash. They are not being helpful in the bank, ignoring me and serving Serbs first. If they refuse to let me have my savings out then at least we will be able to save some of our wages. What do you think?'

Dad was really good at including us all in serious matters. Many men would just take decisions and their family had no choice. Mum said she thought it was a good idea. She also said we might like to think about what we felt was most important to take with us if we had to escape, perhaps even put those precious things into a bag, ready. This seemed as if we were going to be running away very soon and a sense of panic welled up inside me. 'Is this going to happen, like tomorrow or next week? I'm scared Dad.'

'Davud,' said Dad. 'This kind of discussion is necessary in case such a need arises but it is not likely. We must have a plan but also hope we'll never have to use it.'

The next day we received a letter from Mr Dhomi. It had taken a month to get to us and after our discussion it made us realise how serious having no home could be.

A temporary address (I hope)
Clacton
England

Dear Donjeta, Ajshe, Vjolica and Davud,

It has been a long time since we last met and we have missed all of you. Old friends are like gold and we have not made many new ones since we arrived here. That is not to say the people are unfriendly, far from it. They are cheerful and courteous but we find the culture is very different. Not every town has a mosque. Does that shock you? It did surprise us but then this is a predominantly Christian country.

It has been a long arduous journey to get here and I hardly know where to begin to tell you all that has happened.

We began by driving South towards Macedonia but we were forced to leave the car twenty miles from the border, because Serb police stopped us and confiscated it! We could not argue and took what we could carry. The car had made us feel safe but now we were vulnerable and kept close to each other.

Night fell before we reached the border but there was nowhere to shelter. By this time there were hundreds of us crowding the road. Children were crying with exhaustion, hunger and thirst but there was no help anywhere. We just lay in a field and it was so cold we got little sleep. Before dawn there was a commotion and it was the Serb police shouting to everyone to move on. They were brutal, beating anyone who moved too slowly, even the elderly. It took us two days to walk to the border and then there was a long wait whilst everyone's papers were checked; questions were asked. We thought once we entered Macedonia we would travel on or find somewhere to stay but we were not given any options. We were herded into a refugee camp with all of us in one tent. Quite a shock after the beautiful apartment we had, like yours in Pristina!

Our intention was to stay there for a few days, and then ask if we could move on to stay with our relatives. This never happened, not because the authorities refused but because the Red Cross, who ran the medical facility, were desperate for help. I waded in and the need was so great I could not leave. A refugee camp provides food, shelter and there was even a school set up by volunteer teachers but it was not a home. The weather was fine but winter in a tent in Macedonia would be dreadful. I worried about my family.

I explained to the Red Cross that I wanted to make a new life in England and they understood and helped us. Supplies arrived in a variety of ways and some came by sea to Durres in Albania. They had a vehicle going there and we were offered a lift on it. It was a big covered lorry but we were not the only family being helped. In fact it was crowded. The distance was about 250 km and if you drove in a car it could be done in a few hours but it took all night and then there was the usual long wait at the border.

At the port we asked for boats going to England but it was not to be that easy. Durres is a big port but the regular ferries go to Bari in Italy.

We found some lodgings, with a kind old lady, who charged very little. She said her son was a sailor and there were some boats that took refugees. It was cheap, illegal and could be dangerous. I had heard stories of overcrowded boats capsizing or people falling overboard and drowning. I couldn't subject my family to such danger. So we waited and I booked a passage on a ship that went to Italy, deciding to take one step at a time.

I will tell you the rest of the saga when I have a permanent address. I wish you could write back to me so that I know you are all well. Meanwhile I'll pray for your safety,

Your good friend,

Fadil

Vjolica

I don't want to leave here. It's getting harder all the time but this is our home. The Hospital refused to pay Dad and Mum in cash. They said their system was set up for wages to be paid into bank accounts. The only people paid in cash, weekly, were cleaners. If they wanted to be cleaners that was fine by them!

How could they be so nasty to someone so highly qualified as Dad who'd always commanded such respect?

Chapter 3

The Dhomi Family, 1992, in Clacton

Fadil Dhomi ushered his wife and family into the small terraced house. It was shabbily furnished but little Rita ran from room to room shouting, 'Is all this ours?'

She failed to see the peeling paint everywhere, the graffiti on the walls or the filthy cooker. Alek found her in the box room upstairs a delighted smile on her face. 'Can this be my bedroom Alek?'

'I would think so. I can have the one next door and there's a bigger one that Mum and Dad can share. Let's go down now. We should help with the unpacking.'

He followed her down watching her delicate fingers grasping the grimy bannister. He was not surprised to find Mum and Dad in sombre mood in the kitchen; Mum's voice strained with tension. 'Where's that notepad? I must make a shopping list.'

'I've got it here. What do you want?' asked Dad.

'Floor cloth, smaller cloths, scouring powder, floor cleaning liquid and a mop. I can't use this kitchen until it's scoured from top to bottom. How could anyone move out of a house and leave it in this state?'

Fadil put his arms around her but she irritably shrugged away from him. He held up his hands. 'Slow down, Marigana; I know in Pristina we lived in a lovely, spacious apartment but since then we have slept in a field, stayed in just one room and once it was a tent. Stop and give thanks for three bedrooms, a kitchen, a living room, and a bathroom. Don't forget this is temporary. We are lucky to have been given this house and money from the government. In just six months I'll have a work permit. After that I can get a job and we can move somewhere better.'

'You're right, Fadil. I was so disappointed. Somehow I thought England would be smarter than this. I feel so lost. I don't even know where there's a shop to buy these things and I can't ask because I can't speak the language.'

'I can Mum and I saw a shop on the corner when we arrived. It's a very short walk. I'll buy the things on the list.'

'Thank you, Alek. Would you take Rita with you and give us a chance to unpack the clothes?'

Fadil handed him his wallet. 'Don't come back with this empty. It needs to last us a month!'

'I'll be sensible Dad. Come on Rita.'

She skipped happily beside him as they walked by gardens strewn with litter, broken chairs, and plastic crates. Mum was right. England's streets were not paved with gold. They were dirty rubbish dumps. He pushed open the door of the shop and a buzzer went. He was surprised to find it was tidy, clean and the shelves were laden with everything he could think of. He hesitated, suddenly anxious about his ability to speak English but Rita ran about excitedly pulling things off the shelves to fill his trolley.

'Rita! We can only buy what's on the list. Let's put these back and look for the things we need.'

He found the displays made some kind of sense, all cleaning materials and cloths together, milk and other dairy products in a cool cabinet, vegetables were beside fruit. At the check out he listened to what the lady said and found he could understand her. The amount was also displayed. Mum would be able to do this, he thought. The lady helped him pack everything into plastic bags and smiled. He thanked her and as he walked back he thought England was not all bad.

The immigration officials had arranged English lessons at the local Community Centre. The whole family went on the first day and were surprised to find twelve people there already from various countries but no others from Kosovo. The teacher wrote something on a large flip chart saying each word as he wrote, 'My name is Michael Blake.' Then he looked at Fadil, said it again and then pointed to him. Fadil responded by pointing to himself and saying,

'My name is Fadil Dhomi.' Then everyone had to go through the ritual of introducing themselves. After that Michael established how much English the group knew and, as usual, there were people, like Marigana and Rita who knew nothing and Alek who knew quite a lot. Michael then organised them into groups and introduced another teacher and the beginners went into another room.

That day Marigana and Rita learnt to count to ten and were shown pictures of fruit and vegetables and were told the names. They played at going shopping and asking the cost of something. It was very practical and fun. Rita could do it all, learning really quickly but Marigana struggled. Learning English was so important but anxiety took away her confidence. The first lesson lasted an hour and then the family met to walk home.

'Daddy I can count to ten, listen....'

Rita demonstrated and Fadil and Alek smiled at her enthusiasm.

'What about you, my love; was it as hard as you thought?'

Marigana's face twisted with a half smile and grimace. 'I'm much slower than Rita and will need to practice. Janet, our teacher, was very kind and we laughed a lot. I'll not be so worried next week and we have got some work to do at home.'

'We were given some homework too,' said Alek. 'I knew most of the words we were taught today but hearing them spoken by an English person made me realise my teacher in Kosovo didn't pronounce everything correctly.

'You did really well, Alek, and I felt proud of you. I, like Mum, will have to work hard to feel confident. But this was our first lesson and we've got five more so we must make the most of them.'

Rita and I will only have two more, Dad. Michael explained to me that we will have to start school. At the moment the schools are closed because it's now a holiday, called Easter, and the holiday is two weeks. I will have to go to Lonsdale Comprehensive School and Rita to Broad Street Primary. Rita's school is just a bit further than the corner shop but mine is the other side of town and I'll have to use a bus. The bus is free and Michael said next week he'd give me a street map and a bus timetable. It's quite scary.'

'Why is school scary?' asked Rita.

Marigana frowned and assured her that school was not scary and Alek was just worried about missing the bus. She cast Alek a meaningful look and Fadil changed the subject.

'We've all worked hard this morning and it's a lovely day so after lunch I think we should go to the beach.'

Rita cheered and school, for the moment, was forgotten.

In the weeks that followed, the English course covered other aspects of life in England such as the Health Service, financial benefits and how to claim them. They were given useful addresses and encouraged to talk about things that worried them. Fadil asked how he could find out if his medical qualifications were acceptable and was given the address and phone number of the BMA.

When the six weeks were over there would be nothing to do. He did ask about other courses but discovered not everything was free. If he wanted more lessons he would have to go to an evening class and pay. This was impossible. All their money was spent on food and bills.

Before this moment came, however, the children had their first days at school.

Rita had never been to school before so she had no idea what it meant. She had been with her family to the English lessons and thought it would be like that. She cried and clung to Marigana when she realised Mum had to leave. The teacher distracted her with a dolly, picked her up and took her to the home corner. Within seconds Rita wriggled out of the teacher's arms and began to play. Marigana slipped away with tears in her own eyes. How was her little one going to manage when she had so little English?

She need not have worried. At the end of the day Rita emerged with a big smile holding the hand of her new friend, Amanda.

Amanda's mother came up to them. 'Hello. I see our daughters have become friends. How lovely. My name's Diane.'

Suddenly Marigana remembered her English lessons and was able to reply. 'My name is Marigana. I speak little English.'

'Well children don't need to speak to understand each other. Just look at them.'

Marigana didn't understand what she said but was also watching the girls running along the painted lines on the playground. Both women smiled and then simultaneously called their children's names. They laughed and parted at the gate.

When they got home Fadil was delighted to see Marigana smiling and Rita bursting to tell him all about school.

In contrast, Alek had an unpleasant first day. He was shocked by the behaviour of the children on the bus, shouting and moving about, even though the driver threatened to stop the bus and make them walk. The girls' uniforms also disturbed him. Their skirts were very short, their blouses tight across their breasts. It embarrassed him to see such immodesty.

When they arrived at the school, there was much jostling, laughing and some boys kicked a ball about until a bell sounded. They then went into school, through various doors and Alek had no idea where to go. He saw there was a teacher at one door seeing the last children into school so he approached her. 'Excuse me. My name is Alek Dhomi and I am new. I don't know where to go.'

'Right son, come with me. I'll take you to the office.'

Alek followed and at the office he was asked his age and told his form number. The teacher had gone so one of the secretaries showed him where his form was. When he got there he had missed registration and the children were all leaving for a lesson. He was introduced to his form teacher who told him to catch up with the other children because he should be in a maths lesson now. It was utterly bewildering.

In Kosovo the children had almost all their lessons in the one room and the teachers moved around. In this school the teachers stayed in their rooms and the children moved. He was too late to catch up with the others and spent the next ten minutes trying to find his way back to the office. He was mortified to find himself close to tears.

At the office the same secretary looked at an enormous timetable spread across the wall and said his maths lesson was in Room 6B and she would take him. She also gave him a plan of the school with his form room circled. She was kind but when he arrived at the maths lesson it was quiet, the teacher was talking and all eyes swivelled towards him. He squirmed with embarrassment and quickly sat where the teacher indicated.

At first he struggled to understand what the teacher said and then realised his accent was different to the other people in Clacton. Later he was told the man was from Scotland. The lesson was about equations and Alek understood the example going up on the board as the teacher explained. Gradually he was able to tune into the accent and managed to answer all the set questions. The lesson ended when they were given their homework. The bell rang and the class moved on again.

At the end of the morning one of the boys took pity on him. 'Alek, my name is Martin. I was new after Christmas and found it really hard. We are on second sitting for lunch so we go outside for half an hour before we eat. Stick with me and I'll show you where to go.'

'Thank you, Martin. I've never been in a school so big. I think I will never find my way.'

'I felt the same on my first day. Have you got a timetable?'

'No. They gave me a plan of the school in the office.'

'Right, I'll give you mine. Copy it tonight and give it back to me tomorrow.'

'Thanks.'

Alek took the timetable, put it into his bag and then the bell rang for lunch. The dining hall was huge and very noisy. They queued with a tray and were served by ladies in white coats. Alek chose a tuna salad with some bread and butter. When Martin's plate was laden he paid for his but Alek showed a card saying his meals were free.

Martin's kindness made the rest of the day bearable but Alek returned home that night quiet and non-communicative.

In the weeks that followed things improved a little when he was offered the opportunity to play a musical instrument. In Kosovo he had played a guitar but it was over a year since he had touched one. The lessons cost too much but he managed to explain to the teacher that he was not a beginner but could afford neither the lessons, nor an instrument. The teacher handed him a guitar and said, 'Show me what you can do.'

Alek tested the tuning and then played some chords and followed that by picking out a melody.

'So you can play but can you read music?'

He produced a simple book and pointed to a tune. Alek smiled because it was easy. After that he was allowed to come to lessons, free, but he could not borrow a guitar to take home and practice.

As the months went by, Fadil and Marigana cleaned and painted the house, which was immensely satisfying and then, just when they were feeling more comfortable, an official letter arrived. A northern charity had found them permanent accommodation in Leeds and they were to move in August. This was unexpected and unwelcome. Clacton had become their home and Rita would be upset to leave her school and friends but Alek just shrugged.

'Doesn't this bother you, Alek?' asked Fadil.

'Not really. I'm not enjoying being at this school and because you've said it's only temporary I've made no effort to make any real friends.

'But I thought you were enjoying making music again,' said Mum.

'Yes, but that would've been better if I'd had my own instrument. Will you be allowed to apply for jobs in Leeds, wherever that is, Dad?'

'I can apply now, Alek and I've discovered, at the Citizen's Advice Bureau, that Leeds is a very large town in the North Of England, over two hundred miles from here. It's in the middle of the country, so no seaside. I think we should make the most of the coast whilst we have it to hand.'

Every weekend and during the beginning of the school summer holiday, the family went to the beach. It was lovely to see the two children racing around the sand, in and out of the waves, looking healthier than ever before. Fadil wriggled his toes out of the mound Rita had heaped on them and sighed.

'Surely you are not feeling sad, Fadil, this is lovely and the children so happy.'

'No, far from it. I was thinking that we were safe and although our future is uncertain England feels so much better than it did at first. I have written to the British Medical Association to see if my qualifications are acceptable. If they are, I will start applying for jobs. Moving is going to be another upheaval but if I can work it'll make everything better. One of the first things I'd like to do is buy Alek a guitar.'

Rita ran up to them saying she was hungry so they packed up their things and went home.

That evening, when the children were asleep, Fadil said he was going to write to Donjeta Kahshoven and family.

'What are you going to tell them?' asked Marigana.

'The more I hear on the news about Bosnia and Croatia the more I worry. If I tell them about the rest of our journey they could use the same route. The Serbs will be censoring everything, only telling them what they want them to hear. They could soon be in danger if they turn their attention to Kosovo.'

'What if they'd like to write back? We won't be here much longer.'

'That's true. Perhaps I should wait until we've moved.' He sighed. 'You know thinking about them and all that we left behind has made me feel nostalgic. I know we did the right thing to move away but I miss it so. Do you?'

'Yes, but when I look at our children, so healthy and safe I'm happy to be here. Don't have regrets dear. You did make the right decision. There's been no suggestion of war in Kosovo but I think it's only a matter of time.'

Chapter 4

Kosovo

We did not hear from the Dhomi family for over a year. We spoke about them less and assumed they were happy in their new life, had made friends and no longer thought of us. So we were surprised, and pleased, when a letter came.

15 Garden Court
Leeds
England
November 1992

Dear Donjeta, Ajshe, Vjolica and Davud,

I know it has been a long time since I last wrote but I waited until we had an address so you could reply. I promised to tell you about the rest of our journey so here it is.

In my last letter I said we had reached Durres and were trying to find a ferry to take us to Bari in Italy. People were quick to explain the cheaper alternatives but also the dangers so I got tickets on a regular ferry. Once again we arrived in a new country and had to endure immigration.

This time we were housed in a kind of compound but the buildings were solid, no tents! We also had better facilities and were given food and advice. The authorities interviewed us at length to see if we were genuine refugees or just opportunists looking to move to a more affluent country. Can you believe people do that?

It seems we passed the test. When I said we wished to move on and get to England they were delighted and helped us to get bus tickets to Rome. I hoped to fly from there to London. We had been very frugal on our journey and still had traveller cheques but I was not sure I had enough. My ability to speak Italian is limited to musical terms so I could say 'ritardando' but even if they slowed down I still failed to understand!

The immigration people had given us an address in Rome to report to when we arrived. We had to take a bus from the airport into the city and then ask for directions to the address. It was a long walk but a taxi was out of the question.

When we got there it was an office. I had expected it to be a hostel and was looking forward to a rest but it was many hours of processing before we had somewhere to sleep.

In the morning I left the family to find out about flights to England. A travel agent, who could speak English, was very helpful. Unfortunately the price was too high. We would have to spend all that we had with nothing left. I failed to see how we could enter England totally destitute. I had to explain all this, in English, to the travel agent and felt humiliated to be so poor. It was not a pleasant experience but it moved her to look for a solution.

It seems there are charter flights that are much cheaper than the regular, scheduled airlines but they were only available if a plane was not fully booked. She found one but we had to wait a week. I handed over the money. Marigana was happy to stay for a week, even if it was to be a frugal stay. She said it would be good for all of us to have a rest.

What a wonderful support she has been, the children too. Aleksander often carried Rita when she was tired and if I carried her he took my rucksack as well as his own. I felt blessed. I also felt desperate to reach England and have my family secure and happy.

It was frustrating to be in Rome, such an historic and famous city, without enough money to see all the sights. I really want to return, as a tourist, one day.

On the morning of our flight we arrived very early, anxious to find our way around the airport and cope with the language problem. Neither of the children had been on a plane before so they were very excited. We had to wait several hours but they did not tire of watching landings and take offs. I have to admit to a little tingle of anticipation myself. Our new life was about to begin.

I will stop writing now. Before I go I must tell you that the political situation in Kosovo is becoming worse, dangerous. I know everything you hear on the radio is biased propaganda so you may not be aware of this. Please be careful and if you need to leave the country you can follow our route.

If we can help in any way, we will,

Your very good friend,

Fadil Dhomi'

Dad was delighted to hear about their journey and that they were safe so he wrote back immediately. He was able to say we were all well but also to tell him about Granddad and how things were in our country. All our fears of having to leave soon and hiding foreign money in case of an emergency had not been realised, but the Serbian threat increased day by day. We heard many instances of the police forcing people to leave their homes so we were very careful to go into the streets as little as possible and to speak Serbian in public.

The years rolled around to my eleventh birthday but it was not the best I've ever had.

Vjolica

Monday 11th September 1996

Poor Davud. It was his birthday last Saturday and it could hardly be called a celebration. So much had gone wrong I couldn't even write, but now I must. The bank refused to let Dad draw out his money, just like that, no warning. They said they would honour any cheques he'd written for a fortnight and then that was it. All the rest of his savings now belonged to Serbia! That's stealing! Apparently the teller laughed as he said this and Dad, never ever a violent person said he felt so angry he wanted to punch his superior smile right off his face. He didn't.

This meant another family discussion. Dad said he thought he could withdraw some money. Mum asked how and he said there was a patient leaving hospital the next day who was very grateful to him for saving his leg. He'd been told in the emergency department that it would need to be amputated but Dad thought differently. The man was a Serb and offered to help Dad in any way he could, knowing how hard it has become for us Albanians.

Dad would write him a cheque. The man would pay it into his own account and then, a few days later, when the cheque had cleared, he would withdraw cash to give to Dad. This was done four times in the fortnight and then on the fifth occasion the bank was very apologetic and said the account had been closed. At least we had some money but there would be no more. How are we going to manage?

I asked Dad if he had ever thought about my idea of buying gold. He looked very smug and said he had, but that was not to be touched. It was not a huge amount and was to be used only in a dire emergency, like having to leave the country.

Now, dear diary, are you ready for this?

At the end of last week Mum and Dad were both given their notice to quit at work! The hospital had already refused to pay them in cash and now they had no jobs. No wonder there was a family discussion. What's going to happen to us?

Davud

It felt very odd having Mum and Dad around in the mornings. We were used to having Grandma and when we'd done our homework, ready for afternoon school, we would go to the park, help her clean or shop. Now the apartment felt crowded and the atmosphere was grim. Vjolica and I were glad to get away to school after lunch and we felt sorry for Grandma having to stay with them.

There was no need to have worried about her because she suddenly took charge. She had made friends in the market and discovered that there were medical clinics, run by the Red Cross, in poor Albanian areas of the city that desperately needed qualified doctors and nurses. There were plenty of willing volunteers but expertise was lacking. She took Mum and Dad to one clinic where the doctor in charge was delighted to see them. Dad was full of it when he arrived home.

'You should have seen how organised it was Davud. They had four consulting rooms, but only one doctor, two treatment rooms and these could be turned into operating theatres if necessary. They had one qualified nurse and several volunteer auxiliaries that helped with anything and everything. The medical store was also better equipped than I expected. I've made it sound really good haven't I?'

'Yes, I'm waiting for the 'but'.'

He laughed. 'The 'but' was the number of patients. They were standing in the waiting room, crowded together and then overflowed out into the street. There were children crying, some people white with pain, others losing blood from wounds. It was total chaos.'

'So you and Mum helped.'

'Yes,' said Mum. 'We did a triage first and some people got cross when a person behind them was singled out to see the doctor but we explained the most needy must be given priority. Once we had them organised Dad began to see the worst cases whilst I saw people that just needed a wound stitching or a dressing changed.'

'It's been a real experience, like working in A and E,' said Dad, 'I haven't done that since I was a student.'

'The people were so grateful', said Mum. 'They paid what they could for the treatment. Sometimes it was with goods rather than money.'

She picked up her bag and brought out a box of eggs. 'At the end of the day any food given was shared and we had these, so it will be a good meal this evening.'

She smiled and I realised we might have little money, the situation was still uncertain but everything felt better. In my heart I thanked Allah for Grandma's resourcefulness.

The next few months passed with the main issue being money. Mum, Dad and Grandma no longer had breakfast and lunch was a simple bowl of soup made with whatever could be found that was cheap. We all became used to eating less and knew we were still luckier than many others.

Chapter 5

Was this the final straw?

Vjolica

My entries into this diary are sporadic to say the least. I did want to record all my hopes and fears but I find there are few hopes at the moment and too many fears. So I seem to record only momentous happenings. And so, dear diary, are you ready for this one?

Everything has been going well, considering Mum and Dad both lost their jobs. We have very small meals now and I dream about food constantly. Just writing now, without even mentioning stews or sweets sets my mouth watering; pathetic I know. That, of course, is not the reason for this entry.

It seems, despite our efforts to economise, we can no longer afford to live in our apartment! Albanians are targets for unnecessary rent increases and that has happened to us. Where are we going to go? Is this the moment we become refugees? Will we now leave Kosovo? Should I be packing? The last question can be answered with a definite yes, the rest, I don't know.

Grandma, a stalwart when M and D were sacked, has no answers this time. She says she will ask at the market but time is short. We must vacate by the end of next week, just ten days then a blank.

Now would be good time for our prayers to be answered.

Davud

I have packed my schoolbooks, clothes, cuddly rabbit, and just a few toys. It was a hard decision and I watched Mum, tears running down her cheeks, bagging things that could be sold. She included her cheap jewellery, books, cds, the best tea service, much more than could be carried. Dad loaded it all into the car and Vjolica went to be on the stall, they'd booked, with Mum. I stayed with Grandma and when Dad returned we packed the last things into boxes. We cannot take any furniture because we still have nowhere to live. Dad says he has arranged for the women to stay with Fitore Bardici's family. Whilst we worked I asked him if he had any plans for us.

'Davud, I would love to tell you I have solved the problem but the best I can do is for us to stay at the Red Cross clinic. I'm still trying to find a flat but Serbs don't want us, even if we had a lot of money, which we don't. There are very few blocks of flats owned by Albanians so accommodation for us is difficult. We must hope and pray for something to turn up.'

'The clinic is a very long way from school. Will you be able to take me in the car?' Dad looked away from me and paused before replying. 'No, not after next week. I'm taking the car to an auction. It's a luxury we can no longer afford. Your mother knows but I've not been able to bring myself to tell Vjolica or you until now.'

'So how am I going to get to school?'

'Vjolica can go with Fitore but until we find a flat you will not be able to go to school.'

I could hardly believe what he was saying. I thought of my friends, the lessons I was going to miss and in my distress I found myself shouting. 'I'll get behind. I won't know enough to pass the exams. Dad I'm too young to leave school.'

Grandma looked at me, shocked that I could defy my father. 'Davud!' she said, 'that's no way to talk to your father. He has enough problems. You should see the strain he's under and be supportive. How dare you be so lacking in respect.'

I dropped my chin onto my chest. 'I'm sorry. I was just...........'

He put his arms around me and hugged me for a long time. 'I understand your anxiety but whilst you are at the Red Cross I will try to find you a tutor.'

Another aspect Dad forgot to tell me was that without the car Mum would be unable to work at the Red Cross so when would we see each other? There were buses but they cost too much and would be dangerous for an Albanian woman alone.

The following day I went to school deeply upset and although part of me wanted to gobble every crumb of knowledge before I left, a demon inside shrugged and said, what's the point? I took a letter for my teacher who was sympathetic but gave me a glimmer of hope. At teatime he asked me to stay behind for a chat.

'Davud, you're a highly intelligent boy and this letter saddens me.' (Now I wanted to cry) 'But I think I can help you. I have a friend, a teacher, who was attacked by Serbian thugs. He was badly injured and now uses a wheelchair. He could no longer work so he lives near the Red Cross clinic and survives by tutoring people like you. Your parents would need to pay him but he charges very little. Would you like me to contact him?'

I nodded and then found my voice which was just a whisper, 'Thank you sir. I know my father will be pleased if my education could continue.'

'Good. We have a few days left so try to concentrate. Now go and have a break outside.' A weight had lifted and I ran and played until we had to return for the final session.

My last days at school flew past but my teacher kept his word. I was given an introductory letter to give to Mr B. Dushku. His home was a tiny, one bedroom flat only five minutes walk from the clinic. I was also given a parcel of textbooks, several new exercise books and a confidential report about me to give him. Finally he shook my hand and wished me well. I walked away, got into the car for the last time, and cried quietly, hoping Dad would not notice. He said nothing but handed me his handkerchief.

I was at another station on this train journey of life.

Vjolica

Saturday

Hello Diary. I hardly know where to start; so many changes have taken place. Mum, Grandma and I are now living with Mr and Mrs Bardici, Fitore's parents. Grandma has a bed and Mum and I are squeezed together with a double mattress on the floor. It's very cramped and there is little floor space around us but we are very grateful for the room. Mum cried when we were in bed the first night and has done so every night since. Grandma is more stoical and a solid rock of comfort. She has been homeless before, understands the pain but keeps saying all will be well, in time.

When I'm at school it all seems the same, same teachers, same friends, same lessons but when I walk back with Fitore my heart sinks and I would give anything to be returning to our apartment. Her family are very kind but money is tight so they keep apologising for such meagre food. It's hard for them to have guests and not be able to feed them well. Grandma and Mum do their best to help. They wash and iron the clothes, keep the house clean but there is really insufficient work for three experienced housewives. I know Mum misses going to work as well as her own home.

Talking about missing it's horrible to be apart from Dad and Davud. The good thing is Mr Bardici is taking us to see them tomorrow. We are going to spend the whole day together and then in the evening, after supper, he'll collect us again. I think they will enjoy having their home to themselves just as much as we'll enjoy being all together!

I'm really hoping that Dad will have some news of a place to live. I don't even mind missing school for a while and perhaps a tutor could be found for me. Can't wait for tomorrow.

Davud

It felt strange living with Dad in a room at the clinic. He seemed to feel he was on duty all the time and if a patient called after hours he was always willing to see them. I think it was his way of coping, filling his time so he didn't have to dwell on the lowly state we had come to.

'Davud,' he said one evening, 'I feel this mess is my fault. If I had not signed that document and moved us away, like the Dhomi's did, we could all now be living in England, in safety and comfort.'

I felt awkward, embarrassed that my strong father was seeking comfort from me, a boy, but I tried to comfort him.

'You couldn't have known what was going to happen and Serbia may look to another area and leave Kosovo alone now.'

He shook his head. 'If anything, the situation is becoming worse. Our president, Ibrahim Rugova, said some time ago that we have no real army and cannot resist an attack by Serbia so it's better to do nothing and stay alive than resist and be massacred. So far we are safe but the threat still hangs over us. I know it's pointless worrying about things we can't control, and may never happen, so let's look forward to seeing Mum, Vjolica and Grandma tomorrow.'

When they arrived nearly all of us had a few tears. You would have thought we'd been apart for months, not just a week. I showed Vjolica the clinic and it was a chance for us to talk, without our parents.

'So what's it like having a tutor instead of school?'

'It's good because I have his full attention all the time so I'm learning much more each day than I did at school. Of course there's no other children so that's lonely and no proper break times. He's teaching me to play the violin. He plays it really well and that's a change from ordinary lessons.'

'Wow, the violin, Mum will be pleased; she always said you sang well and should play an instrument when you're older.'

'Another thing. We sometimes speak in English even when we're doing another subject!'

'That's hard but I suppose you'll improve quickly. You're probably better than me already.'

Vjolica smiled and I realised it was the first smile I'd seen for some time. It was like a ray of sunshine. I took it away with my next question.

'Is everything ok at Fitore's house?'

She grimaced. 'Well we have somewhere to sleep and they're very kind but food is meagre and we feel we're imposing all the time. It's not comfortable. I wish we could stay here with you and Dad.'

'You've seen our room Vjolica. A family of five wouldn't be able to lie down. We would have to take shifts to sleep.'

We both laughed and went back to our parents to discover Dad had some news.

'I kept this from Davud because I wasn't certain it would come off but I've now found somewhere to live.'

'Hooray! Where is it? Are there lots of rooms? Can I go back to school?'

'Davud, be patient. Here what your father has to say.'

Mum spoke sternly and I realised it was only partial good news.

'The apartment is small, two bedrooms, a kitchen, bathroom and living room.' Dad said. He looked worried that we might think it too poor. ' It's in a small block still owned by Albanians and the previous family only moved out yesterday. After lunch we can go and see it and if you're all happy we will take it.'

Vjolica asked what we were all thinking. 'Can we afford it?'

I was a relieved to see him smile. 'The owner is anxious we stay because his wife is recovering from a severe bout of pneumonia. Mum is going to help him nurse her. He is grateful and says he will keep the rent low enough for us to pay. I think we should give thanks for such a generous spirit.'

We had dinner in a small cafe and all felt unpleasantly full. We were not used to large meals any more but it felt like a celebration. After that we walked to see the apartment. It took about twenty minutes and Grandma walked irritatingly slowly.

'Come on, Grandma,' I called, 'I thought you'd be keen to see our new home.'

'I am Davud, but you're all walking so fast I'm out of breath trying to keep up.'

We slowed down and I noticed Mum and Dad exchange knowing looks. Was Grandma ill?

When we reached the apartment block the owner was there to greet us. He shook hands with all of us and said he had cleaned it thoroughly for our arrival. He handed Dad the key and then left us to explore. It was not furnished. There were blinds at the windows and the kitchen had a cooker, fridge and cupboards but otherwise it was empty. We looked at each other in dismay.

'Well we've got bedding, even if we don't have beds,' said Mum. 'Living here means I can soon return to work so we will have a little extra coming in, but not enough to furnish all of this.'

'Perhaps I could find a job,' offered Vjolica, 'I won't be able to go to school so I should try to help.'

I think she expected Dad to be shocked and refuse, saying she too needed an education but he didn't. 'Thank you for offering; perhaps they'll need some help at the market. We must buy some basics, a frying pan, saucepans, plates, and cups. Let's go there now and we can also ask about work for you. After that we'll need to fetch our things from the Red Cross and Davud and I can move in tonight.'

'I will talk to Mr Bardici this evening and ask if he can bring us tomorrow,' said Mum. Finally things seemed to be improving. We were going to be together again.

When they'd gone back Dad and I moved what we had from the Red Cross. It was not a lot and took only an hour to do. I went straight to bed and saw Dad sitting on the floor with a notepad and a pen.

'What are you doing, Dad?'

'I'm just writing to Fadil Dhomi, Davud, to tell him our new address. Go to sleep now.'

I snuggled down and knew no more until morning.

Monday

Diary, my dear friend. Everything has been changing so fast I feel bewildered. I still can't believe I'm not going to school – understand better how Davud must have felt. I haven't missed it much yet because we've been so busy trying to make our apartment more comfortable. We went to the market and now, are you listening?

I HAVE A JOB!!

I started today. I haven't served any customers yet but I helped load the stalls and made drinks. I hardly sat down the whole time and I'm really tired but that's ok. Tonight I'm sure I'll sleep really well, no matter how hard the floor is.

I feel I'm helping Mum and Dad by doing this and can't wait until Friday when I get paid. Tomorrow Dad is going back to our old apartment. He's going to see if any of our furniture is still there. I hope it is because at the moment it's like we are camping under a roof instead of a tent.

Chapter 6

Leeds

Leeds was a vast city compared to Clacton and the family found it noisy and bewildering at first. They had never experienced a place so full of ethnically varied people. There were many Muslims and they were soon welcomed into the local mosque. It was comforting to be enveloped by familiar rituals and Fadil realised how much he had missed it. He had tried in Clacton to use his prayer mat regularly but it was not the same being Muslim with no support. Marigana had never emerged from the house without wearing hijab even on the beach but it would have been tempting to discard it when all other women were wearing the skimpiest swim wear.

Fadil thought back to their arrival in Clacton two years ago and how lost they all felt. Despite the size of Leeds, this arrival was much easier. The house they were renting was in good order so there was no panic or disgust. The schools were close by and both children had settled well into their studies. At home, Rita now prattled in a lovely mixture of Albanian and English. Marigana worried that she would forget her native language in time, especially as Fadil had suggested they all speak English at home. She compensated by still singing Albanian songs and was happy when they all joined in.

Rita found new friends quickly but Alek was more reserved. He concentrated on his studies and had been disappointed to be told guitar lessons were costly and he needed his own instrument. The family had barely enough to live on so there was nothing left for luxuries. Why was it so hard for Dad to get a job? He felt angry, frustrated and became withdrawn at home. He spent hours in his room studying, got excellent marks in tests and exams but was an unhappy, friendless boy.

One Saturday, when he was lounging on his bed reading a set book, his Mum called him down. He sighed and decided not to have heard. Her footsteps sounded on the stairs; she paused half way up and shouted.

'Alek can you hear me?'

'Yes.'

'Well if you can hear me please come down. I need you to go to the corner shop for some bread.'

He dragged himself off the bed and went down slowly. Marigana ignored his attitude, perilously close to insolence. 'There are a couple of other things too. Here's the list and some money. Be as quick as you can because I've made soup and it's almost ready.'

He took the money, list, thrust the shopping bag under his arm and left without a word. Marigana watched him amble along the street, his head down. What was wrong with him?

At the corner shop Alek filled a basket and then queued for the till. Whilst he waited he read various notices on the wall and one charged him with excitement.

Are you an early riser?
Wanted, boy or girl to deliver papers six days a week.
Talk to any cashier if you're interested.

When Alek reached the counter he asked about the job.

'Yes we still need someone. Are you interested?'

His heart was thumping and he jigged from foot to foot. 'Yes I am.'

'Ok,' she smiled, 'Jot down your name address, telephone, age whilst I serve these people.'

He moved to the side, picked up the pen she'd indicated and found his hand was shaking. He took a deep breath and filled in the form. When she was free he handed it to her.

She glanced at it, 'Right, Alek, the rate is £4 a week for six mornings. Don't worry about the route; Max will take you out in the van a couple of times and you'll soon get the hang of it. Can you start on Monday?'

'Yes. What time?'

'You'll need to be here at seven, prompt.'

'Thanks; I'll be there,' Alek said as he left the shop.

Once outside he punched the air with delight and ran home, the shopping bag swinging dangerously from side to side.

Marigana noticed the difference as soon as she saw him. 'Did you get the bread and other bits?'

'Yes but I got more than that, Mum. I got a job as a paper boy.'

He was still breathless as he told her about it and she smiled to see him so animated, but his face lost the glow when they discussed his wages.

'We need all the money we can get just to be able to pay the bills and eat, Alek. You know that. You've got to be grown up about this and be proud you can contribute.'

His face grew red with anger and frustration. 'Are you telling me that I'm to get up hours earlier than usual, traipse around the town lugging heavy bags of papers and have nothing for my effort? '

'Alek! Don't talk to me like that.'

He was feeling rising panic, but managed to quash it. 'I'm sorry. I'm really disappointed. I saw this job as a chance to save towards a guitar. I don't want lunch I'm going out.'

The door slammed behind him and Marigana sighed.

Fadil and Rita returned from the library whilst Alek was out. Marigana wanted to tell him about Alek but it could wait.

'That library is amazing, Marigana. I've never seen so many books and to think they charge nothing to borrow them. We started in the children's section and I thought of getting a child's book for myself because the vocabulary was simple but when I explored the rest I couldn't resist this. He held up a history book. It seems wrong to live in a country so steeped in history and yet be so ignorant of it.'

'I got a storybook, Mum. Dad said you might like to read it with me.'

Marigana grimaced as she took it from her and flicked through the brightly coloured pages. 'I will try, Rita. I know I need to read and write in English but I don't seem to learn as quickly as you.'

'That's because you don't go to school like me.'

'That's probably true but you have youth on your side. Anyway it's time for lunch. Alek went to the shop for me and bought some bread but he's decided to skip lunch and go into town.'

There was silence whilst they savoured the food and then Fadil spoke. 'I don't know what to do Marigana. Every job I apply for; they don't even consider me. Perhaps I should stop trying to be a doctor and go for a manual job.'

"I don't think it's your nationality that stands in your way because this town is multiracial. Perhaps there are a lot of people who have also specialised in orthopaedics. A manual job would be much less money than you could get as a doctor and may not be better than the benefits the government give us.'

'That's a good point so what do you think I should do?'

'What about trying for a family doctor post. Could you do that? Are you qualified?'

'I don't know if I am. I had to study all aspects in Kosovo and then specialise. It's probably the same here. I'll find out.'

After lunch Rita helped Mum clear away and wash the dishes whilst Fadil wrote to the BMA again.

He was just about to go and post his letter when Alek arrived home wearing his usual sullen expression.

'What's that? Another application for a job? Well whilst you keep writing useless letters I got a job this morning. 'Expect Mum told you.'

Fadil's face reddened and he frowned. 'If you want to tell me about it you'd better change your tone.'

Alek did but with no joy in his voice this time. 'I hoped I'd be able to keep the money or at least some of it to save towards a guitar.'

'That is something your mother and I will discuss. Now Aleksander I think you should go up to your room.'

'But I'm starving. I missed lunch.'

Fadil made as if to rise from his chair and Alek ran upstairs.

He was allowed to come down when the evening meal was ready and tried to be pleasanter by asking Rita about her trip to the library. She happily told him. His parents kept a stony silence and there had been no mention of his wages when Alek went to bed. He trudged up the stairs, threw himself on the bed, fully clothed and found tears springing to his eyes. He bunched his fists, willing them to stop but they flowed giving him some relief.

Monday arrived and Alek was out of bed as soon as his alarm went off. When he arrived at the shop he met Max who glanced up briefly, grunted and returned to marking all the papers with the house number. When he'd finished he stood up, easing his back and said, 'Right Alek this morning and tomorrow I'll take you round in my car then on Wednesday you're on your own. Pick up those bags lad and follow me. The bags were very heavy and Alek was not sure he would be able to carry them around for an hour but he had no time to worry because they were in the car and he had to remember the route.

When they arrived back at the shop he had just enough time to run home, change into his uniform and go to school. Breakfast had been forgotten and by break time he was very hungry. The time seemed to drag until he could refuel at lunchtime. He decided to get up even earlier the next day so he could eat something.

The following morning Max was friendlier and offered to drive him a third time if he was unsure but Alek assured him he could do it.

'Good. I'll check over your bicycle, and it'll be ready when you arrive.'

'Bike?' said Alek. 'I thought I had to walk it.'

'Nay lad you'd never get round in time and the bags are too heavy to carry.' Alek stood still with shock.

''You'd best be off, clock's tickin'.'

Alek shook himself into action. 'Yes, bye.'

He left feeling his heart thumping. I can't ride a bike. What am I going to do? Should I go back and tell Max I can't do the job? He shuddered and dismissed that thought. How can I learn to ride a bicycle when I don't have one, in just twenty-four hours?

He said nothing whilst eating his breakfast and Marigana asked if he was feeling poorly. He shook his head and gave her a look that said leave me alone.

At school he was so distracted the maths teacher shouted at him to wake up. The other children smirked because Alek was seen as a boring 'geek'. He never had a cross word from a teacher. At lunch he stood in the queue beside a boy in his class called Peter. He was several inches taller than Alek, broad in the chest, athletic with an attractive face topped by thick wavy fair hair.

'What was up with you this morning? You never get told off.'

Alek turned to look at him with a wry grin. 'I've just got a paper round and found out I've got to use a bike. I thought I'd have to walk it.'

'They'll give you a bike won't they, if you don't have one?'

'Yes. I don't have one and my problem is I've never ridden a bike before.'

'Where do you live? If it's not too far I could bring my bike round tonight and you could practice. I'm sure you'd soon get the hang of it.'

Alek grinned with surprise and pleasure. 'Thanks that'd be great.'

Suddenly Alek had his appetite back and asked for extra potato. They took their laden trays and sat down together.

They exchanged addresses and Peter lived close enough to come that evening.

Alek faced the afternoon lessons with a lighter heart. When he got home he told Mum and Dad about Peter and his need for cycling lessons.

Peter arrived about four thirty and Mum offered him a drink and some cake.

'No thanks Mrs Dhomi I haven't time 'cause my Mum will have dinner ready at six and I've no idea how long Alek will need. We'd best get started right away.'

The boys went out to the street and Peter gave a demonstration then Alek sat astride the bike. The saddle was too high and he could barely touch the ground with his toes. He pushed off and then wobbled to a frightened stop.

'You made it look easy!'

More advice followed and he tried again with several turns of the pedals before he lost his balance. Half an hour later he was pedalling with confidence. He brought the bicycle back to Peter grinning happily. 'That was brill. Thanks Pete. You're a real mate.'

'No probs.' Peter mounted the bike. 'I'd better be off. Say bye to your parents for me.' He set off and waved a hand as he rounded the bend. Alek went in, now looking forward to his paper round in the morning.

When he got to the shop, a little early, Max was ready with the papers and showed him his bicycle that had a basket on the front.

'Get on it so I can see if you need the saddle raised.' Alek did so and found it was much lower than Peter's.

'I think it's ok, Max.'

'Good. Now I'll put your second bag in the basket and you need to put the strap of the first one over your head and hang it on one side. It will affect your balance at first so take it steady until you get used to it.'

He watched as Alek set off straining to push the pedals down. He wavered at first with the extra weight but he managed to remember his route and rode back with both bags empty and time to spare. Only three more days and he would get his first wage, ever.

Saturday soon came and Alek arrived home to have breakfast waving a plastic bag containing four pounds. 'Look, Dad, My first wage packet.'

He handed it to his mother.

'Thank you dear. Now eat your breakfast.'

Alek sat at the table, poured cereal into his bowl and said, 'Last Saturday I went into town and looked at second hand guitars. They let me try some and there was one...... It had a lovely tone and was only £20.'

His eyes shone with excitement and Fadil was overwhelmed by the desire to give him the money, but food had to come first. 'I would love to buy it for you Alek but you know how carefully we have to budget.'

Alek's face lost its glow.

'I'm also humbled that you've managed to get a job whilst I'm still struggling. I think, as a reward for your enterprise, you should keep your first wage packet completely. After that give half to the family to help with food.'

Alek dropped his spoon into his bowl, stood up, nearly knocking his chair backwards and hugged Dad, his Mum and finally Rita. 'If it's not sold, I'll be able to buy it in just two months. Brill!'

'An excellent compromise,' said Mum. 'I'll look forward to hearing that guitar when you get it.'

That evening Fadil wrote to his friends in Kosovo giving them his English address. He felt a sense of permanency for the first time.

Chapter 7

Kosovo

Davud

When Dad came home last night from his visit to our old apartment he was laden under the weight of small things he'd been able to carry. He put the bags down, stood up and grinned at us all as we waited expectantly for his news. Vjolica could not wait. She rushed to peer into the bags and pulled out the electric kettle, cups, plates and a set of saucepans. That got Mum up from the floor (we still had no chairs) and she picked up the saucepans to take them into the little kitchen. Tears streamed down her face, as she asked, 'Was there any furniture or has it all been cleared out?'

Dad smiled, 'As far as I could see everything was as we'd left it. The landlord was pleased to see me and he's not quite as bad as we thought. He wants us to take what furniture we need because he can then offer the apartment to someone else. He asked why we hadn't given him a forwarding address?'

'That's because we didn't have one. If he'd given us more time we could have stayed there and............'

'Yes Vjolica but no good comes from an, 'if', like that. We must look forwards and the good news is we can take as much as will fit into this little place.'

Mum moved to the kitchen and put the kettle on, then returned. 'How are we going to bring large pieces of furniture? It will cost a lot to hire a van.'

Dad put his arms around her. 'I have an agreement with the landlord. He wants the apartment cleared so he will pay for a removal company to bring whatever we need here, and then he can have the value of what is left. All we have to do is decide what we need and then it can be arranged. Let's have a cup of tea and make a list.

'Could I have some of my toys and books? I really miss them.'

'Davud, we have to be sensible. There's so little space here but I'm sure a few, especially precious, things can come for all of us. We must be selective.'

The list was made, we had bread and cheese for supper and I went to bed.

Vjolica

Friday 1st November

I've been working for weeks now and I'm so tired I haven't been able to write, sorry. I'm getting used to the early start and clearing everything away when it gets dark. I'm glad it's November and the days are shorter! But I'm earning money and everything is better now. Mum and Grandma have a bed each and Davud, Dad and I have mattresses we just lay down at night. We have 5 dining chairs and a tiny table that used to be in our old kitchen, just for eating breakfast. We also have one easy chair for Grandma. Just between us, dear diary, I'm worried about her. She moves so slowly now; all the efficient bustle gone. Dad says it's angina and I know that's not good. She has a spray to inhale if she gets a pain.

Now it's time for a confession. I'm feeling really envious of Davud. Are you shocked? I know I'm older and perhaps he wishes he could work and bring in money to help, but I had hopes and plans. I wanted to do well at school and go to university. I'm not sure if I want to be a nurse like Mum and maybe I'm not clever enough to be a doctor, but I could be a teacher. Children are so gorgeous, innocent and they absorb knowledge so easily. I'm sure I'd love it.

It's good that you accept me and aren't critical. I have a conscience for that! If Mum read this she would say I was selfish, and she would be right.

That's more than enough moaning. I need to make my bed up (Sick of doing that every night – moaning again!) and get some sleep.

Davud

I was home earlier than everyone else and Grandma gave me a drink and a sweet cake she 'd made. It was good to see her baking again, even if she has to have frequent rests. When the others arrived home, Vjolica the last, Grandma produced a letter that had arrived from Mr Dhomi. Dad took it from her eagerly.

'It means he must have got mine with our new address.' He tore open the envelope and there was one page of tiny writing. Dad read it out to us.

15 Garden Court
Leeds
England

Dear Donjeta, Ajshe, Vjolica and Davud,

Your letter telling about your change of fortune moved me greatly. When I think of you all I see you working in the hospital and your lovely, spacious apartment. Now I must try to picture you working for next to nothing at the Red Cross clinic and living in a tiny flat with only two bedrooms! But your letter seemed buoyant, enjoying your work, Davud having a tutor and doing well.

'Thanks Dad for telling him that.'
'Don't interrupt Davud. Go on dear.'

Dad continued,

Vjolica working in the market! She has become a grown woman overnight and you must be proud of her.

Dad stopped reading and looked at her. 'I am proud of you. He's right.'
Vjolica went pink and looked down modestly but I knew she would want to punch the air and shout, 'Yes!'
Dad went back to the letter.

I believe that when you are roughly shaken from a comfortable, possibly complaisant life, you become stronger. This happened to us and it is easier to tell our story now we are living in safety and comfort.

The hardest thing for me has been finding work. I have applied for jobs but not even got an interview. I am persevering but then Alek put me to shame by getting one! He is still working hard at school but now he delivers newspapers every morning. It has helped his self-confidence and he seems to be happier than he was.

You would hardly recognize Rita now. She is so tall and beautiful and full of life. She chats away in English as if she was born to it! Marigana still finds the language barrier difficult, especially now we no longer have lessons, but I am trying to help this by insisting we all speak English at home. It does not work very well and we end up speaking Anglo-banian!

We all laughed and Dad said, 'He still has that wonderful sense of humour.'

Then he turned back to the letter.

I have noticed in our news that the Kosovo Liberation Army is trying to fight the Serbs by attacking the police. I thought Rugova wanted non-violence and this seems to me like 'waving a red rag to a bull'. Surely the KLA have not the strength, or sufficient weapons to tackle such a large, experienced force.

'We were talking about that weren't we Dad.'

'Yes Davud and the rest of the letter is not good. I'm not sure I should read it out.'

'Whatever it says, dear, we all have a right to know. If the situation worsens and we have to leave we should have some warning.'

Mum looked very serious. He didn't argue, just read the rest of the letter.

Slobodan Milosevic is a formidable man and will not be lenient. So far the reprisals have taken place in villages where they think KLA members are hiding. They are shelling these villages or rounding up the men and shooting them. The situation is dangerous and I worry it will escalate. I tell you this not to frighten you but to make you aware, knowing the news you get is not always the true facts.

I wish you would leave now and come to England. Nothing would please us better than to have you as our neighbours again.

I pray everyday for Allah to protect you and your family.

Your good friend,

Fadil

Dad looked up as he finished and Vjolica voiced all our thoughts. 'They are such lovely people. I really miss them.'

'We miss them too Vjolica,' said Mum. 'I just wish he hadn't put in that piece at the end about how dangerous it is here. I know he meant it kindly but there are rumours......' Before she could say any more Dad changed the subject. 'I'm famished, Ajeshe, what's for supper?'

Vjolica

It was lovely having the Milad un Nabi holiday from work last week. We, that is Mum and I, celebrated the Prophet's Birthday at the Red Cross clinic. There were a few Christians there but they were happy for us to do it. We set up a stall in the morning for gifts of food to be given to the poor and many people came. Some were traders in the market and I knew them all. The only uncomfortable moment was when Erind came. He runs the hardware stall and was kind to us when we moved and had nothing. He makes me feel uncomfortable. I always look down, as I should, never look him in the eye, but he seems to send out an aura that scares me. Anyway he gave his gift and soon went away. Everyone was generous, considering these difficult times, and my heart went out to the people that came to collect the food.

Some of the children were dreadfully thin, their clothes in tatters, usually clutching a precious, filthy toy.

Whilst we were doing that, Dad and Davud went to the mosque to pray. In the past we would have had a good evening meal to end the celebration but we had given away most of the food we had so it was bread, cheese and a small piece of Kadaif, deliciously sweet and crunchy with walnuts, to finish.

I forgot to say that Grandma stayed at home whilst all this was going on. Her back aches now if she has to stand for any length of time. We were all quite surprised and pleased that she had managed to do some baking. Her Kadaif was gorgeous. It seems an age since she showed me how to make bread when I was little.

So that's it. I've nothing more exciting to report. Back to work tomorrow and so it goes on. To think, if this really is the start of my working life and I never go to school or college again, I shall be working forever. Not a good thought. Perhaps I'll marry and become a mother. Whoa!

I hope Mum and Dad aren't thinking of arranging a marriage for me! What if they chose someone like Erind? He's old, fat and his beard is straggly. When he's close there is an unwashed smell about him. They wouldn't do that, would they?

Help!!

Davud

It was a lovely spring day and Mr Dushku and I went out. We don't often do this because he cannot walk and managing a wheelchair is difficult. Around his home he can manoeuvre because there's nothing wrong with his arms but the pavements are cracked and uneven and he needs help then. I'm not strong enough to help him, even though he is very thin, so he arranged for a friend to come with us.

We went to a park, not far from our old apartment, so it was a long walk. As we went along he asked me if I had heard of the Kosovo Liberation Army.

'I have heard of it but my Dad said Ibrahim Rugova did not feel we were strong enough to fight the Serbs so we shouldn't try.'

'Yes, Davud, that's true but still the KLA is getting bigger. A lot of young Albanians are angry at the way we've been treated and are secretly joining it. You may have noticed I did not introduce my carer to you by name. That's because he has now joined them and twice a week he goes for training.'

I looked at the man with interest. He did not look tough enough to be a soldier, being thin and not very tall. 'What do you do when you train?'

He smiled as he said, 'It's all rather primitive. We use sticks as pretend guns and do a lot of marching. We also run, climb, do press-ups and other things to make us fitter. New men are joining every day but there are very few weapons. I have had two weaponry training sessions; one firing a rifle and the other an automatic gun.'

'Wow I'd love to try shooting a gun. When I'm older I might join. Have you fought anyone for real; not training I mean?'

'No but I think my first time will come soon. Our targets are the police. You know what they did to Bamir and his sister. I mean to avenge my friend and all the other people they've hurt or killed.'

'They attacked my Granddad. He refused to leave his home and tried to fight them. He died. Now Grandma lives with us.'

'I'm sorry for your loss. This has happened to many people and is still happening.'

Mr Dushku changed the subject as we got to the gates of the park. 'I think we must get back to Davud's education now so no more talk of soldiers. Take me towards those woods please and we will identify trees, woodland flowers and mini beasts.

Inside the small wood the sound of traffic was reduced to a muffled rumble and we could hear birds singing, the flapping of their wings and the wind swishing through the trees, making them shake. I forgot the discussion of soldier training and enjoyed bark rubbing, gathering acorns and oak leaves to draw later and throwing ash keys into the air. A small stream ran through the wood and we stood quietly on a wooden bridge watching a kingfisher darting into the water and flapping out with a minnow in its beak. It was magical and as we walked back, at the end of the afternoon, I wished all lessons could be like that one.

Chapter 8

Leeds

Just as they were finishing breakfast the postman pushed a letter through the door. Rita rushed to pick it up and gave it to Dad.

'Thank you, Rita. I wonder what this is?' He opened it slowly and read it.

Marigana watched his concentration and could not wait. 'Well what is it? It looks important.'

Fadil looked up with a broad smile. 'They say I can apply for jobs as a GP. Yes!'

He dropped the letter onto the table, gripped his hands together and shook them over his head. Everyone was smiling, although Rita didn't really understand what they were all so happy about. Then Dad lowered his arms, stood and chivvied the children to get ready to go to school. There was a scramble of activity and then quiet descended in the house. When they had gone he fetched the latest medical journal and scanned it for posts in Leeds. There was only one. He was not familiar with the area but presumed it would be possible to go by bus. He sat down and wrote a letter requesting an application form and had just finished when Marigana came home from taking Rita to school. He showed her the advertisement.

'We should walk into the centre and buy a map of Leeds, then we could find out where it is and the bus route,' she said.

'That's a good idea. I wish I could buy you lunch out to celebrate, but...'

'Fadil. You don't have to explain or worry. I know there's not enough money for luxuries but I have a feeling things are looking better. Today has been a turning point. Come on, I'm ready.'

The centre was busy, as it always was, but they were in a buoyant mood as they jostled to cross the road to the large stationers. The travel section was at the far end of the shop and they soon found a street map of Leeds and opened it out.

'There it is,' said Fadil and that's where we live. Too far to walk as I suspected. ' They decided not to buy the map, not wanting to spend any money, and set off to the bus station, arm in arm. Fadil stopped abruptly, pulling Marigana backwards.

'What's the matter?' she asked.

'What if I get an interview? I don't have a suit, smart shirt or tie. Even my shoes won't polish to look good after all these years. I just don't have the money to buy any of this. What can I do?'

'Is it possible to borrow money from, say, a bank?'

'A bank would want me to own my own house and have a job before they'd lend me anything. I'm not a good risk.'

'I don't get it Fadil. Why will they only lend money to people that have money?'

He smiled and explained. She listened patiently and then made another suggestion.

'Alek has nearly saved his twenty pounds...............'

'We can't do that to him after all his hard work, Marigana. How could you even think that?'

Alek tipped the money out of the tin, and counted it. He already knew how much there should be but needed to check. He had eighteen pounds. On Saturday he could buy his guitar, if it was still in the shop. He found Mum in the kitchen.

'I'll have enough money to buy that guitar on Saturday. I can't wait.'

'That's excellent Alek. You've done well to be so focused, not spending it on anything else.' She took a deep breath. "I know how much you want it but........'

He sighed audibly; a 'but' didn't bode well. 'What? Can't I go on Saturday?'

'Alek I wouldn't ask this if there was any other way, but Dad needs your savings to buy some smart clothes for his interview.'

Alex clenched his fists. His face reddened. 'It's the first I've heard that he's got an interview. When did that letter come?'

This was not going well.

'He hasn't got an interview yet but when he does he needs to look smart and he has no suit, or anything.'

Alek snorted. 'So he thinks he can buy a suit, shirt, tie and all that with just eighteen pounds? He's not living on the same planet. I can't believe you want me to give him my savings for a possible, not even certain, interview. Shit Mum that's not fair!'

'Don't you dare swear at me. I don't care how stressed you are we don't swear in this house. Go to your room.'

Alek lifted his chin, did not apologise or move. They

stood equal in height and anger as Fadil strode into the kitchen.

'What's going on in here? I'm surprised you haven't woken Rita with all that shouting.'

Alek was still standing defiant, like stone, so Mum explained.

Fadil turned to look at his son. 'I'm sorry Alek but I do need your money. Think of it as an investment for your future. If I get this job I will buy you a guitar with my first wage. Now I would like you to go upstairs and bring down the money.'

Alek was rooted to the spot.

'Alek!'

He turned, went upstairs came down immediately and threw the money on the work surface. Still without a word he went back up to his bedroom, fell on to the bed and let the tears of frustration and disappointment flow.

At breakfast the next morning he was morose and Mum and Dad avoided any possible confrontation. Marigana was just grateful that he had still done his paper round.

When she returned from her walk to school Fadil was getting his coat on. She looked at him eyebrows raised.

'I thought I'd see what eighteen pounds will buy. Do you want to come?'

She hesitated. 'I didn't realise you were going today so I've agreed to go for a coffee with Sarah Glover. You're all ready to go dear so go without me.'

He kissed her and left the house. When he had gone Marigana's smile faded. How she wished she could give Alek a guitar and her husband a job. She needed a genie or a magic wand. As that was impossible she would trust in Allah and get ready to visit Sarah.

Fadil looked in the window of the first men's shop he came to and quickly realised that Alek was right. He didn't have enough money for a suit. He felt deflated but then saw a sign in another shop, displaying models dressed for a wedding, that suits could be hired. He went in but came out after asking the price. He could afford the suit and shirt but it would take all the money and would only do one interview. Uncertain what to do next he wandered away from the smart stores selling designer brands and stopped outside a charity shop. He went inside and asked but they had no suits.

'We only have shirts and jumpers at the moment but we do get suits in.'

Fadil looked though the rail of shirts, picked out two and took them to the counter. 'I don't know what my size is so can I try these on please?'

'This one will be far too big with a neck size of 18 inches but the other one might fit. I'll show you where you can try it.'

In a curtained alcove he put it on and looked at himself in the mirror. It was a long time since he had looked so smart, at least from the waist up. He took it off and bought it but before leaving the shop he asked about other charity shops. She gave him directions and he hurried along the road. He still had sixteen pounds.

As Marigana walked to Sarah's house she hoped her English would be good enough to hold a conversation for an hour. There was no doubt she had gained confidence in the last couple of years. When she arrived, she was pleased to see that it was no great mansion, just one of a terrace, like hers. She rang the bell and Sarah opened it, smiling broadly.

She was shorter than Marigana, plump with a round face, stubby nose and long brown hair hanging loose.

'Come in, come in. No don't worry about taking your shoes off, but let me hang up your jacket.'

She led Marigana into a living room and the smell of coffee wafted from the kitchen.

'That smells lovely.'

'Yes, I've put the machine on so we can have another cup if we want to. I love proper filter coffee but only make it when we have visitors otherwise it's instant. What am I thinking of? Please sit down and I'll go and pour it.'

She bustled away and Marigana looked around. Sarah had lots of lovely things including an enormous television set. There were paintings on the walls and an elegant vase of flowers standing on a solid wood dresser. The dresser displayed matching plates and delicate china cups. The exterior of the house might look like hers but inside it was like Aladdin's cave. It made her realise just how poor she was.

The coffee arrived and a plate laden with slices of buttered sultana loaf. 'You must try this cake. It's a new recipe. I love baking. I expect you can tell that by looking at me.'

She laughed; Marigana smiled, took a piece of cake and nibbled a corner. 'It's lovely Sarah.' She ate another piece. 'I'd like the recipe. I bake the things I was taught by my mother in Kosovo and I really want to make English cakes. I'm sure my family would enjoy this.'

'I'll copy out the recipe and give it to you at school on Monday but I'll also cut a few pieces for you to take home and they can try it.'

'That's really kind. Thank you.'

'Now, I want to ask you about Kosovo and why you left, but you don't need to tell me if it will hurt you.'

Marigana told her new friend who listened with sympathy. When it was time to leave she thanked Sarah and tentatively invited her to come to her house next week.

'I'll bake an Albanian cake for you to try.'

They stood, just outside the door and as she turned to go Sarah called out. 'I'll see you before Monday because Rita's coming to Ellen's party tomorrow.'

'Of course! See you tomorrow then. Bye'.

She walked away, her head held high her heart soaring with pleasure. She had a friend.

When she got home Marigana wrapped the little present Rita was taking to the party. They had bought it together and Rita had chosen the pretty hair clip, explaining that Ellen's long brown hair was so thick and wavy she always had to wear it pulled into a ponytail or clipped into place.

Marigana had worried about a party dress but Rita had explained that party dresses were not cool. She would go in her clean jeans and pink T-shirt with the sparkly bits.

As she finished she heard Fadil opening the front door. He came in smiling, carrying a large bag.

'You've had some success, then.'

'Yes. I can see lunch isn't ready so I'll try it all on and show you.'

He went upstairs whilst she buttered bread and unwrapped Sarah's cake. By the time he emerged lunch was ready.

'Oh you look........splendid.' Her eyes brimmed with tears. 'You look like a slimmer version of my husband, the Kosovar doctor. Turn around.'

He obliged and she felt the fabric of the suit. 'This is lovely. It must have cost a great deal.'

'It's a designer label, apparently, but all told I spent £16, in a charity shop. It's amazing what people will discard when there's still so much wear left.'

He changed into comfortable clothes, after carefully hanging his new clothes up, fervently hoping that he would need to wear them soon.

Over lunch they talked about Alek, his need for money and his general attitude.

'I think his attitude is influenced by his peers and also the frustration of not being able to buy the guitar,' said Marigana.

'It's possible to buy some things and pay for them on credit. Usually it means for something that costs £20 you eventually pay £30 for the privilege. I don't really like the idea but it would help him get the guitar quicker.'

'No Fadil it's not worth paying so much extra. In just a few weeks it'll be the school summer holiday and lessons will not be available then until September. I think we should give him back the money that's left and let him keep all his earnings from now on.'

'Agreed. It will do him no harm to wait a while longer. I'll speak to him this evening.'

Alek arrived home and went straight upstairs without greeting his parents or Rita. Fadil sighed and followed him. Alek was sitting on the side of the bed, his school bag open.

'We need to talk Alek.'

'I've got homework.'

'It'll wait until I've had my say. Now look at me and listen.'

Alek continued to look at the floor so Fadil sat on the chair bringing his eyes on a level with Alek's. 'First I want to thank you for lending me your money. I will pay it back with interest when I get a job.'

He ignored the rude 'huh' and pressed on. At the end he gave him the money and went back downstairs.

'How did he take it?

'Better than I expected. I just hope I get that job. I'm sick of being poor and having to put my son through all this.'

Marigana put her hand over his. Then Rita broke the sombre mood.

'I can't wait until the party tomorrow. Ellen says they're having a real disco, flashing lights and everything. Her mum's baked this amazing cake. It's a huge number 10 with pink icing, and we're not having normal party food, you know, like sandwiches, crisps and jelly. We're having hot dogs with ketchup!'

'That sounds like fun, but now it's homework time for you before tea.'

'But it's Friday. I've got all Saturday and Sunday before I need to do it.'

'Please don't argue Rita. You'll enjoy the weekend better if it's not hanging over you.'

She made a face but got her books out.

Saturday was warm and sunny, the sort of day everyone expects, but seldom gets, in an English July. It raised Fadil's spirits and he felt even happier when he had a letter enclosing a long application form for the job. He wanted to fill it in immediately but decided to wait until the afternoon when Rita would be at the party.

It was even quieter than he expected because Alek declared he needed to go to the library to do some research. He managed to get a dig in about other students having their own computers but Fadil didn't rise to it. Marigana knew he needed time alone so she busied herself in the kitchen.

He was worried about spelling mistakes so he borrowed Alek's dictionary and wrote all his answers on a piece of paper first. After an hour the form was complete and he then wrote a covering letter. He knew he should have a CV but the form was so searching he really had nothing else to add. Finally he stood up and called out that he was going to post his letter. Marigana leant out of the kitchen door and asked him to collect Rita. The party was due to finish in fifteen minutes.

'Where is it?'

'St Andrew's church hall.'

He left, walking briskly, happy to be making another step towards employment. As he neared the church hall he could hear the disco's thumping rhythms long before he got there. Inside they had closed the curtains and he could hardly distinguish Rita from all the other bouncing bodies.

'Hello, have you come to collect someone? I'm Sarah Glover, Ellen's mum.'

'I'm Fadil Dhomi....'

'Rita's Dad, good to meet you. Marigana came for coffee and told me about your escape from Kosovo. It must be so hard starting a new life. The party is just ending so I'll fetch Rita for you.'

She moved towards the disc jockey and he handed her a microphone, whilst fading out the music.

'Well, everyone, I hope you've had a good time.'

The children responded wildly with whoops and cheers.

'That's good. Before you go please show Jason here,' and she gestured to the DJ, 'how much you've enjoyed it.'

The children clapped and cheered again.

'There are party bags for you all so don't go without one. Thank you all for coming.'

She gave the microphone back and went around the hall pulling open the curtains letting in the sunshine. Rita then spotted her Dad and ran to him. He gave her a hug and she showed him the party bag.

''What's in it?'

She opened it up to look. 'There's a packet of sweets, birthday cake, a book and a bracelet.'

'That's great. I'm glad you've had a good time. Have you said thank you?'

'Not yet; there's Mrs Glover.'

He watched her run across the hall, proud of her confidence.

Chapter 9

Tension building

Vjolica

At work today everyone was talking about Albania. There's been a financial crisis and the government has collapsed! There have been riots because people have lost all their money and there's no police or army to control it. The United Nations has sent forces in to try and get order. There are rumours that lots of weapons have been acquired from Albania to arm the Kosovo Liberation Army.

It seems scary but also exciting. Is it possible that we could fight the Serbs?

I really want the current situation to change. The Serbian 'police' are cruel thugs and living here is getting harder. Everyone seems to live in constant fear. I used to be able to walk along a street with a girl friend or Mum. Now we daren't do that unless we have Dad with us. We know Albanians, like us, are targets and the police like nothing better than to beat us. They don't even bother to invent an excuse.

At home, we don't really discuss politics, just talk about the patients M and D have treated and I talk about the incidents in the market, like someone caught stealing. Perhaps I should be the one to bring the subject up. If we had to leave Kosovo in a hurry would we be able to get a ferry from Durres? Surely it would be too dangerous.

Sometimes, diary, I wish you were a person and could discuss these worries. It's no good I'll have to talk to Dad tomorrow.

Davud

Vjolica seems to think we are going to war! She asked Dad about it at breakfast and his face took on a pained expression. We all knew he hated talking about the political situation but he answered her.

'I've heard about Albania's financial problems and I feel very sorry for the ordinary people who've lost everything. I also know that when people are desperate and don't know where to turn they want to have revenge on the police, government, anyone in authority. At this moment southern Albania is a dangerous place to be.'

'But Dad what will happen if there's a war here? I heard that the KLO has been able to buy lots of cheap weapons from Albania.'

As Vjolica said that I thought of Mr Dushku's carer and wondered if he had a gun instead of a stick and if he'd been involved in attacking Serbian police. I hoped so. I cannot understand or forgive them for what they did to Granddad.

Vjolica went on, 'Instead of little skirmishes could they now fight the Serbs? I've been thinking if it turns into a proper war we might have to leave like the Dhomi family. In that case we can't travel through Albania to Durres like they did. What would we do? I'm scared Dad.'

'That's why we've not discussed this before. Mum and I didn't want to have you and Davud worried if there was no need. For now we carry on as we are, working, studying,

(He looked at me) and living as best we can. You hear rumours Vjolica but the Red Cross have access to accurate information. Please trust me. If I find out there is real danger your Mum and I will tell you and we will go. There are other routes than Albania, if that should still be too dangerous.'

'I'm sorry to have had to ask but I hear such a lot at the market. I've been really anxious. I feel a bit better now. Shall I make some tea?'

'That would be lovely. Thank you,' said Mum.

Grandma heaved herself out of her chair to go and help. She made it seem a great effort but she must weigh less than Vjolica; her face has shrunk under her cheekbones and her skin hangs thin and wrinkly. It is only a few years since she was fat and jolly. Grandma's body seems to show the effect of all that has happened more than anyone's.

'It's ok, Grandma. I don't need any help,' said Vjolica.

'I know, dear, but I thought I'd clear up the kitchen. I need to feel useful and I slept well last night.'

When they had gone Dad surprised me by asking about Mr Dushku. 'I understand he's having to manage on his own now his friend and carer has gone.'

'I didn't know he was on his own. He hasn't said anything to me Dad.'

I felt guilty I had not told him about our conversation in the park. Did Dad know his carer was in the KLA? Luckily he stopped talking about it when Vjolica bought in the tea.

Vjolica

I know it's several months since I wrote and I'm sorry but sometimes I have little energy or enthusiasm after a day at work. Anyway, here I go.....

When I got to the market this morning I was told to see the supervisor. She said I was old enough to earn more and take the responsibility of running a stall if the owner was poorly or just needed extra help. It would mean more money and I was really pleased but then she said the stall I had to help with today was Erind's hardware. He does get really busy but I'd rather work on any stall but his. Anyway, I had to do it and it was not as bad as I expected. We served at different ends and hardly spoke. One man that came was desperate, living rough and possessing nothing. He wanted a pan to boil water, a cup, plate and cutlery. Erind said the price and the man's face sagged, his eyes filled with tears. He didn't have that much.

'What can you pay?' Erind asked. The man unclenched his hand and showed the coins, two Deutsche Marks and a few dinars.

'Is that all you have?

The response was a shrug. He turned to move away but Erind called him back. 'Hey, don't go. I'll help you. Give me the dinars but keep the Marks for some food. Do you know about the soup kitchen?' The man nodded. 'Good. Ask there about somewhere to sleep. Allah be with you.'

For the first time the man smiled, showing his few yellow teeth, and turned away clasping his purchases.

Erind was so kind. Why do I feel anxious when he comes too close?

Anyway I went home that night and told Mum and Dad about my new status. Neither of them was sure about me working for Erind. Dad wanted to know more about him. When I explained, Mum remembered how kind he'd been when we first moved here with nothing. She said he was good and probably honourable but she was still uncertain. Dad said he would come to the market at lunchtime tomorrow and have a word with the supervisor and possibly Erind himself. I'm glad I told them but not sure I want Dad to interfere.

Enough of all that. I'm looking forward to my 15th birthday, just five days to go. I don't expect much in the way of presents but Mum's had some eggs given and refuses to cook them. I think, hope, she might make kajmaçin, sweet baked eggs. My mouth is drooling just thinking of it, truly luscious.

Vjolica

Dad did come to the market. The supervisor, Lule, said she was acting like a chaperone for me and he need not worry about Erind asking for my help. He also came to our stall and I felt uncomfortable but it was fine, really. They seemed to get on quite well, although I couldn't hear everything they were saying because I was serving customers.

When Dad had gone Erind seemed really cheerful. He kept having a little chuckle to himself as if he was remembering a joke. Sometimes he rubbed his hands together and looked directly at me. I looked demure and felt that wave of anxiety again. I think, no, I know, he fancies me. This is not the way a good Muslim girl should think. Glad no one reads this but me!

Vjolica

It's only a few days since I wrote but things are not going very well. It seems I'm expected to work with Erind every day now.

It's not fun and not fair. I know my wage has increased and I'll probably be pleased at the end of the week, but...............

This morning he asked me to look after the stall whilst he went out for an hour. He didn't say where he was going but as he passed me his hands squeezed the cheeks of my bottom. I gasped and he laughed. Whilst he was gone I was very busy serving but then he returned and passed me in the same way as before. He seemed in excellent spirits, laughing and joking with everyone and every time he said something funny he looked at me to see if I was laughing. I kept my eyes down but could still see him from under my lashes and I'm sure he was disappointed by my lack of humour.

I do have a sense of humour but I felt everything he was doing was for my benefit and I had no intention of encouraging him. How could I ask the supervisor to move me? I would have to say why and I can't do that. It would shame him and me, especially as she assured Dad she's my chaperone. Would a good chaperone allow him to touch me like that? If I complained I might even lose my job!

Davud

It's Vjolica's birthday tomorrow and I mentioned it to Mr Dushku today. He asked how old she would be. When I said fifteen he said she was now a young lady and had I got something pretty to give her. I said I had no money to buy a gift, which he knew, and he told me to open the bottom drawer in his bedroom.

'That drawer is too low for me to reach in my wheelchair so it only has things in that I don't need.' I opened the drawer and it was full of fine silk ladies scarves and clothes. 'Choose a scarf you think she'll like Davud. They belonged to my sister and until now I couldn't bear to part with them.'

I chose a beautiful green one that I knew she would love but was not sure if I should accept such a gift. I took it to show him. He smiled and said he remembered how beautiful his sister looked in it and then showed me a photograph of her.

'Are you sure you want me to have this for Vjolica. I don't want to take it if it will make you sad.'

'Davud that scarf was made to be worn and seen. What good is it doing gathering dust in my drawer? Please take it and make her happy.'

I folded it into a tiny square and hid it in my violin case. I felt excited because she wouldn't expect any gift from me.

Vjolica

My birthday

This should've been such a happy day for me. Mum and Grandma made the pudding I longed for. Grandma had sewn me a really pretty bag and Davud gave me a beautiful silk scarf. So what spoiled it?

Dad? No, not Dad, Erind.

He went to see Dad yesterday, whilst I manned his stall. He has no living family to help him choose a wife so he has done it on his own and asked Dad if he could have me!!!

When Dad told me I trembled so much I had to sit down.

He was very gentle and asked me what I thought of Erind. I said he was kind, and generous to people in need, but he made me feel very uncomfortable and anxious. I couldn't say I didn't like him touching me or I just didn't like him. Dad didn't understand.

'Why do you feel anxious?' he asked.

Well this was really hard. I squirmed. I couldn't say, because I think he fancies me and wants sex! I mumbled something like, 'I don't know.' Then he said, Thank you Vjolica I'll give this some thought and speak to your mother.'

I was so angry I hadn't thought to say he was too old for me. He must be forty at least. I was also scared because Erind has much more money than us. He makes a good living at the market and rumour has it the apartment he lives in is beautiful. Many women would consider him a catch.

What would they decide? This is my whole life teetering on the balance. What shall I do if they say I must marry him? Work for the rest of my life on that stall? Bear his children? I feel sick. Help! I can't bear it.

Davud

When I saw Mr Dushku this morning he asked if Vjolica had liked the scarf.

'She thought it was beautiful and tried it on straight away.'

'I'm pleased she liked it and I assume she had a lovely day.'

So I told him, ending with, 'Now she's frightened and waiting for their decision. When I left this morning they still hadn't spoken to her and she was already late for the market.'

'Have you met this man, Erind, Davud?'

'Yes'

'Would you like him for a brother?'

'A brother? I hadn't thought of that. He's too old. I think he's old enough to be my father.'

Mr Dushku looked sad. 'I'm so sorry for her and all of you, Davud but there's nothing I can do to help.'

Chapter 10

Leeds

The atmosphere continued to be strained with Alek morose and non-communicative. It wasn't fair. All his friends had more than him. Look at that Peter with his flashy bike. No doubt he'd have a computer, a huge television, his dad would have a car and they'd holiday every year, abroad. His resentful thoughts haunted his time at home. Dad had spent his hard earned guitar money and still hadn't even got an interview. The summer holiday was nearly there and he hated the thought of the long days to come, at home.

He asked at the shop where he did his paper round but they said they did not need holiday cover. Max said he would ask around but did not sound very hopeful. Alek scanned the local papers when he delivered them and found a grass cutting company that wanted help for just a couple of weeks. He went to a phone box and called before breakfast.

'Hello, 'Short and Sweet' gardeners, Marcia here.'

'Hello, Marcia, my name is Alek Dhomi and I'm ringing about the grass cutting job.'

'Wow you don't let the grass grow under your feet do you.' She giggled. 'Sorry about the pun. The advert only came out this morning.'

'I know I deliver the papers.'

'Right, Alek, do you have any experience?'

'No, but I'm strong, quick to learn and desperate to earn money to buy a guitar.'

Everything came out in a rush and he felt he was making a mess of things but Marcia liked his honesty. 'Ok, well the job will only be for three weeks starting Monday, if you can. They are long days, start at eight and finish at six. What do you think?'

Alek's heart sank. 'I really want to do this Marcia but I don't finish my paper round until just after eight and I'd still have to get a bus to wherever you are.'

'Hm. You wouldn't need to get a bus because we could pick you up. Where do you live?'

Alek told her and she said it was quite close to their yard. The call ended with Marcia saying she would discuss it with Geoff and if Alek rang back about five-thirty she could tell him if they were willing to start later.

He went home feeling hopeful but did not talk about it in case it fell through. Marigana noticed that he was not hanging his head down and he even spoke to Rita asking if she was looking forward to her last day before the holidays.

They went off to school and when she got home Marigana asked Fadil if he had noticed a slight improvement.

'Yes but I think it's too early to start relaxing. That boy cannot forgive me for taking his money, and I can't blame him really.'

'Well I can. It was disappointing for him but we have only delayed it, not stopped him buying a guitar altogether and it will do him no harm to learn a little selflessness.'

Fadil held up his hands. 'You are talking to one who agrees with you. Don't get all steamed up.'

She was about to retort when a letter arrived. Fadil reached the front door first and opened it eagerly. 'Yes, Yes, Yes!' With each repetition he punched the air.

Marigana 's smile filled her face. 'You've got an interview?'

'Yes. I was so pleased I only read the first sentence. Let me read it slowly now. It's next week on Thursday, 10am and it will be at the surgery. I'm nervous already. Let's celebrate.'

He pulled her towards him and twirled her around humming a tune they used to dance to in Kosovo. Marigana laughed and he stopped dancing and hugged her with delight.

'Do you know what I'd like to do today?' She shook her head. 'I'd like to go to the music shop and put a deposit on that guitar to hold it for a few weeks.'

'It's a lovely idea. You might not get this job but it would mean Alek could have the one he's set his heart on.'

The sun was shining, and they both walked, heads held high, full of hope for the future.

The music shop was crammed with instruments of every type festooning the walls and hanging from the ceiling. Someone was playing jazz on a grand piano and the very air seemed to be crammed with music and possibilities. They wandered around until they found the guitars and then their euphoria evaporated. How could they know which one Alek had chosen? They were not even sure if it had been an acoustic or electric one. There were also several marked at £20. Finally, Fadil went to the counter. 'I wonder if you can help me? My son has been here a couple of times and set his heart on a guitar. We want to put a deposit on it to hold it for him but don't know which one it is.'

'Would it have been a Saturday?'

'Yes.'

'Wait a moment and I'll fetch Sandy. He works most Saturdays and might remember him.'

She returned with a young man that physically matched his name. Fadil explained his problem.

'Ah. I think I know who you mean. He had an accent like yours and stood about as tall as your wife, black hair, slim.'

'That sounds like him.'

'In that case I can show you the one he chose. We still have it. Lots of kids go for the electric ones but your lad knew a good tone when he heard it.'

As he spoke he was reaching to unhook the instrument from the wall and then he handed it to Fadil.

'I can't play, unfortunately, but I'd like to hold it for my son. He's saving up for it.'

'That's fine. We usually ask for ten per cent deposit so that will be two pounds.'

Fadil was given a receipt and a 'deposit paid' notice was placed on the guitar. They left the shop, pleased with themselves and walked home.

When the children were both home from school Fadil told them about his interview. Rita immediately responded to the excited atmosphere but Alek barely managed, 'Now you can wear the suit I paid for.'

They ignored his attitude, not wanting to spoil the pleasure of the moment.

It was the end of term and Rita had handed Mum lots of pictures so she took them into the kitchen and stuck them on the wall. It looked as if both her children had a talent for drawing, she thought. She began to cook the evening meal and was just going to announce it was nearly ready when the front door banged. She went into the living room.

'Has Alek gone out?' Fadil nodded.

'Before you ask he didn't say a word so I've no idea where he's going or when he's coming back. Can you hold the dinner for half an hour?'

'Yes. It won't spoil but we're going to have to talk to him. He should be courteous enough to tell us what he's doing.'

Fadil sighed. 'Ok I'll do it after dinner.'

Ten minutes later Alek arrived home again with a broad smile on his face. Everyone looked at him, surprised and expectant. 'I've just got a summer job for three weeks! You're now looking at a grass cutter. I start on Monday straight after my paper round. They're picking me up at eight fifteen.'

'That's fantastic Alek. How did you hear about it?'

He told them about his phone calls and then apologised for rushing out without a word, explaining his anxiety to get the job.

'We really have something to celebrate today so let's eat. I've made an English fruit loaf for pudding.'

It was a lovely meal, full of chatter, with an air of hope and possibilities, they had not felt for years.

On Monday Marigana made Alek two packed meals, breakfast and lunch and she watched him get into the van feeling a wave of love for him. She lingered a moment until the van and trailer had turned the corner and then bustled around the kitchen making a picnic for a trip to the park with Rita and Ellen.

Alek sat in the van, anxious but excited. 'Would it be ok if I ate my breakfast? I don't suppose there'll be time when we arrive.'

'Carry on lad, you've five minutes, tops, then it's all go.'

Alek ate quickly but found his sandwich hard to swallow and decided to save the rest until lunchtime.

They arrived at a private house with wrought iron gates and a sweeping drive leading to an impressive brick house with colonnades flanking the front door. Alek thought they would be cutting the grass at the front, either side of the drive but they swept round to the back and parked near the stables. They both got out and Geoff let down the back of the trailer.

'Right Alek, give us a hand'

There were two petrol driven mowers and Alek had his first lesson beginning with the lawn at the back of the house. They had to move some garden furniture and then Geoff watched whilst Alek made his first run, turned at the bottom and drove the mower back. He asked Alek to stop by raising his hand.

'Am I doing something wrong, Geoff?'

'No, it's fine, lovely straight line there. As you've got the idea I'm taking the other mower round the front. You'll finish before me so then you've to trim the edges. I'll show you how the strimmer works now and then we can both get on.'

The strimmer was also petrol driven and the technique to start it was not easy, but once he had success Geoff left him to it. Alek got back on the mower and drove it up and down, concentrating carefully. By the time he had finished and got the strimmer working he had decided this job was fun. It was mid morning when they had finished and Geoff set off for the next one. Before they got there he stopped in a lay-by and got out a flask and a snack.

'You're doing all right, Alek, but there's one thing puzzling me. Why haven't you asked about the pay?'

Alek's cheeks felt hot with embarrassment. 'I forgot. I wanted the job so much it seemed whatever I was paid it was a whole lot better than nothing.'

Geoff laughed. 'Well it won't be nothing. What do you say to one pound?'

'How long do I have to work to earn a pound?'

'An hour, lad. Most manual jobs are paid by the hour.'

'Oh. How many hours a day do we work?'

'It depends on the weather but if it's good, eight or nine.'

'That's nine pounds a day, five days a week, forty five pounds!'

'You know your tables then. You can bump that up a bit too if you work Saturdays because we pay time and a half. Anyway finish that biscuit 'cos we must get this next one done before lunch.'

The day went by quickly and when he arrived home Marigana thought her son had grown taller. Then she realised he was standing upright, his head held high. She saw the man he was going to be.

Chapter 11

Davud

When I got home from school Vjolica was there with Grandma. Vjolica should have been at the market so I knew the decision had been made but was it yes or no? Vjolica's face was blotchy with crying, relief? I didn't think so.

'So are you going to tell me?' I asked.

Vjolica could not speak so Grandma answered. 'It has been decided that Vjolica will marry Erind.'

'She can't! He's too old for her, fat and ugly. How could they think he was right for her?'

Grandma stood up, her face wincing. 'The decision was theirs and they've made it. I'm going to make some tea.'

She went into the kitchen and shut the door, allowing us to talk. Nothing I could say could make this horror go away so I tried to put my arms around her. She shook me off. 'You can't make this right, Davud. I want to kill myself. I'll just go out into the street and wait until some Serb soldiers find me. They'll rape me then they'll kill me and it'll be done. Better than a life time of misery.'

'No, please Vjolica. Don't even think like that. Has Erind been told?'

'Yes, I assume. Dad said he would go straight to the market this morning and invite him to a meal in a few days to discuss.........'

This time she allowed me to hug her as she sobbed. Grandma brought in the tea. She said nothing but her mouth was pursed and I felt she did not approve of the decision.

I desperately wanted to help but knew neither my entreaty nor Vjolica's tears could change an agreement once it had been made. I wanted the Serbs to attack Erind. In my mind I saw them beating him and when he fell down kicking him and stamping with their boots on his face. I'm not proud of such thoughts but I do love my sister.

Eventually Mum and Dad came home. Grandma asked me to come into the kitchen to help with the meal. I didn't move. I needed to be with Vjolica.

'Davud please leave us and help Grandma, now.'

The emphasis was on the 'now' and I had no choice but my face at least showed them I hated their decision.

Vjolica

25th June 1997

I'm sorry. I have neglected to write for nearly a month. This diary is supposed to contain all the important events in my life and the greatest one so far has been so awful I couldn't bring myself to speak about it even to you.

Dad told Erind he was pleased and flattered he wanted to marry me. He then said a final decision would be easier if he knew him better. So Dad has invited him to come for a meal every week. Tonight will be the third one. Needless to say he's been absolutely charming and it's obvious that Mum's fallen for it but Mum won't have to spend her life with him.

He is a total creep all smarmy and nice so he can legally get into my knickers! I'm sure tonight he'll push for a wedding date and Dad will rush to name one. I just hope it's months away.

Wrong. I hope it'll be never!

Perhaps tonight I should behave badly so he thinks he's getting a wild cat. What could I do? I might just blurt out the truth that I don't want to marry such an old man.

Have to do something to save myself.

Davud

'So how is your family getting on with Erind?' asked Mr Dushku.

'We've all been falling over ourselves to be pleasant and Mum's been making Vjolica cook and then she tells him, 'Vjolica made the pudding; she's a good cook,' as if she's trying to sell her! I hate him. Everything he does and says is an act to ingratiate himself with Mum and Dad.'

'How is Vjolica behaving?'

I smiled. 'Well up until last night she was demure, eyes down, just as a potential bride should be. Last night she was rude and so unpleasant I was almost ashamed of her.'

Mr Dushku chuckled. 'I wish I'd been there.'

'She brought food to the table and put the dishes down so clumsily juices spilt onto the table cloth. Then she deliberately burnt the sauce and served it with a shrug. She refused to clear the table, when asked, suggesting I should do it. I stood up and Dad shouted at me to sit down and Vjolica to do as she was told.'

'And did she?'

Mr Dushku's eyes were twinkling with enjoyment.

'No she refused saying, 'Why should I do everything you ask so Erind thinks I'm an obedient girl? He should see me as I really am, wilful, disobedient, an awful cook and a real bitch!'

He laughed loudly at this. 'So she gave it to them with all guns blazing. Good for her. I hope it puts him off, for no woman should be made to marry someone she cannot love.'

'Unfortunately, Erind laughed at her outburst and said he could hardly wait to tame this shrew. So I don't know what's going to happen next.'

Mr Dushku said he was looking forward to the next instalment of my family drama and then made me sit and translate an English text.

Vjolica

26th June 1997

It didn't work. Now Erind sees me as an exciting challenge. I dread to think what method he would use to 'tame' me. I feel like running away but that's impossible. I've no money, no friends close by. I'm getting desperate. Dad's furious with me and is going to have 'words' with me tonight. Even Grandma is refusing to talk to me and Mum's the same. Only Davud understands but even he was red with embarrassment at my outburst. I still have to work on his stall everyday and it seems he's told everyone at the market we're betrothed. Now he feels he can take even more liberties with me and puts his arm lovingly around me when he wants to, showing the world how happy he is. Why can't he see my misery? I never smile. I'm monosyllabic, yet still he wants to marry me.

27th June 1997

It was awful. Dad strode up and down the room shouting and everything he said was true. I'd been rude in front of a guest. I had shamed my family. My behaviour was unforgivable (but I think it was justified). Finally he ran out of steam, sank onto the armchair and just looked at me.

'Well? Have you nothing to say?'

I knew I should say I was sorry but it came out all wrong. 'I had to behave like that because I just can't marry him. He's too old, he's ugly, he's fat. I hate him. How could you make me marry someone I hate? I thought you loved me...........'

Needless to say that ended in unstoppable tears but my, usually loving, father was not to be put off by a display of feminine weakness. All he took on board was the phrase, 'I had to behave like that' and the tirade started all over again.

'There is no had to about it. Nobody has to behave badly. I brought you up better than that, or so I thought.'

He went on and on and on. Finally he strode out after shouting at me to go to bed. I wasn't allowed to eat, just given a glass of water, by Davud. Even he had been forbidden to talk to me. Could things get any worse?

It seems they could. This morning I was told that when I got to the market I had to apologize to Erind. I bristled and steeled myself to refuse or just disobey then Dad said he was coming with me to make certain I did so.

I went through with it – had to. Needless to say Erind was nice-as-pie and they made arrangements for another meal in two weeks time to discuss dates and wedding arrangements. They both looked at me to see my reaction to this but I just stood there, fists clenched, eyes down, stony.

Davud

July 1997

'So,' said Mr Dushku. 'Any more dramas in the family?'

'Not really. Vjolica says nothing, just nods or shakes her head. Mum, Dad and Grandma behave as if this is normal and ignore her. I'm beginning to think the wedding date will be set very soon so they can get rid of her.'

'I'm sorry this situation has arisen Davud but arranged marriages often work out. Our parents know us really well and tend to choose a husband that's suitable. I'm sure your parents are wise to get to know Erind better before making the final decision. When's he coming to dinner again?'

'Next week. Mum's been planning the menu with Grandma and normally Vjolica would be involved but after last time she is being excluded. I think they fear she would salt the pudding and sweeten the savoury dishes.'

Mr Dushku laughed. 'I've never met your sister but I like her spirit. I'll pray for a kind resolution to her problem. Now I must set you some work or your parents will be wondering why they pay me for your education.' He chuckled, 'Sometimes I think it is you who are educating me with your insights into family life.'

I struggled with maths and science that day but we finished with music and for the first time I felt my violin and I were one. There was no scratchy tone, my bow didn't catch on other strings and the melody soared with a confidence I've never had before.

'Well done Davud. That was lovely, perfectly in tune. I need to find you something more challenging. He rummaged through piles of music and chose a piece by Mozart. Until now we had only played folk tunes and study exercises and scales. Was I ready to play something by such a famous musician? We looked at the opening bars and excitement welled up as I realised I would be able to play it, with a lot of practice. For the first time I had to move my left hand up and down the finger board to access a greater range of notes. He was right it was a challenge.

Normally after a personal achievement I would run home with the news and everyone would be pleased for me. Not this time. I went home and said nothing.

All the talk was about the arrangement they would make with Erind. Mum and Dad were worried about how much a wedding would cost and Vjolica looked interested for the first time when they said they would have to save. They settled on Thursday 6th November.

Erind arrived for the meal and Vjolica was quiet but polite. She did nothing to upset Mum and Dad and we were all relieved. I wondered if she was finally accepting her fate and trying to make the best of it. As the meal drew to a close, Vjolica stood to clear the dishes and Dad turned to Erind.

'I am pleased to say that I am happy for your marriage to go ahead. You show great courtesy and patience with Vjolica and we feel she will make you a good wife.'

Something fell and smashed on the floor in the kitchen and Mum went to investigate, shutting the door behind her.

'That's good news,' said Erind. 'Can we now discuss a date?'

His face fell when he realised he would still have to wait three months but by the time he left he seemed to have accepted it.

Vjolica

August 5th 1997

I'm not going through with it and now it's time for desperate measures. I'm being good, behaving as a bride should, except I can't get excited. I think I've lulled M and D and even Grandma into believing I've accepted my fate.

So this is the plan.

I've been writing to Fitore now and again so I'm going to step this up. Make out my engagement is fantastic and get her to invite me to stay, some time before the wedding, a last chance for us to be teenage girls together. I think M and D will go for it. I can pack a bag with more than just overnight stuff and I will never return.

I'll need some money so I'll ask if I can keep some of my wages. Not sure yet what reason I can give, perhaps I want to buy my husband a gift? Perhaps better to say I want to buy some smart underwear!

My problem, once I get to Fitore's house, is where to go next? There's nowhere safe for a Muslim woman alone. Even if I tell Fitore she can't allow me to stay there because Dad will just come and fetch me back. Perhaps I could join the KLA, become a soldier!

Chapter 12

'Oh, Daddy, you do look smart,' said Rita as Fadil came down dressed for his interview.

'Thank you Rita,' he said smiling. 'It's a big day today and I want to make a good impression.'

'Well, if looks were what they went by, you'd get the job instantly,' said Marigana. She went to him and kissed him. 'I've been thinking. Don't forget to mention the months you spent at the immigration camp working at the clinic. That was very close to being a GP wasn't it?'

'Yes, I'll certainly get that in if I can.' He looked at the clock. I'd better be going. I may not be home for lunch so have a lovely day both of you.'

He went out of the door and Marigana prayed he would do well. Rita then broke into her thoughts by asking what they were going to do that day. She smiled down at her. 'Well we must start by tidying and cleaning the bedrooms and then we can go to the swings.'

Rita was happy helping, particularly if there was a reward at the end of it.

Fadil reached the surgery with ten minutes to spare. It was just one storey, red brick and obviously purpose built. A sign said the car park was at the rear so he walked around to it and was surprised. The building was much bigger than the frontage suggested. He went back to the front and read the list of doctors printed on the shiny brass plate. There were seven but he suspected some of them might be part-time. He took a deep breath, entered, and made himself known to the receptionist. She gave him a friendly smile and said, 'They're having coffee at the moment Dr Dhomi so I'll take you to join them.'

She opened the door to a large room. People were standing, chatting, holding cups of coffee. He was introduced to a tall man, slightly stooping, with receding, light brown hair.

'Dr Green this is Dr Dhomi.'

They shook hands and the receptionist left the room. Dr Green offered him a coffee but he refused, not wanting to be interviewed juggling a cup and saucer.

'In that case I think we could make a start.' He raised his voice. 'Right everyone, let me introduce you to Fadil Dhomi and can you take your places.'

There was a general welcoming murmur and then they moved to chairs behind tables leaving Fadil to take the lonely one in front of them. A wave of anxiety hit him and he felt sweat prickling under his arms.

The interview was long and searching. He was pleased to have the opportunity to talk about his time in the refugee camp and was surprised when they asked him if he was a practising Muslim.

'Can I ask why that's relevant?' he said, frowning slightly.

'It's important because at least thirty per cent of our patients are Muslim and we need someone who fully understands their religion.'

Fadil nodded. 'I can see the need but there are Sunni, Shia and different cultures, depending on the country they come from.'

'Yes I appreciate that but most of them are English born, so their heritage will be tempered, I suspect.'

Fadil decided he liked Dr Green. He seemed caring and sensitive to the needs of his patients.

When the interview was over he thought he would be going straight home but they asked him to wait for a few minutes and he was shown to an empty treatment room. He could not sit still and wandered around, opening cupboards and drawers. It was well equipped, clean and bright. He wished it was his. The window looked out onto the car park and he was looking that way when the door opened. He turned to see Dr Green smiling.

'I have a favour to ask of you. We're short staffed and wondered if you would help out this afternoon?'

'I'll happily give you a hand but I'm not familiar with your patient record system.'

'Don't worry about that we can show you at lunch time and Nurse Roberts, Jenny, will be working next door so you can pop into her if you're stuck. Now come and have something to eat with us.'

The large room, where they had had the interview, was now laid out with sandwiches and cakes. Fadil was introduced to Jenny.

'I don't want you to think we have lunch like this everyday,' she said, her eyes twinkling. 'It's in your honour. We do it for all candidates so we can chat socially.'

'That's a good idea. Have you had a lot of applicants for this job?'

'I don't know but we short-listed it to four and you are the last to be interviewed. Shame really, I've been enjoying these lunches.'

She laughed and steered him to meet and chat to some of the others. He wanted to know if all the candidates had been asked to help and if this was all part of the process. The opportunity failed to arrive but he knew it was not really important.

Afternoon surgery finished at six if you gave each patient exactly the set number of minutes. It was half past six when Fadil shut the door behind his last one. He stretched, tidied the room and was about to leave, when there was a brief knock and Dr Green came in.

'So how did that go, Fadil?'

'I've had a great afternoon. It felt really good being a doctor again after such a long break.'

'I'm glad you enjoyed it because whilst you were taking my place I was discussing all the candidates with my colleagues. We've decided to offer you the job, so, congratulations. Now I need to know if you're going to accept it.'

Fadil struggled to compose himself and then smiled broadly, 'Thank you; thank you very much. Of course I'll accept it. When do I start?'

'Well it is a bit complicated. One of my younger colleagues is going overseas to work and his job begins on the first of January.' Fadil's face fell. 'No let me finish. We also have a part time doctor, Elaine, due to go on maternity leave next month. The full time job will be yours in January but meanwhile you could do the part time job, if you agree.'

'I want to work as soon as possible so I'll happily accept the part time one whilst I wait. What will the hours be and when do I take over from Elaine?'

'Well we must get it all on an official footing so a letter offering you the job will come your way and you must formally accept it. I'll also include the details of the part time job, that I can offer on a locum's salary. Elaine works on a Monday so you can begin the first one in September?'

Fadil nodded. 'That's fine by me. Thank you again.'

They shook hands and Fadil left the surgery. He was so relieved tears ran down his cheeks. He walked straight past his bus stop and then had to retrace his steps. Wouldn't it be great to be able to take his family out to celebrate? He sighed, knowing it would have to wait until he had some money. On his new salary there would be all kinds of things they could buy. As he sat on the bus he imagined driving a car along the busy streets. Alek was not the only one who longed to be able to buy something.

When he got home the family looked at him expectantly. Fadil clasped his hands over his head and shouted, 'You're all looking at Dr Dhomi! I got the job!'

'Hooray!' Shouted back Rita and they all rushed to have a family hug. Marigana was so pleased she couldn't stop crying and Fadil laughed as she gave him his dinner, saying it would now be too salty.

'Not salty, but a little dried having waited so long.'

'This will be the best meal ever to me, thank you. I'm really hungry.'

As he ate he told them about his day and the people he had met that would now be his colleagues.

Everyone went to bed that night feeling tired but very happy.

Alek's grass cutting job finished after three weeks and he had never felt so rich. He had worked every Saturday and had not had the opportunity to buy his guitar even though he had had more than enough money after his first week.

It was Monday. He returned from his paper round, had breakfast and said, 'I'm going out to buy that guitar now.

'You certainly deserve it, Alek,' said Mum. 'I'm proud of the efforts you've made, continuing to get up early to do your papers and then working a long day cutting grass.'

'I just hope they still have the one I saw. I'll be gutted if it's gone.'

'It should be there because Dad put a deposit on it.'

'Wow. I hope he got the right one.'

He stood up so quickly his chair fell over backwards. Oops. I'd better go now before I break something. Where's Dad? I don't know how much deposit he paid.'

'He's gone out, not sure why, anyway it was two pounds.'

'Ok, thanks. Bye.'

Alek entered the music shop, excitement mounting, and went straight to the guitar display. He was so anxious he missed it at first and had to look again more carefully. There, with a deposit paid sticker, it hung next to a bright blue electric one. He hesitated. There was plenty of money for an electric one. He lifted it down and took it to the counter to ask if he could try it. The shop was not busy so the girl plugged it into a sound system and left him to experiment. The first twang was shockingly loud so he turned it down and looked around to see if anyone was going to tell him off. Reassured he tried again and had fun, imagining he was Eric Clapton.

After ten minutes he unplugged it, returned it to it's place on the wall and took down the one he originally wanted. He strummed it and then picked out a simple tune. The mellow tone was lovely and he knew it had to be that one. He took it to the counter. The girl found the case and asked him if he wanted anything else. It struck him he could afford some sheet music and a music stand, so he left the shop having spent thirty pounds.

He was tempted to get a bus home but the habit of frugality went deep, so he walked.

Whilst Alek was walking home Dad was in a car show room. He had not even begun his new job but he just had to see what cars cost and get some advice about a driving licence. He wandered around the second hand cars and a Ford Escort caught his eye. It was £500, seemed in excellent condition and he sat in the driver's seat, gazing at the controls.

'Can I help you, sir?'

Donjeta looked up and a suited salesman was beaming at him. 'An excellent choice sir, if I may say so, one point two litre, leather seats, superb radio. Even the mileage isn't bad for a 1991 reg.'

He got out of the car and was pleased to find he could look down on the pushy salesman. 'I haven't made up my mind yet but I would like to know what a car like this would cost paying monthly.'

'Come inside sir and we'll work it out. A lot depends on how quickly you want to pay it off.'

Half an hour later Donjeta emerged having resisted buying the car. He had the address of the DVLA in his pocket and the desire to save for the car rather than waste so much money on interest. It worried him he would be expected to have a car to make home visits.

He arrived home in thoughtful mood but as he opened the door the dulcet tone of the guitar welcomed him.

'Daddy, Daddy Alek's got a guitar.'

He put his arm around Rita and let her lead him into the living room where Alek was strumming. 'That sounds lovely. Are you pleased with it?'

The look of happiness on his son's face did not need words.

'I remember you used to play a folk song in Kosovo. Can you remember it?'

Alek went straight into the simple melody. Donjeta pulled Marigana onto her feet and they danced.

'Oh Alek,' she said, as the tune finished. 'You've made me cry. That was so lovely and reminded me of home.'

'I can't wait to go back to school now so I can have lessons, but I bought some music too, so I can practice.'

'Don't wish your summer holiday away dear, enjoy it. We can't afford to go away but at least now you're not grass cutting you can relax. Why don't you go and see that boy who helped you ride a bike? What was his name?'

'Peter. I could do. Yes, I'll go round there after lunch.'

It was a lovely day so Mum made sandwiches and they sat out in the garden on a blanket, to eat. She sighed, 'I'd really like to do something with this garden. It's small but such a mess. Grass and weeds were poking through cracks in the concrete and there was no lawn. I suppose you'd call it a yard rather than a garden.'

'Why don't you draw what you'd like to have, and when I get my first wage, we'll make a start. It will be autumn then and a good time to do it, when it's cooler. Now Alek is something of a gardener he can give us a hand.'

He ruffled Alek's hair.'

'Fine by me,' said Alek, standing up. 'I'll go and see if Peter's in now, if that's ok?'

Mum nodded. 'Rita will give me a hand clearing up.'

Peter answered the door and seemed pleased.

'Hi, Alek. Are you as bored as me?'

'Well, not exactly. This is the first day of the holidays I've had nothing to do. Anyway if you're bored let's walk to the park near school.'

'Great, wait there while I tell them where I'm going.'

He came out a few minutes later with a football in a plastic bag and they talked easily. Alek related his grass-cutting job and Peter a week's holiday in Blackpool.

'Blackpool sounds fun but very expensive.'

'It is, if you go on everything in the funfairs, but you can go and just enjoy the beach, fish and chips and all that.'

'Before we came to Leeds we lived in a seaside town called Clacton. Have you heard of it?'

'Yes but never been. It's in the South. What's it like?'

'I think it's a bit like Blackpool by the sound of it. We liked going to the beach there and loved fish and chips.'

They arrived at the park and met some girls and boys from school so the game of football became a mixed three a side. They laughed a lot and there was some decidedly illegal tackling, resulting in a draw. Near the entrance to the park was an ice-cream van and they bought a cornet each and lounged on the grass in the sunshine. Alek realised he was happy and revelled in it.

On the way home Peter asked what he was going to do with the money he'd earned.

'I've done what I wanted to do. I bought an acoustic guitar, this morning.'

'I've got a guitar, electric bass.'

The boys grinned at each other.

'Can you play it?' They said in unison and laughed.

'I can play a bit but I'm rusty,' said Alek. 'What about you?'

'I have lessons at school and doing ok, I think. I'd like to start a group. Do you want to join it?'

Alek put up his hands as if to stop him. 'You're going too fast for me. I'm probably not in your league.'

'There's only one way to find out,' said Peter. 'Let's get together and see. Tomorrow ok?'

'Yes. Your place or mine?'

'It'd be easier for me if you came here because I'd have to bring the amplifier as well as the guitar.'

The arrangements were made and the boys parted company at Peter's front door. Alek desperately wanted to be good enough to join a group. His world seemed to have expanded in just one day.

When he got home Alek went up into his bedroom and counted his money, took half of it and went to find his dad. He was reading a book and looked up with a smile.

'Did you have a good afternoon?'

'It was great. We went to the park, played football with friends from school and had a laugh. Peter has a guitar too and I'm going over to his house tomorrow morning and we're going to play together.'

'I'm pleased you're making friends and music, at last. What's that for?'

Alek was holding out his money. 'I want us to have a telephone. You'll need one when you start work and I want to be able to ring Peter. I still have enough money left to buy some casual clothes so I'm hoping this'll be enough.'

'Thank you, Alek.'

He stood up. 'I'll go and organise it right now.'

He felt in his pocket for change and went out to the public phone box. Only ten minutes later he was back. Alek looked at him eyebrows raised.

'That's organised; BT is coming to connect our line tomorrow and all we have to do is buy a phone. I'll take

Mum and Rita into town tomorrow afternoon and do that. We have to pay line rental every month and then calls are on top. We definitely could not have afforded to do this before and we'll have to use it sparingly, until I get paid. Thanks again, Alek.'

Mum popped her head around the door and announced the meal was ready so, when they were all sitting at the table, Dad talked about the phone.

'Oh I'll be able to ring Sarah when I want to invite her and Ellen over. This is so exciting.'

Mum got up from her chair and gave Alek a hug. 'You're a star,' she said.

Chapter 13

Vjolica

September 20th

It's worked! Fitore has written inviting me to stay for a week's holiday. I'm to go next Friday. She seems to be very excited about my wedding and I'm pretending I'm looking forward to it. She thinks Erind is the love of my life! Yuk.

I'm still not sure what to do once I'm there. Should I tell Fitore the truth? How can I escape from her house? How can I contact the KLA to become a recruit? That should be easier in the centre of Pristina but I really don't know who I can trust. Before that I need Erind and M and D to allow me to go.

One step at a time.

September 21st

M and D are happy for me to have a holiday before I enter married life. Now I must ask permission from my husband-to-be, (he hopes).

Davud

Vjolica is going to have a holiday with Fitore. I'm really envious that she should have fun especially when she's the total centre of attention all the time at home. It's been all

112

wedding talk and now holiday talk. What shall she wear? What gift can she take to the family? I'm really sick of it. The only good thing is, when she's away we can see what it will feel like without her. For a start there will be more room and one less mouth to feed. On the down side, she gives Mum all of her wages and that will make it much harder for us.

It has just occurred to me that I might be expected to work. I hope I'm still too young at eleven.

Vjolica

Thursday 24th September

Erind agreed! How can he be so kind to me, when I'm such a bitch?

Anyway, there's no work today so I've had time to pack my case. I've put extra underwear in, my warm coat with a hood and gloves because I don't know where I'll be this winter. Mum has allowed me to keep my wages for last week to buy a nighty and some underwear for the wedding. I felt so guilty when I thanked her for it, knowing I had no intention of buying those things.

I've also got a large bag of fruit and vegetables that Erind bought me to give to Fitore's parents as a gift. I'm feeling guilty about hurting him too. Sometimes I think about just giving in and becoming his wife but then I feel really, physically, sick. I can't do it. We'll get to the wedding night and I'll be throwing up before he lays a hand on me!

So now I'm ready. I just have to stop writing and put this diary in the bag too. The next time I write I will have left home.

The last time Vjolica visited Fitore's house had been an emergency sleepover when her Granddad was attacked. She remembered feeling slightly superior because the apartment was smaller and their furniture shabby compared to hers. As she was welcomed in this time it seemed spacious, genteel and made her feel humble. Her own family was now much poorer than her friend's. The tables had turned.

Fitore fussed, with excitement, showing Vjolica where to sleep and where to hang her clothes. If she was surprised at the quantity her friend had packed she did not show it as she sat on the bed talking so quickly she hardly seemed to draw breath. 'I'll have to go to school whilst you're here and I wondered if you'd like to come and meet all your old friends again. I'm sure the teachers would be pleased to see you too.'

'I'd love to see everyone but my education stopped when I left school and I doubt if I'd be able to do the work.'

'You'll be fine. The only tricky lesson would probably be maths but you'll be able to sit with me and I'll help you.'

'In that case, I will. At least I can come for one day and if I feel too out of place I needn't go again.'

'Excellent.' Fitore suddenly lowered her voice to a whisper. 'I'm going to tell you something you mustn't mention to my parents. On Wednesday there's going to be a student protest march and I'm going to join it.'

'What's the protest about?'

'It's about Albanians being unable to attend university and the sacking of Albanian teachers and lecturers. We're being prevented from going on to higher education and it's not fair. We're all Kosovars and there should be no discrimination.'

'You're right but I don't see your parents letting you do this.'

'They know about the march but I've told them our age group are not involved. I didn't give them a letter from school saying that the upper school was going to close for the day so all the teachers and pupils could join the protest.'

Vjolica smiled in admiration for her friend's deceitfulness and bravery. 'So if I go to school with you I could join the protest too.'

'That'd be great. We're going to meet...........'

She stopped speaking as her mother pushed open the bedroom door to announce that lunch was ready.

They went into the dining room and ate soup with fresh bread and that was followed by deliciously sweet baclava.

'That was wonderful,' said Vjolica. 'If you keep feeding me like this I won't want to go home.'

Everyone laughed, pleased with her compliment. When the meal was over she insisted on helping her friend clear the plates and wash up. In the kitchen Fitore hugged her and said,

'I'm so pleased you could come. Now you must tell me all about Erind.'

Vjolica felt uncomfortable. Fitore had entrusted her with an enormous secret but she hesitated to tell the whole truth. 'I'm afraid it's not as rosy a picture as I painted in my letters. I knew your parents would want to hear all about it so I made it sound wonderful.'

'And it's not?' asked Fitore.

'No. Some of it was true but I missed out that he's a least forty-five, fat, doesn't wash often enough and I can't bear to be near him.' Her voice rose to a squeak. Fitore put her arms around her and they both cried.

'Why have your parents arranged this marriage when you must have said how you felt?'

'I don't know but it may be because he has a smart apartment and makes a good living out of the market stall.'

She blew her nose and then related her rude behaviour when Erind visited. Fitore looked aghast and laughed.

By this time, they had tidied the kitchen, and private conversation ceased as they joined Fitore's parents. They wanted to know all about the Red Cross clinic and how Davud was faring with his private tutor. This was safe ground and the conversation was enjoyable for everyone.

When they went to bed there was no opportunity to say more because they were in separate bedrooms.

The weekend passed quickly and Vjolica had to face going back to school. She had mixed feelings but the strongest one was nervousness. Would she be embarrassed being so far behind the others?

Vjolica

Fitore's House

At last, a chance to write in my diary. I'm having such a wonderful time here. They've made me so welcome and even going to school was better than I expected. The teachers were so helpful and I realised how much I'd missed girls of my own age to chat to. Most of them seemed to be full of admiration for me because I was working, betrothed, and so, an adult. That was difficult but I assured them I didn't feel grown up most of the time.

It was lovely to study different subjects, to realise how much there was in the world and how small and cramped my current life has become. My brain wanted to soar and capture every crumb of knowledge while I could. It made me even more determined <u>not</u> to be trapped into a life with

Erind, and the market stall, forever. He said he was going to phone me tomorrow to see how I was getting on. I hope he does, when I'm out.

Tomorrow is our BIG LIE day. We are going to school as usual and then setting off for the university to join the march. We should be safe because all our teachers are going with us. I don't know what'll happen when our parents find out!

The upper schoolgirls were divided into groups of ten with a teacher or parent supervising. They set off to walk towards the Velania district and after just half a mile they joined crowds, surging and it became difficult to stay together. It was only just gone nine in the morning but the Serbian police were everywhere, a threatening presence, truncheons in their hands, ready. Two young men were carrying a banner, 'Education for All'. Vjolica, a little taller than Fitore, saw them ahead and then watched, pressed by the crowd and helpless, as two policemen shoved their way through and beat them viscously. As the bloodied men collapsed the police tore up the banner shouting, 'Banners are forbidden. Banners are forbidden,' as if to justify their attack on the peaceful protesters.

'Did you see that? It was horrible. I've never seen anything like it. Oh look. People are coming out of their houses to help them.'

Vjolica watched, standing on tiptoes, as a man and a woman dragged an unconscious man to the safety of their home. When they came out to help the other one the police were there, bloody truncheons raised and they rained blows on the couple. This was too much for the crowd and several people rushed to help, putting themselves in the path of the police and pushing the couple, with their burden back into their house. Once the door was shut, everyone safe, Vjolica realised she had been holding her breath and let it out with a gasp.

'I'm not sure we're doing the right thing, Fitore. Maybe we should go back.'

There was no reply and when she looked behind and around, her friend was not there. 'Fitore, Fitore!' she shouted.

Fear welled up, making her breathless. She tried to go back but the crush of bodies around her was too great. She was propelled forward, alone amidst thousands. The mood of the crowd was calm, but determined. It was pointless to struggle against it so she allowed herself to be taken along, hoping to find Fitore, or other school friends, when they got there.

They arrived at Velania just before ten thirty, when the march was to begin. The police were a daunting sight, several hundred of them lined up supported by two armoured cars. There was even a helicopter circling overhead. The march could not proceed peacefully whilst the barrier of police stood there. What was going to happen?

Everyone was looking towards the police and a high-ranking officer get up onto a platform, with a megaphone in his hand, to address the crowd. A hush descended as he told them they had no chance of marching and had just thirty minutes to disperse. Vjolica looked around for an escape route, desperate to get away from the square. She saw no way out, but she did see Fitore. Her friend's face was white and tears were running down her face. Vjolica shoved through the people to get to her and they clung together.

'I was so scared when I saw you ahead of me and people pushed in front and then you'd gone.'

'I felt the same. I spoke to you and you weren't there. I'm so glad we've found each other. We must hold hands now so we don't get separated again. We've been told to disperse but nobody seems to be leaving.'

Suddenly, as if they were synchronised, students began to sit on the ground. Teachers and lecturers followed suit. Finally the only people standing were supporters and onlookers. This quiet action seemed to incense the police and the unfortunate ones at the front were beaten with truncheons then dragged out of the way so the police could move forwards.

Fitore and Vjolica were sat, terrified by the violence they were witnessing, but unable to see how they could escape out of the crowd. Then their fear was increased with the sound of the helicopter droning louder and louder, lower and lower, till at the last minute it pulled up after jettisoning some canisters. They burst amongst the people knocking some unconscious and tear gas exploded out. The noxious cloud drifted, encompassing everyone. The police had donned gas masks and watched to see if it would start the exodus. To make sure, more gas was fired from the armoured cars.

Vjolica's eyes burned, tears no relief. Her skin was scorched. She couldn't breathe. Her eyes tight shut, she could hear people screaming, crying, and moaning. Those at the back ran to find fresh air, water and safety. Those in the middle pushed and shoved blindly, trying to escape. Those slow to stand were trampled in the panic and the girls, stood, clinging together crying and gasping.

Chapter 14

September 1997

Fadil had been working for a year and another school summer holiday was nearly over. Rita was looking forward to changing schools and life was more comfortable than it had ever been.

The postman brought a letter from Donjeta and as Fadil read it quickly his eyes widened. Rita was watching him,

'What is it Dad? Who's written to you?'

'It's from Donjeta Kahshoven. Haven't heard from him for ages. Where's Mum? I think she'd like to hear this.'

Rita found Mum, making beds. She told her, Alek heard, and they all went into in the sitting room.

'Read it out then,' said Mum as she sat down.

Fadil began, but when he got to the part about Vjolica's engagement, there was so much noise, he had to stop reading.

'Engaged? How old is she?'

'She's about two years younger than me so that makes her fourteen or maybe just fifteen,' said Alek.

Mum smiled, 'Well England must be influencing me because that seems far too young. She should still be at school, not getting married.'

Everyone laughed because marrying young was not that unusual for Muslims in Kosovo.

'If you remember, dear, she had to stop going to school when they moved. She works in the market, so I suppose love must have blossomed as they worked together,' said Fadil.

'Was there any more in the letter Dad?'

Fadil read some more. 'Not really, Davud is improving on the violin and Vjolica is going to stay with her friend Fitore for a few days. They are all well. That's it.'

'Anyway it's good to hear from them. When you write back, perhaps you should give them our telephone number. The political situation seems to be getting worse and there is a lot of Serbian focus on Kosovo now.'

'Yes I will. We should also send a wedding present. If we were there we'd give money so I could send them Deutsche Marks. I'll write back tonight but we can wait a while before sending the money because the marriage doesn't take place until November.'

'Whilst we're all together,' said Alek, 'I need to tell you that I'm going to stop my paper round. I'll really miss having my own cash but I might be able to get a holiday job, like the grass cutting that pays so much better and doesn't have to be done early every morning.'

'Why now?' asked Rita.

'It won't be long before I have to take 'A' level exams and I want more time and energy to study.'

'It seems a sensible decision to me and I think now I should share some of my wages with both of you,' said Dad

Rita sat up tall. 'All my friends get pocket money. Is that what you mean?'

Dad nodded. 'I cannot give, without something in return, so you will, in effect be earning it.'

She slumped back into her chair. 'I knew there'd be a catch.'

'Rita don't be rude, especially when your father's offering to give you some money.'

She made a face that negated her apology but Mum let it go, not wanting to spoil Fadil's generous moment.

Dad went on. ' I thought a reasonable amount for Rita would be £5 to be given every Saturday morning. In return she must, willingly, help her mother as required, particularly the ironing.'

He looked at her expectantly and was not disappointed. She went over to him and gave him a hug, 'Thank you. I've never had any money of my own before.'

'I'm not sure what the going rate for you would be, Alek, but for now I'll give you £10. In return for that you must keep the garden tidy during the growing season and clean the car every week.'

'Brilliant, thanks Dad. I'll tell the shop I'm finishing at the end of the month and that'll give them time to find someone else.'

'Aren't you forgetting something? What about the Christmas gifts you got last year? You got chocolates and money. Wouldn't it be better to stop after Christmas?'

Alek conceded Dad had a good point but he thought he would tell the shop anyway so they could advertise for someone.

Christmas 1997 was to be exciting for Alek. The drama department at school normally put on a show but they wanted something different. They consulted with the music teachers and decided to do a concert of short sketches with musical acts in between.

Peter was asked to work at filling two ten-minute slots with his group and they could choose what to play. It was the first time they had performed to an audience and it was nerve wracking.

Mrs Hurst, who taught French and helped Mr Newsome with music, ran the school choir, and Rita was going to sing in that, so Fadil and Marigana were looking forward to it.

Peter's group normally rehearsed once a week, in the music room, at lunchtime. Mr Newsome helped by playing keyboard and arranging music. They were hoping to find another student good enough to take over keyboard. There were only three members so far, Peter on bass guitar, Alek acoustic guitar, usually picking out the melody, or strumming and singing. Then there was Sam, short for Samantha, on drums.

Now, faced with a concert, they needed to meet more often so Mr Newsome said they could play after school, until he was ready to go home.

The first problem was what pieces to play. Peter thought of doing all the Christmas hits but they had never played any of them and felt it would be too much to learn. Mr Newsome agreed and suggested their first slot should be three pieces they knew well already, to give them confidence. Peter was designated to think of something to say in between each piece.

'What about the second slot, right at the end?' asked Sam. 'It should be something really loud and lively.'

'I like Whigfield's 'Saturday Night' and we're performing on a Saturday night,' said Alek.

'That's a great idea,' said Mr Newsome. 'I'll get hold of the sheet music and put the idea to the other members of staff to make it a big finish number. Everyone who has performed coming on stage and joining in singing or dancing.

'No pressure then,' said Peter, and they all laughed.

They did feel under pressure and whilst waiting for the music to arrive they worked hard on the other pieces. The Dhomi family were soon humming melodies to themselves that they heard Alek playing, over and over again. Then Rita began singing Saturday night along with Alek playing so they knew that too.

'We don't need to go to the concert. We've heard it all already,' said Dad, a twinkle in his eye.

'Oh you have to come Dad,' said Rita. Once you get the drums and everyone singing it's brill.'

Despite Rita's confidence Fadil and Marigana settled onto the upright school chairs feeling apprehensive for both their children. Rita had been in little concerts at her primary school but the audience that night was huge in comparison. Would she cope when she saw the sea of faces?

The choir opened the show. They sang some popular Christmas songs and Rita looked tiny on the front row but she never took her eyes off the conductor and sang with a face shining with enjoyment. Marigana felt her eyes pricking with tears and as they clapped at the end she saw Fadil was similarly moved.

A sketch followed that was very funny; everyone applauded enthusiastically and then Peter's group took up their positions. Alek had never felt so nervous but once they began to play he concentrated and relaxed.

After the first number Peter announced what they had just played and what they were going to play next.

After the second piece he addressed the audience again.

'Thank you everyone. Before our last piece in this half, I want your help. We are such a new group we have yet to decide on a name. This is where you come in. I've put some pieces of paper and pencils in the entrance. Please write your suggestions for a name for us. If you put your name and telephone number there would be a small prize for the one chosen.'

The audience reacted well, despite the slightly shocking volume of the last rock piece and then it was the interval. In the classrooms close to the hall there were soft drinks for the students. They were so excited, but still tense because they all had to perform again in the second half.

This time the choir sang some Negro spiritual songs ending with a happy one where they clapped and moved and the audience took up the beat and joined in. The sketch followed and then it was the group's last appearance and the finale.

As they began to play Saturday Night the choir came in behind them and joined in followed by the actors who danced. The audience began tapping their feet and then clapping along and it was exhilarating for everyone on the stage. The applause went on and on and when they eventually left the stage to pack up to go home the mood was euphoric.

Peter remembered to collect the papers from the entrance hall and was pleased to see a lot of different suggestions.

The Dhomi family went home and celebrated the end of a lovely evening with hot drinks and biscuits.

'I'm too excited to go to bed,' said Rita, yawning.

'Well I think you'll find when your head touches the pillow you will sleep. It's very late,' said Mum.

They went upstairs and Dad looked at Alek. 'I was impressed by your group and was wondering if you could find other places to perform.'

'Like a club?'

'Yes. I think the phrase is, 'do a gig'.'

Alek laughed. 'It's the right word but I think we've a long way to go before we're ready for that. We need a much bigger repertoire and a keyboard player. I can't see Mr Newsome wanting to play at a club. I think I'll go to bed now. Paper round in the morning but it's the last one. Night Dad.'

Alek went upstairs as Mum came down and Fadil heard them murmuring their goodnights. Mum came into the living room, sank onto the settee and put her feet up with a contented sigh. 'We are so lucky,' she said. 'Two lovely, talented children, enough money to even contemplate a holiday next year and we are safe. I can honestly say I'm happy. Thank you dear for getting us away from Kosovo when you did.'

Chapter 15

Kosovo

Erind was missing Vjolica. She brightened his day even when she seemed quiet and withdrawn. She was soon to be his bride and he constantly imagined her naked body laying on his bed waiting for him. He saw her response to him, willing but nervous. He would tell her not to worry. He'd be gentle, take it slowly. He'd caress her silken skin, cup and kiss her soft..............

'I'll take over now Erind if you want to make that call.'

He snapped out of his dream, left the market manager in charge of his stall and went to the office to phone the Bardici house. When someone answered he said, 'This is Erind, Vjolica's fiancée. Are you Mr Bardici?'

'Yes. I expect you want to speak to her but I'm sorry, Erind, she's at school with Fitore.'

'But I thought all the schools were closed today because of the student demonstration.'

'No, Fitore said only the oldest children were going and she could still go to school.'

'I'm worried, Mr Bardici. Are you sure they didn't go to the march? The radio said all schools were closed.'

'We didn't listen to the radio. I'll go to the school right now, check, and ring you back.'

'No don't ring me back because I'm going to see for myself. If they're not there I'm going to search for them.'

He made arrangements with the market manager and drove to the school. From the van he could see the gates were padlocked. He fought the rising panic, parked and began to run towards the Velania district.

Before he could see the crowd he could hear moaning, and crying. He ran faster but had to slow to a walk as people with streaming eyes, coughing and wheezing pushed blindly past him. There was a chemical, acrid smell and his eyes began to smart. Was he being stupid? Should he go back? No Vjolica might be trapped, gassed, terrified. He had to go on. His throat hurt and he fumbled for a handkerchief holding it over his nose and mouth.

The street opened out into a square flanked by tall houses. Most of the demonstrators were helpless, hunched over as they fought for breath or staggering blindly to find a way out. He stood tall to see above them trying to keep calm as all around him were crying, groaning or whimpering. At the end of the square was a broad road. Armoured cars, dozens of policemen wearing gas masks and holding riot shields, blocked it. They were treating the people laying or sitting near them very roughly, pulling them to their feet or dragging them to one side.

'Help me please, help me I can't see!'

It was a young woman, possibly a friend of Vjolica's. 'Here hold my hand. I'll guide you. Do you know a girl about your age called Vjolica?'

'Yes, she was in our group but we all got separated by the crowd.'

He pulled her along as fast as he could and then stopped when the air seemed fresher. 'You're going away from the gas now. Keep going straight down this street. I must leave you and find her.'

She moved slowly forward feeling her way along the wall of a building and he ran back to the crowd. In just those few moments the violence had escalated. He could hear the sickening crack of metal truncheons on unprotected heads. The moans and wails became screams. Most of the people were male, students and teachers but he could see several women, conspicuous by their headscarves. He thought he saw Vjolica's favourite green one. Now he became less gentle and considerate, thrusting his way towards the flash of green. No, please. Don't hurt them. A policeman was close to her. He seemed to be as intent as Erind was to reach her but the policeman got there first. He raised his truncheon but it was the girl next to her who was hit. Was it Fitore? Erind was close. He could hear Vjolica. 'Fitore! No. Don't you hit her again.'

She jumped upon the policeman's back. He swung round, yanked her hands from around his neck and as she fell he raised his truncheon. Erind threw himself at the policeman. His breath was rasping but he put all his strength behind a punch to the stomach. The man doubled over. Erind grabbed his gas mask and pulled it off. 'Let's see how you like it you bully!'

He raised his fist again.

'Erind, look out!'

More policemen turned their attention onto him. No one got away with attacking one of their own. When Erind collapsed to the ground from blows to his head and abdomen they kicked and stamped with their steel capped boots.

A kind couple, damp cloths over their faces, tried to pull the girls into the safety of their home.

'No, no, please help him. Erind!'

Vjolica pulled away from them and hurled herself at the legs of the nearest policeman. He fell heavily to the ground, lashing out at her, but she rolled away. The man who had taken Fitore into his home now picked Vjolica up and carried her away from the fight. She was too dazed to argue as he kicked the door shut behind them and gently lowered her into a chair.

'Are you hurt, let me see.' said a gentle female voice. Fitore allowed her headscarf to be removed.

The woman tutted, 'You will live my dear. Hold this cool cloth to your eyes and I will bathe your cuts.

Fitore tried to do as she was told but realised there was something wrong. 'I can't move my hand.'

The woman slid the sleeve back to reveal a red, swollen arm oddly shaped just above the wrist. 'You poor thing you must be in agony.'

'My eyes hurt more. I can't really feel my arm. Is it broken?'

'Erind. I must go to him. Please help me.'

Vjolica threw down the damp cloth she had been holding over her eyes, forced them open and started for the door.

'No, please. It's not safe!'

Hearing her shout, the woman's husband came and blocked the door. 'I can't let you go out. Let me look and see if I can help the man.'

'It's not just a man it's Erind, my fiancée.'

'Go back into the room and I will try.'

She allowed herself to be led back but was too agitated to sit down. Her own discomfort, Fitore's injuries meant nothing. Erind had tried to save her. They'd beaten him. He fell. She could still hear the thud of their boots on his body.

Was he outside the door writhing in agony, calling for her? Was he unconscious? Was he dead?

Whilst Vjolica wallowed in misery and fear, Fitore was able to give her phone number to the gentle woman.

'I will leave you for a moment and telephone your father.'

When she had gone Fitore struggled to her feet, cradling her arm. It was throbbing now and she felt sick. She went to Vjolica and leant against her. Vjolica put her arms gently round her friend and they both sobbed. They didn't hear the woman come back.

'Your father is coming.'

The girls moved away from each other and Fitore sank onto a chair again. 'Thank you for all you've done for us.'

There was no reply because a shout from her husband caused her and Vjolica to rush to the door. 'I've found him but he's unconscious and I can't move him on my own. He's too heavy.'

Before he had finished speaking Vjolica flew out of the door. The square was almost empty, no police nearby and there he was, curled up on his side, his head in a pool of blood. Vjolica dragged off her scarf and tried to wrap it round his head calling his name. The man and woman both came to her and he knelt and felt for a pulse. He was still for a long time and then said gently.

'There's no pulse. I'm so sorry.'

'No! Erind, oh Erind; Please, forgive me.'

She laid her head upon Erind's lifeless body, heaving with distress. But they had made too much noise and attracted the attention of a policeman. He was striding towards them and beckoned to another as the couple pulled Vjolica away. 'The police. Quick. We must go in.

Once inside the door was bolted. 'We can do no more now. Fitore's father will be here soon to collect you. I've explained your injuries and he's going to take you straight to the Red Cross clinic.'

'Thank you. My friend Vjolica's parents work there.'

'She is only suffering from the tear gas and shock but she looks much worse.' The woman turned to Vjolica. 'Come my dear, let me clean you up before your parents see you.'

Erind's blood was soon washed off her hands and arms but there was nothing they could do with her clothes.

Moments later Mr Bardici arrived and both girls were helped into his van. The area had cleared of people, the police had gone but it was littered with rubbish. Vjolica forced her eyes open, searching for Erind but his body was gone.

The clinic was inundated with patients suffering from the effects of gas and beatings. Ajeshe was assessing them outside, sending home those just suffering from the gas, assuring them the effects would soon go. There was nothing they could do for bruises but gashes were sewn and bandaged and people with broken limbs were being given painkillers whilst they waited. She was exhausted but driven on by the desperate need.

Her efficiency collapsed when she recognised her daughter's, tear streaked face and blood stained clothes. Fitore was silent, ashen with pain. All other patients were ignored as she rushed to take them into the clinic. 'Donjeta, quick it's Vjolica.'

He rushed to her side and she collapsed into his arms, crying and, between sobs, she told him about Erind's heroism.

'Erind's dead? I can't believe it. He died saving you and Fitore.'

As he said the name he turned to look at her, just as she fainted, caught by her own father before she hit the floor. 'Poor girl let's set that arm. She must have been in agony.'

When Fitore was ready to go home Donjeta thanked her father. 'I'm so grateful to you for collecting the girls. I can't understand what made them lie to you and join that demonstration, but I think we both owe Erind our deepest thanks. If he hadn't rushed to save them we might have been looking for our daughters in the morgue.'

Mr Bardici nodded. 'He was a hero. I don't know what's happened to his body. The police will deny it if we ask and we may suffer the consequences. I don't think there's anything we can do. We both have families to look after.'

Donjeta nodded and waved as they drove away.

Vjolica was calmer when he saw her next and only her blotchy face and puffy eyes showed the effects of tear gas and guilt stricken grief.

'I'm sorry but Mum and I cannot take you home yet, because there are still so many patients to see. I'm afraid you'll need to wait for us.'

'It doesn't matter. I'll help. I'm sure I can make tea or sort out the gassed people from those with other injuries.'

'Well if you are not too exhausted............'

'I need to do it. If I just sit doing nothing I'll think about it all.'

She stood up and went outside where the queue was considerably less. The first patient she saw was a friend from school with severe teargas effects. She had been vomiting but when she saw Vjolica she said she felt better. They spoke briefly about the horror of their experience, hugged, and she went home.

Vjolica moved on to the next patient and within an hour there was no queue. Mum and Dad walked her home without talking, but the silence was broken, by her sobbing. What could anyone say to ease the burden of such guilt, shock and loss?

Davud

Grandma and I had heard about the student demonstration on the radio so we did not expect Mum and Dad to come home on time. When they did come in, Vjolica was with them. Her face was swollen, her clothes covered in blood and I jumped up to help her. We thought she was safe with the Bardici family and were horrified to hear her story.

Poor Erind. Poor Vjolica. I know she couldn't love him but he didn't deserve to die so violently. Grandma was shaken too. She went very white and had to have her inhaler. I think it made her think of Granddad being beaten. I made cups of tea for everyone and then started to cook the meal. It was much later than we usually ate and I was starving. There was salad and I boiled some potatoes and looked around for something else. Eggs. There were five so I hard-boiled them too. It was not a feast but it would do. Mum came out to help. 'Well done Davud. It's been a day we'll never forget and I needed that tea and a sit down before starting the meal. Now there is nothing for me to do except lay the table.'

We sat down to eat but it was not a comfortable meal. Vjolica had a couple of mouthfuls, said she felt sick, and just got to the bathroom in time. Mum jumped up to help her and we all put our cutlery down as we heard the sound of vomiting.

Vjolica was helped to bed with a glass of water to ease her sore throat. We tried to continue the meal but the sound of her crying made it almost impossible. Dad managed to finish his but the rest of us gave up and Mum cleared away the plates. After that we all went to bed, exhausted and anxious.

Vjolica

October 2nd

I can't believe Erind is dead. I've stopped crying at the moment but my eyes still feel raw. I want to see Fitore more than anything.

What's going to happen now? I can't go back to the market. They'll all blame me. Did he have any brothers or sisters? What will they do with his stall and stock? What will happen to all his things, his house, his furniture and his clothes? So many questions and I'm so tired. I couldn't sleep last night and Dad gave me a sleeping pill at two in the morning! It's nearly time to get up and for everyone else it's business as usual. Davud will go to Mr Dushku, Mum and Dad will go to the clinic and I suppose I'll stay here with Grandma.

I wanted to get out of marrying Erind. I was prepared to run away from everyone I love to prevent the marriage, but I never wanted him hurt or killed. He was a good man.

Crying again now; must stop writing.

Davud

Vjolica looked a little better this morning. Dad said he would ring Mr Bardici to see how Fitore was and to ask if he and Vjolica could go to their house to collect her clothes.

She was really pleased at that. My day was to be as usual, lessons with Mr Dushku.

I suppose I feel a mixture of jealousy and sympathy with my sister. She has been through an awful experience and could have been killed, but still she gets all the attention. It will lessen now I suppose. There will be no wedding. Am I a really bad person for thinking like this?

Chapter 16

Leeds

It was just after the New Year celebration that a letter came from Donjeta Kahshoven. It was a cold, wet Saturday morning so the family were all in. Mum was ironing, watching the morning cooking programme on television and Rita was curled up reading a book. Alek was upstairs playing his guitar and Fadil had been reading the newspaper.

'Alek, we've had a letter from Donjeta. Do you want to come down and hear it?'

'Be right down.'

Mum turned the television off and when Alek was settled Dad began reading.

'Dear Fadil, Marigana, Alek and Rita,

I must begin by apologising for not writing sooner, especially as you sent Vjolica such a generous gift. Your gift could not be used as intended because there was no wedding.

'Oh no. Whatever could've happened?'

Fadil looked over his glasses at Rita and said, 'If you're a little more patient I expect we'll find out.' He continued to read,

On the 1st of October there was a student demonstration and Vjolica was staying with her friend Fitore at that time. They pretended they were going to school and then went to the demonstration............

He stopped reading and looked up. Everyone's eyes were on him, expectantly.

'I'm not reading the rest out loud because the details are far too upsetting. I will just tell you that Erind was killed.

'What about Vjolica and Fitore?' asked Marigana.

Fadil finished reading the letter, and then explained.

'Poor Vjolica,' said Rita. How awful for her fiancé to die saving her life.'

The mood of the family now matched the weather; the rain on the windows dripped down like tears.

'It's certainly not an easy letter to answer,' said Fadil with a sigh. He decided to wait whilst he thought about it.

About a week later he wrote, pleading with them to leave, and sending some money to help with the journey.

As the year progressed Kosovo, whilst not making the headlines, appeared more frequently in the newspapers.

Fadil read out an excerpt he'd read, *'US diplomat Robert Gelbard publicly calls KLA, 'Without question a terrorist group......'*

'Oh that's so unfair,' said Marigana, 'There would've been no need for the KLA if the Serbs had not been so greedy and aggressive.'

He nodded, 'That statement is also really dangerous, you know. It lends support to Slobodan Milosevic, encouraging him to proceed against Kosovo and the KLA.'

'It's also disappointing to think that the Americans seem ignorant about the ethnic cleansing that's been going on for so long,' said Marigana. 'Atrocities are continuously happening, against our people, and I worry about Ajshe and Donjeta.'

'So do I but there's nothing we can do about it, just read the papers, listen to the news and wait.'

Alek, Peter and Sam were arguing about the name they should choose for their group. There had been about twenty suggestions and they were now down to four.

'Perhaps we should put them into a hat and agree to go with whatever one comes out,' said Sam. She was twiddling strands of shaggy black hair, a habit she resorted to when agitated or bored. At the moment she was afflicted with the latter. Her suggestion was met with silence.

'I take it you don't like that idea. Well I'll tell you what. I'm going home now and then it's up to you two. I really don't care a shit.'

She stormed out of the music room and the boys grinned at each other.

'Let's look at them again,' said Peter. 'Rockin' Rebels, Max Mix, The Scorchers, Pete's Pizzazz. I'm not sure about Rockin' Rebels because we're not really bucking the establishment are we?'

'No, I agree that's one less.'

Alek screwed up the slip of paper and dropped it in the bin. 'I don't really like The Scorchers. I know it implies we're hot but we play a real mix of things, not all loud, rock numbers.'

'Ok, so that leaves just two. Well you said we play a real mixture of styles so what about Max Mix?'

'It's not bad but I think I prefer Pete's Pizzazz. I looked it up and pizzazz means we play with style and I like the alliteration. I suspect you wouldn't pick that because it has your name but why not? The group was your idea.'

'You're right, I was reluctant to pick that one, but I do like it.'

Davud screwed up all the slips and said, 'That's agreed then. We can tell Sam tomorrow.'

At that moment Mr Newsome came in. He frowned when he saw them. 'I was just coming to collect my bag to go home. Don't you have homes to go to?'

'Yes sir, but we've been trying to decide which name we liked best for our group and we've finally agreed. It's 'Pete's Pizzazz'. What do you think?'

'Great name. Right get off home.'

They left the music room together and Alek said, 'I've had an idea about finding someone to join us playing keyboard. Why don't we send a letter to the music departments of all the schools in Leeds? Now we have a name it sounds like we're established and it might encourage someone to come forward.'

'That's brilliant! I'll write it this weekend.'

They parted to go home and Alek felt almost high with excitement. He knew it was unlikely he could have a career in music but he loved it.

A career was very much on his mind because he had applied to several Universities and had two interviews to face in the next few weeks. He wanted to be an architect and was soon to sit 'A' level exams in Maths, Physics and Art and Design. His first interview was at Leeds Beckett University and a few weeks after that he had one in Bath. He was torn between wanting to stand on his own feet, a long way from home, or staying local, where he could save money by living at home. If Peter and Sam stayed around they could continue playing together. He felt the chances of this were unlikely.

Peter wanted to be a teacher and hoped to teach maths with music as a second subject. He had also applied to Leeds University and had an interview pending and others in Wakefield and Liverpool. Both boys felt they were reaching an important milestone and were anxious to do well.

It was early February when Peter arrived at school, found Alek and showed him a letter. 'It's from a lad called Mark, reckons he'd like to join us.'

Alek read it. 'He's got Grade seven on the piano and has his own keyboard. He could be good. The only problem is where to meet and practice with him. We always play at school and I don't know if he could get here between four and five.'

'Finding somewhere else to practice would be difficult. He's given us his number so I'll ring him tonight.'

When school was over Alek told Dad about Mark, and the difficulty of practising together.

'I think the neighbours would have something to say, if you played here,' said Fadil, smiling. 'But I do have an idea where you could play. The surgery has a basement. It's used for storage. There are shelves all around but there's plenty of room. I would think, being below ground, you could make plenty of noise. Leave it with me and I'll ask. How many times a week would you want it? Don't forget you need study time.'

'That sounds brill' Dad. Twice would be good but once would be better than nothing.'

Within a week they had a practise room and permission to leave the drum kit. The room had a lock and Alek was entrusted with a key. They could only use the room during surgery hours so they chose Saturday mornings and a Wednesday after school from 4.30 until 6.00.

The first day they all met there, was an icy Saturday, towards the end of February. They agreed to meet outside the surgery and Alek arrived first, quickly followed by Sam. She was all hunched up in a parka with a fur hood and had been dropped off, with all her kit, music stands and music, by her Mum.

They chatted and shivered, waiting for Peter, but it was Mark who came first. They saw an overweight, tall, black lad coming towards them carrying an enormous case with considerable ease but had no idea who he was until he stopped in front of them. 'Hi, I'm Mark. Are you Peter?'

'No I'm Alek, acoustic guitar and this is Sam, drums, as you can see. Oh and that's Peter coming now.'

Peter was running lop-sidedly down the street his guitar case clenched in one hand and an amplifier weighing him down on the other.

'Phew. It's further than I thought. I walked from the bus station.' His breath was coming in steamy gasps as he turned to Mark. Introductions were quickly made and they trouped, thankfully, into the warmth of the surgery. Alek led the way to the stairs and they all descended into a chillier atmosphere. As he put the key into the lock he said, apologising, 'I didn't realise the basement wasn't heated.'

'We'll create our own heat when we start playing;' said Sam, 'and we can keep our coats on. This looks great. Where are the plugs?'

It took a while to get set up with the amplifier, keyboard and drum kit. Then Alek realised they had no chairs and went upstairs to ask if there were any spare ones they could have. As he returned with some folding ones, he opened the door to the stairs and heard the others playing. It had been almost inaudible until he opened the door so they really could let it rip. He felt a thrill of excitement as he heard the keyboard. Mark was good.

When everyone was seated they sorted out some of the pieces they knew well and gave Mark his music. He looked at it all, carefully, nodded and said, 'I'll have to practise some of this but a lot of it I can sight read.'

Peter chose the one with the simplest keyboard part and they got started. When it was done Sam whooped and Alek clapped Mark on the shoulder. 'That was brill; welcome to Pete's Pizzazz!'

At the end of the practise they packed their instruments away whilst Sam covered her drums to keep them clean.

'Mark looked at them all, grinned, and said, 'We're quite politically correct aren't we. I was born here but my parents come from Ghana, and Alek you're not English are you?'

'No I'm from Kosovo and I'm a Muslim, so we do make an interesting group. As far as I know Sam and Peter are English.'

Sam's head snapped up. 'Not so, Alek, I'm Welsh and proud of it.'

'You've not got a very Welsh name; shouldn't you be called Myfanwey or Bronwen?' Peter's voice lilted in the Welsh way and he waited for the explosion.

'Go to Hell!'

Everyone laughed, including Sam, and they left the surgery, looking forward to their next practise.

Alek arrived home to find Mum and Rita arguing. He was not surprised. Rita was almost a teenager, suffering from mild acne and pleased and embarrassed that she was developing breasts. Marigana had to keep reminding her now that Muslim women did not wear short skirts and she could not follow the fashion trends favoured by her friends at school. Whilst understanding the reasons for this, Rita objected, frequently. 'I don't want to be different to everyone else. I want to be accepted Mum.'

Marigana sighed. 'You make it sound as if you're the only Muslim girl in your class and I know that's not true. What you're really concerned about is Ellen. When I see the way she dresses I'm surprised Sarah allows it. She dresses like a much older girl, and, being tall, she could pass for fifteen or sixteen easily, when not in her school uniform. I find it quite shocking.'

They both looked up as Alek entered and Mum was relieved when he launched into a description of Mark and how well the practise went.

A few months later another letter arrived from the Kahshoven family.

Chapter 17

Davud

It seems the whole world has reacted to the student demonstration. The United States and the European Union condemned the violence and said they held President Milosevic responsible. Something positive had come out of that disaster. Perhaps we were not alone after all, but if these powers were going to help when would they get involved? How many more innocent people had to die whilst the politicians discussed the Kosovo crisis? Whilst I was thinking of this, Grandma brought in a tray and I jumped up to take it from her. She shook quite a bit and keeping the tea in the cups was a problem.

'So, Vjolica,' said Dad. 'You need a job to get you out of Grandma's hair and we need you to earn some money. I suppose you wouldn't want to go back to the market?'

'I know I should go and see everyone there but it will be hard. They will all know about Erind and will be sympathetic. It makes me cry when people are kind but I'll go tomorrow.'

Dad stood up and touched her shoulder. 'That's brave and just the right thing to do. I'm proud of you.'

Vjolica

Tuesday 4th November

I did it. I went to the market and faced everyone. They were lovely to me, so very kind. Of course I cried but it didn't seem to matter. I feel so guilty that everyone assumes I was in love with Erind. Anyway I saw that his stall was still closed and I asked why it hadn't been taken over by anyone.

'We were waiting for you to come back Vjolica. Erind had no other relatives so there is no one to run it or officially close it. We all felt you should have it.'

I had to write those words down, just as she said them, because it was so wonderful and generous. The manager could so easily have offered it out, but she waited, for me. I'm crying now as I write this. Erind loved me and would have wanted me to have it; so his stall was now mine.

I opened it straight away and customers were so pleased to see me and to have it up and running again. Pristina is a big city but the area we live in is like an Albanian village within it.

It's only just occurring to me that I no longer get a wage at the end of the week. I must buy new stock, keep careful records and only take the money that's left over. The more I sell the more I'll make. I feel excited, and a bit overwhelmed, with the responsibility.

M, D and everyone were pleased for me, and probably relieved too, because I will be contributing to our housekeeping money again.

I wonder what happened to Erind's apartment? Everyone rents, so I suppose the landlord will simply let it again, after helping himself to Erind's personal possessions.

That was a mean thought. He might give stuff away to the poor. Ha Ha.

It's time to stop writing when I'm being so cynical!

Davud

I try to live in the present. If I spend time thinking of how things were, before the chaos we are in now, it makes me sad and resentful. But at this moment I'm looking back with relief.

Vjolica had no time to think, being so busy running her own business. She seemed happier than I'd seen her for a long time.

Dad and Mum were also run off their feet, with so many casualties coming in, as the KLA stepped up its skirmishes against the Serbs.

Mr Dushku's friend and carer, was one of those. He suffered multiple gun shot wounds and it was uncertain he would live, but he did. His left hand was such a mess it couldn't be saved. Another bullet had smashed his knee, so he walked with a strange, hop-along gait.

Mr Dushku was really upset, at first, but his friend's misfortune had a brighter side. A disability like that meant he couldn't fight again, so he was safe; well, as safe as anyone here. Their relationship changed and they now looked after each other.

Another letter from Mr Dhomi made us all think very carefully about our current life.

Dear Donjeta, Ajeshe, Vjolica and Davud,

I cannot tell you how sad we were to hear your news, so soon after hearing about Vjolic's engagement. I hope the pain will lessen with the passing of time.

England is proving to be everything we had hoped. There is a wonderful health service and you only pay for prescriptions. Children and the elderly get those free too! There are plenty of restrictions for immigrants but you are given money to survive until you can apply for a job.

The general standard of living is far higher than we aspired to in Kosovo. I have been in full time employment for less than a year but I have been able to buy a TV, radio and cassette player, second hand car and am now saving for a computer. The children use computers in school and having one at home will help them.

This is <u>not</u> a boasting exercise. I have written this to try my hardest to persuade you to leave Kosovo <u>now</u>. It is obviously a dangerous place and not good for a family to grow up in.

I have enclosed some Deutsche marks because they are acceptable currency everywhere in Europe. I know you still have the money I sent for Vjolica's wedding. But, in the light of what has happened, and may still happen, you could need it.

If you do decide to leave, and money becomes a problem, you have my number so ring me and I will find a way to help.

Please come. We worry about you constantly,

Your true friend,

Fadil

Dad finished reading and counted the money. 'A very generous amount! How do you all feel?'

Nobody rushed to answer so he turned to Vjolica. 'You have experienced violence first hand. Do you want to leave Kosovo?'

Her reaction was not helpful. 'I don't know. Can you start with Davud?'

Dad looked at me eyebrows raised.

'I don't know either. I'm very happy being taught by Mr Dushku but I miss playing football, and having friends of my own age, like I did at school. I'm scared of leaving but Mr Dhomi makes England sound good. I'd like a television and you could have a car again Dad.'

'That sounds like a yes vote. Ajeshe?'

'I feel the same as Davud. I enjoy working at the clinic, but what happened to Vjolica and Fitore really scared me. You, and our children, are everything to me and I can be happy anywhere, with all of you.'

'So that's another yes vote. Grandma?'

'I'm sorry Donjeta I'm too old to start a new life. You've all been wonderful to me since I've been a widow but I don't want to die in a strange country.'

Dad nodded, but frowned. I felt he was annoyed with her. If Grandma refused to move how could we leave her? She couldn't cope on her own.

'What about you Dad?' I asked.

'I could pack and leave tomorrow because, like Mum said, you are all the people I love and I want to protect you from harm. I feel we should go, but I'm aware that Grandma can't leave, and we can't leave her. I think we will save these Deutsch Marks, just in case we are forced to flee, but for now we'll stay put.'

'You mean you'll wait until I'm dead. I'll try not to linger too long.'

Grandma heaved herself out of her chair and muttered something about making a cup of tea. When she had gone into the kitchen there was a moment of silence. We all felt upset. There was nothing we could say to make her feel better.

Vjolica stood up. 'I haven't had my say and I want to now. What happened to Erind was the cruellest thing I've ever seen, and a war would be worse. England seems to be a stable place and Mr Dhomi does make it sound good. I'm enjoying running the stall, but things are getting more dangerous here. I vote yes.'

'Thank you dear. So we're all agreed, in principle, which makes it easier when the time comes. I'll write back to Fadil and explain our position. I'll assure him that should our circumstances change, we will leave for England.'

Since that discussion I thought a lot about leaving and going to England and, I am ashamed to say, I looked at Grandma to see if she was getting worse. She slept more during the day, but, apart from that, she still managed to help at home. Her breathing became more laboured and her angina pain more frequent, but she just used her inhaler and carried on. I really loved her, but I was getting scared. I saw people everywhere with injuries inflicted by the Serb police or accidentally caught in the cross fire of a KLA attack. It could happen to anyone of my family as they went to work or to shop. Nowhere in Kosovo was safe.

I needed something to take my mind off the situation and Vjolica came to my rescue. 'Davud I'm run off my feet at the weekends. Would you come and give me a hand?'

I was really surprised, but pleased, she thought me capable. 'Yes. Will I have to serve customers?'

'Not straight away but you can do lots of other tasks, like restocking and making tea. Sometimes I go all day without a hot drink because it's so busy.'

The following day I woke feeling excited. My life was quite restricted, confined to Mr Dushku's house and our own. Today it would be different.

'Hurry Davud', called Vjolica, 'It's nearly time to go and you haven't eaten.'

I gobbled my breakfast, amused to see Mum frown at my table manners, and followed my sister out.

When we got to the market, Vjolica introduced me to the Manager and some of the other stallholders. Everyone made me welcome, and by the afternoon, I was general tea boy. Vjolica reminded me she had started like that, and was happy for me to help the others too. By the end of the day I ached with exhaustion.

Vjolica laughed. 'If you did this everyday you'd be a lot fitter and would soon get used to it.'

She tucked my arm into hers as we walked home but when we entered the apartment block she stopped, before we got to our front door. 'Here. You've earned this.'

She handed me two Deutsch Marks. 'Thank you. I didn't expect to be paid.'

'It's not much Davud but I keep a little for myself and the rest I give to Mum for housekeeping.'

'Can I show Mum and Dad?'

'Of course you can. It's not a secret.'

We went in and I proudly showed them my first wage, ever.

'Did he really earn that money?' asked Dad.

'If you look at him I think you'll see he did.'

Everyone laughed because I was yawning, slumped on a dining room chair, almost asleep.

After the evening meal I felt better and asked Vjolica if I was to come regularly when not at school.

'I'd be pleased if you did Davud. It made a big difference having you there and I had some kind remarks from some of the other stall holders about you.'

I grinned, 'What did they say?'

'Oh, Just things like you were willing to help and worked hard.'

She made a wry face. 'I was quite proud of you.'

My grin stretched from ear to ear.

'That's enough praise, Vjolica,' said Dad. 'He'll get a big head.'

We all laughed and I went to bed, exhausted, but happy. The prospect of a war was momentarily forgotten.

Chapter 18

Leeds

In April they had a letter from Donjeta Kahshoven. Fadil decided not to read it out to the family, waiting until Rita was asleep and Alek out before showing it to Marigana.

'You've kept that hidden all day. Why didn't you read it out loud like you usually do?' she asked.

'I just felt it might contain something unpleasant and the children don't need to be shocked by what they hear. We can then tell them or read it out tomorrow if it's ok.'

He tore open the envelope and took out a couple of sheets of writing paper and began,

March 10th 1998

Dear Fadil, Marigana, Alek and Rita,

I hope you are all well and Allah continues to bless you with good fortune.

Our house has been a happier one since Vjolica took on a job that takes all her energy, leaving her no time to dwell on the loss of her fiancé. The clinic has kept Ajeshe and me very busy, dealing with gunshot wounds and injuries from explosions, as well as the usual ailments.

I expect you know by now about the Serbian attack on the Jashari family. He was leader of the KLA and would have

been a target but he was in his own home, with all his family and some neighbours with him. He was killed with mortars and machine gun fire along with over fifty family and friends, including children. It really was a war crime and someday I hope Milosevic will be held accountable. Jashari's house, as you may know, was in Prekaz, north west of Pristina, not far from where Ajeshe's mother lived. Apparently she knew some members of Jashari's family, cousins, and the shock of their death affected her so deeply she collapsed with a heart attack.

'Oh no, that poor woman. Ajeshe must be so worried. Sorry dear read the rest.'

Fadil continued.

At this moment she is still alive, but very weak, unable to get out of bed. Ajeshe has had to give up working at the clinic to look after her. We are all praying that she will get stronger but it will be a slow process.

We have decided that we will join you in England, but obviously we cannot leave whilst Ajeshe's mother needs us.'

'Well, that's good news,' interrupted Marigana again. 'I really want them safely here with us. Sorry dear, finish the letter.'

'There isn't much more,' said Fadil and he read to the end.

I feel guilty that I want her to die, so I can start the journey and get us all to safety. I would like to follow your route but am not sure about the Albanian situation, at the moment. If you have any ideas, or knowledge that would help, please let me know.

Your very good friend,

Donjeta

He lowered the letter and looked at Marigana and saw tears glistening in her eyes. 'I remember Ajeshe's mother, so fat and jolly, a typical countrywoman. She made such delicious cheese. The whole family used to decamp to her house for the summer and they all came back healthy and happy. Why do things have to change Fadil?'

'Well everyone dies at some time, of course, but you didn't mean that did you?'

She shook her head. 'I meant all this violence and hatred towards our people. I don't understand why it's happening.'

'Nor do I and there's nothing I can say that'll make you feel better.'

He put his hand on her shoulder and she leant her head against it. 'I think I'll write to the British Embassy. If I say Donjeta is a highly qualified, and respected surgeon, it might persuade them to allow him in. It may also speed the processing. He may not have to wait so long to apply for a job.'

'That's a good idea. Do you know anything about the situation in Albania?'

He shook his head. I believe we can trust the news on the BBC and in the papers but when the initial sensation is over they forget about it and move onto something else. I assume things must have improved there or we'd have heard.'

'I hope so.'

With that Marigana picked up her embroidery and Fadil began his letter to the embassy. It was very quiet. They worked in companionable silence and Marigana thought how lucky they were to be safe and happy.

Their peace was interrupted when Alek burst in bringing a chill draught and chatter into the room. 'It's been brill at the Youth Club. We played for half an hour and everyone danced and clapped. When we stopped they shouted for more so we played the first piece again as an encore. I think it's Sam on those drums that really gets them going. She's fantastic and Mark keeps standing up as he plays. He says he feels the rhythm and he likes to move, like Little Richard, in Rock and Roll days. I'd never heard of him but it looks good.'

He paused for breath and saw his dad's indulgent smile. 'Sorry. I'm a bit excited. I don't think I'll sleep a wink. We've been asked to play again in a fortnight so we've got to learn a new piece. Peter's going to the music shop to look for something.'

'I'm glad you've had a good night, Alek. I thought your sheet music came from school. It's not cheap. Who's going to pay for it?'

'We're all going to chip in this time but George, the Youth Club leader, says he'll put a hat on the floor for donations, next time we play and that'll help.'

The door opened and a sleep tousled Rita came in, eyes crinkled against the bright light. 'What's all the noise about? You woke me up.'

She sunk onto the settee with a sulky look. Mum put her embroidery down and got to her feet. 'I'm going to make a drink, tea for us and hot milk for you two. Hopefully that'll calm you down Alek and then we'll all go to bed.'

She left the room and Alek sat down next to Rita. 'I didn't mean to be so noisy, but they loved us at the Youth Club.'

'I wish I could come. How old do you have to be?'

'I don't know. I didn't see any other kids from your class. I'll find out.'

The next morning Dad told the children about the letter from Donjeta and was disappointed by their reaction.

'I'm not bothered any more if they come here or not. I can't remember what they look like now,' said Rita. Alek was also relatively unmoved, but he did say he was sorry to hear that their Grandma was so ill.

When they had gone to school and Fadil was shrugging into his jacket Marigana said, 'I suppose their reaction is not that surprising. Alek is so busy studying and enjoying playing with the group. Kosovo is now just a memory.'

'You're right. Most young people are selfish and ours are no different. I'm off to work and I'll post my letter to the embassy.'

He kissed her cheek and left.

Several months went by before they heard from Donjeta again.

June 15th 1998

Dear Fadil, Marigana, Alek and Rita,

Thank you for writing to the embassy on my behalf. Please let me know if you have an answer. It would be good to be received kindly by the authorities.

I am writing to tell you that Ajeshe's mother's health has not improved. She seems to sleep more than she is awake and reluctant to eat. It's possible she is giving up and wants to hasten the end by depriving herself of food. The children have never seen anyone slowly dying, let alone someone they love, and it has hit them hard. Vjolica is coping better because she is older and also she has witnessed violent death. It was a very tough life experience but it seems to be helping her now.

Davud mopes at home after school. He seems to have lost interest in his studies and needs pushing to do his homework. Mr Dushku, his tutor, is very kind and says we are not to put too much pressure on him during this difficult time.

You know the political information we receive is sparse and unreliable, but I was able to have some current knowledge recently.

An American journalist was brought in, on a stretcher, to our clinic. He had been observing a fierce battle, between Serbs and the KLA, and was knocked unconscious by falling masonry. When he was able to talk, he told me about an American politician called Richard Holbrook. He'd been having talks with Milosevic about something called, 'The Christmas Warning', when President Bush told him he should not abuse the human rights of the Albanians of Kosovo. (I assume that did not move him, because nothing has changed!)

Apparently Milosevic agreed to have talks with Rugova and his colleagues, provided they came to his palace at Belgrade. They went to the talks so perhaps there is hope.

All this happened in May, apparently, and I knew nothing about it.

The journalist's name is Greg Jackson. He is still very weak and that is all he told me this evening, just before I left to go home. He will not be well enough to get up for a

*few days so I hope to find out more, before he leaves us.
How I long for proper information. If I thought there was
a real chance of a peaceful solution I would stay.*

May Allah keep you all safe,

Your very good friend,

Donjeta.

'Do you think there's a chance that Milosevic would agree
to let Kosovo be independent?' asked Marigana.

'Not a chance. He had to cave in, under great pressure
from America, over Bosnia and Croatia but we're different.
Our country has two distinct cultures with different
languages. All Bosnians speak Bosnian and Croatians
speak Croatian. Our country is unique, in Yugoslavia,
and because many Serbs live there, Milosevic wants to
incorporate it into his own country.'

Fadil looked worried as he moved to the sideboard and
took out his writing pad and pen. 'I'm going to write back
to him now and tell him what the embassy said.'

Chapter 19

Davud

I feel it's my fault. I was willing Grandma to die because she was stopping us leaving. Now she's really ill. Mum looks at her lying there, so still and white, and I can see how upset she is. I didn't understand, when I had those thoughts, just how it would affect everyone, particularly Mum.

Vjolica is out all day, and she must balance her books in the evenings, so she doesn't have time to worry about Mum or Grandma. Dad is swamped by work at the clinic and often comes home very late.

I'm finding it really hard to do my homework for Mr Dushku, in a room full of misery. My only escape is, once a week, when I go to work on the stall. Vjolica says people are attracted to stalls where the owners are friendly and cheerful so I have to try when I'm there.

Vjolica

July 20th

Life is never simple. I'd just got used to running the stall when Grandma collapsed and turned our household upside down again. Mum is nursing her day and night and looks ill herself. I'll help her tomorrow, because the market's shut.

I've never wanted to be a nurse. When Grandma wets herself, or worse I want to run away, not help her. So far

I've just had to give her a drink, or try to feed her, but she keeps turning her head away. Sometimes I make quite a mess dropping food onto the pillow or smearing it in her hair! It all makes a lot more washing, no wonder Mum's exhausted.

I'm cooking tonight and am going to make a vegetable stew. They were selling off the veg that wouldn't last another two days. I got potatoes, carrots, turnips and onions. The last day of the working week is always hard for people selling food and I'm glad I run a hardware stall. Nothing to go mouldy.

Dad spoke last night about an American with head injuries. He was saying things might improve here. I hope he's right. Must stop writing now and get this stew on.

Davud

When Dad arrived home he looked tired and miserable. He said nothing but went straight to Mum and they hugged for ages. Vjolica was dishing up dinner and Dad said he would tell us about his day after we'd eaten. I was just wiping up the last drop of gravy with some bread when he spoke.

'I told you yesterday about Greg, the American. Well he was telling me more today about the high-powered talks and it seems things are not so good after all. A second meeting was arranged but before that could happen the Serbs attacked a town in the west and our Albanian politicians refused to come to any more talks. I can't blame them but I'm disappointed.'

'At least this Greg has shown us that America is concerned. Perhaps they'll send troops to help us.'

Mum looked hopeful but Dad just shrugged. 'I don't know. How's your Mum?'

'She's just the same; refused breakfast but did have a small amount of bread softened in milk at lunch time.'

'I tried to get her to eat my stew but she wouldn't.' said Vjolica.

Dad nodded. It seemed the conversation was over so I stood up to clear the table, but Mum flapped at me to sit down. 'I let Dad tell us his news, but we've had a letter from Fadil Dhomi. Davud, will you get it for me? I put it on the shelf.' I did so and Mum went to hand it to Dad to read. He shook his head, 'You read it dear.'

She began.

July 1998

Dear Donjeta, Ajeshe, Vjolica and Davud,

You asked me to write if I heard from the British Embassy. I did receive a letter and it was neither good, nor bad. It said that they would normally welcome skilled refugees but a large number were coming into Europe from Kosovo and they were not sure if the government would restrict the numbers coming to Britain.

It said all the details I had given them, of you and your family, would be noted and filed, so if you came they could match them to you and it may speed your case.

America does seem to be showing a lot of interest in the situation, In a few days, on the 6th July, a Kosovo Diplomatic Observer Mission is going to begin. I assume this means they will have people in our country watching and reporting what they see. Surely this will promote some action to help us. I cannot believe they can just watch the killing of whole families and the destruction of villages, without intervening.

Here, in Leeds, we are also about to experience some family changes. Alek has taken his final school examinations, called A levels, and has applied to go to university. He wants to take a course to enable him to become an architect. If he was accepted by Leeds we would be pleased, because he could then live at home, and save money. But he has also applied to other universities and he may have to live away.

If that happens it will bring his music group to an end and this would be a shame. He has a friend called Peter who plays bass guitar and runs the group that they call, Pete's Pizzazz. They play at the local youth club and are well received. I know Davud is musical and I had hoped if you came over that he could join the group.

'Wow, I like that idea,' I said. 'I'd better practise harder if there's a chance I could join a group.'

Mum smiled at me and finished the letter.

Marigana and I were very sad to hear about Ajeshe's mother. It is hard to nurse someone you love and watch them slowly deteriorating.

You are all in our prayers,

Fadil

'They seem to be having such a lovely life in England,' said Vjolica. 'I envy Alek, and his friend Peter, having the chance to go to university. They play music together, go to a youth club; they are really enjoying themselves. Our lives are so confined, narrow and dangerous. We never have any fun now.'

Mum and Dad's faces looked sad and guilty because everything Vjolica said was true. If we had moved when the Dhomi family did, we could have been offered those opportunities too.

Dad sighed. 'There's nothing we can do about anything, whilst Grandma is so ill. Please be patient Vjolica. I promise we will go to England as soon as it's possible. I would go tomorrow if we could. Anyway, changing the subject. I wondered about inviting Greg to come here for a meal. It would aid his recovery to have a few hours away from the clinic and he did say he would like to interview some ordinary Albanians. He wants to hear how their lives have changed, instead of focussing on guerrilla fighting, with the KLA.' He turned to Mum. 'Do you think we could feed him, perhaps try to make something sweet too? I understand Americans love sweet things.'

Mum smiled, and I realised it had been a long time since I had seen her do that. 'It would be lovely to have a guest. Give us a couple of days to find some ingredients.'

'I'll get what we need but it will cost a bit more than usual,' said Vjolica. She seemed happier too, with the prospect of a guest. I started my homework as they worked in the kitchen, their voices eagerly discussing menus. I found it easier to concentrate with the lifting of the gloom.

Vjolica

24th July

Greg Jackson came to dinner last night. His head was bandaged and there were minor scratches on his face. He apologised for not shaving but said it was still too painful. He was not as tall as I expected, after all, everything is big in America! He seemed older than his thirty-four years but I think this is because of all the awful things he's seen, as a journalist. This is not the first war he's covered and I'm glad he didn't tell us too much about the horrors he's had to report.

It was a hot, humid day so we welcomed him with a cold glass of homemade lemonade. Dad apologised because we hadn't got anything alcoholic but he said he didn't expect it in a Muslim household. He chatted to Dad, whilst Mum and I finished the main course, 'Speca te mbushuru', served with a tomato, cucumber and feta cheese salad. This was my idea because I knew I could get the green peppers and salad ingredients from the market. It did look lovely when we bought it to the table, the peppers stuffed with tomato flavoured rice and the fresh, cool salad. Greg said it was the tastiest meal he'd had since arriving in Kosovo, so we were pleased.

The main course was followed by Halvah, soft, sweet and almondy. He rolled his eyes in a comic way and asked for seconds of that!

After we'd eaten I cleared away the dishes and Davud helped me wash them so we didn't hear what they talked about, but when we came back in, Greg had a notebook and was busy writing in it. His writing was odd squiggles and I asked what language it was.

'It's called short hand and is much quicker than writing every word. Most interviews are recorded on tape but that's difficult in a war zone.'

Dad said he'd told Greg what had happened to us, Granddad dying, losing their jobs, the bank closing their account and keeping our money.

'You haven't mentioned Davud and I having to leave our schools and being evicted from our apartment because we couldn't afford the rent.'

'That's true', said Dad. 'I think he should also be told about the student demonstration. Could you do that?'

I nodded, and as I spoke Greg didn't comment, but kept noting everything down. It was strange to relate our story. It could have made us feel sad, but somehow it felt more of a relief. We seemed to off-load some of our resentment.

When it was time for him to go, Greg stood up and swayed, unable to balance. Dad held onto his arm. 'I think you have done a bit too much, so soon after your injury. I'll help you back to the clinic.'

I enjoyed the evening and wished we could have visitors more often.

Davud

Naturally, having had Greg come for a meal, we were all keen to hear how he was getting on. Just a few days later Dad said he was well enough to leave the clinic. He was going back to work and would be observing with the KLA. He had heard they were making their way towards Pristina, currently in Orahovac, and were going to take over a village called Retimlije. The Serbs controlled all of the villages in that region but the KLA was making progress, liberating them.

Dad said Greg gave the impression that the fighting was getting closer and had hinted that it may not be safe soon in Pristina itself.

He looked at Mum. 'What about asking the clinic if they'd nurse Grandma?'

'And what sort of nursing do you think she'd get there? They haven't the time to see to an old lady and you know they need all the beds for injured people.' She was really angry.

'I'm sorry. I shouldn't have asked. Greg's made me even more anxious to leave.'

Mum's voice whispered, but I could just hear her. 'I don't think you'll wait much longer. Listen to her breathing.'

They both went into see Grandma and when they came out Mum looked pale and exhausted.

But Mum was wrong. Grandma lingered on and on.

We got some news through the Red Cross and the situation waxed and waned. In October the Serbs agreed to withdraw troops and thousands of people who had fled from their villages into the hills were allowed to return safely. They were saved from a severe winter that would surely have killed them.

Everyone relaxed a little, but after the Christian Christmas festival, there was another massacre. This time in Racak and Milosevic was blamed, on television, apparently. They were even talking about a war crime, so why were the Americans holding back? How many more people like Erind had to die before they would help us?

By the end of January Grandma was near to the end and Mum was so thin I wondered if they would go together. The gloom outside and in our house was affecting us all.

Vjolica

February 1999

I can't bear it. I just want her to die. She's killing Mum and we're all in a constant state of waiting. I love the Grandma we used to have, but this skeletal form, lying in the bed, refusing to die is not the same person. It's awful at work too. Many stall holders have left and customers too. They all say it's too dangerous. NATO is bombing Belgrade to try and persuade Serbian troops to leave Kosovo. As a result of that the police and soldiers here, have been even more vicious. Just a few streets away people have been forced to leave their homes and loaded onto trains to Albania. Albania must be flooded with refugees. The pressure is huge like we're being crushed, and it'll be our turn next.

I'm scared, not strong enough, really frightened, terrified!

Chapter 20

Leeds

The phone rang and Alek got to it first.

'Hi Pete.' There was silence as he listened, then his face creased into a grin. 'That's brill, really great. Congrats and all that.' Another pause and he said, 'Not yet and I'm getting worried. I thought I did really well in the interview at Leeds but so far nothing. Not sure if I should contact them and ask.'

The conversation ended soon after that and he looked at his expectant family. 'Pete's got a place at Uni, Bretton Hall in Wakefield. He's well pleased 'cause it's not that far from home.'

'That's good news, Alek. I'm surprised you haven't heard anything yet,' said Dad. 'What are you going to do if you don't get a place?'

'I can ask to go into the clearing system or have a year out to work or travel and try again next year.'

Rita looked up from her book. 'What about Pete's Pizzazz? Even if you could find another bass player it wouldn't be Pete's anymore would it?'

'No. I don't know what's going to happen. The youth club want us to play next week so we'll decide what to do at Saturday's practise.'

'It 'll be a shame if it has to fold, Alek, but if you decided to travel you couldn't be there either,' said Mum.

'I'll phone Leeds' Uni tomorrow, then I'll know.'

Alek phoned and was told he had not got a place on the course. It had been very popular and there had been enough students, with even higher grades than his, to fill it. He put the phone down feeling flat and miserable. Mum was in. Rita was at school and Dad at the surgery. He told Mum.

'Oh Alek, I'm so sorry.' She put her arms around him and hugged him, wishing she could take away his disappointment. His voice was muffled in her shoulder. 'I don't know what to do.' He lifted his head and pulled away from her. 'Even if I want to travel, I'll have to get a job first because I've no money. Who'll want to employ me? All I'm good at is playing the guitar and making neat drawings of buildings.'

'That's not........'

'No Mum. There's nothing you can say that'll make this any better. I'm going for a walk.'

It was drizzling, weather to march his mood, so he put on an anorak, flicked up the hood, and set off with quick, irritable strides towards the newsagents. He bought a local paper and a large bar of chocolate; comfort food. He walked on towards the park, found a damp bench, skimmed through the paper until he reached the Job adverts, pulled that section out, and sat on the rest. He opened his chocolate bar, took a huge bite, and read whilst he chewed. Most of them seemed to be part time, cleaning, or office work in small companies, nothing that would bring in a reasonable amount of money or look good on a CV.

'Hey you.' Sam grinned down at him, eyebrows raised.

He smiled back and jerked his head towards the space next to him. She made a face and shook her head. 'I'm not sitting on that. Why would I want a wet bum?'

'Sorry, didn't think.' He jumped up and opened out the newspaper so they could share it. She sat, pulling down her short skirt before crossing her legs. 'So, what are you doing, sitting out here, in the rain reading the paper? Had a row with your Mum?

'No. I'm pissed off. Pete's got a place at Wakefield and I've not got a place at Leeds. What about you?'

'My grades were only so-so. Didn't really expect to be accepted anywhere but your grades were good weren't they?' He nodded and she went on, 'So, what're you gonna do? Have you been applying for jobs?' He flipped the paper towards her.

'You won't find owt in there,' she said. 'Get yourself to the job centre. I did and I start next week.'

'Doing what?'

'Trainee manager in a supermarket. The pay's crap but after the training it's better and there'll be opportunities to move up; it being a big company.' She turned to look at him, anxious not to see disapproval. He put an arm around her and pulled her towards him.

'That's brill. A job with prospects. That's what I need.'

She pulled away from his arm, as she thought of something. 'If Pete's off to Wakefield, he's not going to be able to play with us is he? Is this the end of Pete's Pizzazz?'

'Don't know yet. We'll talk about it at practise on Saturday. See you there?'

They both stood up, he gathered up the soggy paper and dropped it into a bin.

'Yea. Better make the most of it. See yer.'

Alek caught a bus into the city, his mind buzzing. At the job centre he had to queue for a few minutes and then sat at a desk before a young woman. She took notes onto a computer and had a look for jobs there and then.

'Have you got a driving licence?'

'No.'

'That's a big disadvantage, would you consider taking lessons?'

'If it would help me get a job, yes.' She nodded and kept staring at the screen and clicking. Then she sighed, 'There's not much at the moment, office junior in a solicitors, minimum wage. I have several restaurants wanting people to wait on tables. There's nothing at the moment that you could class as a help to your career. I've got all your contact details, so I'll get back to you, or you can pop in again in a day or two. New positions are coming in all the time.'

'Right, Thank you.' Alek felt he had done something towards his future, but was disappointed to be going home without a job prospect. He decided to walk back to get some exercise and to think. What about travelling? How could he find the money? He'd have to find work. He passed a travel agents, then turned back and went in. He asked about round the world tickets. The agent was very helpful and he emerged half an hour later with brochures, different routes, prices and ideas for cheap accommodation. He felt excited and scared.

Mum was there when he arrived home. He told her about his morning whilst they ate lunch. She was pleased he had done something positive and, just in case he got a job quickly, she asked him to help in the garden. He moved a very heavy pot to a sheltered spot to protect the delicate plant from frost and then dug a weedy area of the small vegetable patch.

'You can pull up the courgette plant too if you would. I don't think we'll get any more. He peered through the large papery leaves. 'You might not get any more Mum but you've a huge marrow here!'

He took it in both hands, twisted and lifted it up, triumphantly, 'Ta-da'.

'That's solved the problem of what to cook for dinner. We'll stuff it with spicy lamb mince.'

She took the marrow from him and walked towards the kitchen door. 'When you've pulled up the plant, just a quick dig where it was, and that'll be enough for today. Thanks, Alek.'

Mum kicked off her boots and went in leaving him to think again about his future. Had he the nerve to travel on his own so far from home? Should he find someone to go with him? A picture of Sam sprang into his mind. She'd be perfect, not scared of anything or anyone. Then he remembered her vulnerable face, when she told him of her job. Underneath, he realised, she was just as insecure as he was. It would be easier to go with a boy. Life got complicated with girls. He thought of Pete but knew he would never defer his Uni place to travel. He wanted to teach and couldn't wait to get started.

As Alek put the spade back in the shed and swept the soil that had landed on the path he wondered about Mark. Mark had not got all the grades he needed but was still hopeful. He would talk to him on Saturday.

The rest of the week dragged until the job centre came up with an interview. It was on Friday at an accountancy company. They had, apparently, been impressed with his maths 'A' level grade. He felt less confident than he had at the interview for Leeds Uni and it did not go well. The truth was, he could not see himself as an accountant. That must have been evident, because he failed to get it.

On Saturday he went to the practice feeling despondent; almost not wishing to see Pete.

They plugged all the instruments in and played something they knew really well with plenty of beat and noise. It was satisfying and Alek's mood lifted. They sorted out a set of pieces to play at the youth club and played them all before they stopped for a chat.

'I think they'll really be jumping with those,' said Pete. 'I want us to be at our best because it'll probably be our last gig for some time.'

Mark shuffled in his seat. 'It's not just you that's got a place Pete. I've got one but it's miles away in Exeter so I'll have to leave next week too.'

Everyone congratulated Mark, and Alek suppressed another pang of envy. How come they could do it and he couldn't?

Rita was allowed to come to the youth centre to hear her brother play with Pete's Pizzazz for the last time. She intended to sit still and listen but soon she was up and dancing with everyone else. Alek and his friends were forgotten as she gave herself up to the rhythm and danced until she was breathless. When they walked home together she hung onto the arm that was not holding the guitar.

'I know your pissed off about the others having their futures sorted but this evening you all played brilliantly. I know it's pathetic to admit, but I was really proud you were my brother.'

'Wow! That's rich coming from you.' He was pleased and it helped to salve the wound left by the ending of the group.

A few weeks later Dad was reading the paper and suddenly sat up straight.

'Mute the tele for a minute will you Rita?'

'Oh Dad I'll miss the end of Neighbours.' He lowered his paper, looked at her over the top of his glasses, but before he spoke again, Mum said, "Dad wouldn't ask unless it was important. Do as you're told.'

Rita pouted but pressed mute, her eyes never leaving the screen.

'I've just read that the UN Security Council have approved something called Resolution 1199. Apparently this demands that Serbia withdraw their soldiers from Kosovo, refugees must be allowed to return and if this is not done they will apply, 'additional measures'.'

Mum frowned. 'What do you think additional measures means?'

'I'm not sure but it's obviously a threat. Perhaps they'll send troops or tanks. I don't know whether it's good or bad. It'd be good if Serbia agreed, and withdrew, but if not?'

'Things might get even worse,' said Alek.

Just two weeks later the news was even more worrying.

'It seems Serbia has no intention of withdrawing,' said Dad. 'There's been fighting near the village of Gornje Obrinje, just West of Pristina. Police and army surrounded some KLA forces in the woods nearby and in the battle several Serbian police were killed. They then attacked the people in the village itself, who were unarmed farmers, and massacred thirty-five villagers, twenty-one of them from a single family.'

This had really upset him. He stood up, looking serious. 'I'd like to write to Donjeta again but it's no good worrying them. They can't leave whilst Ajeshe's mother is so ill. I wish there was more we could do.'

He looked at Alek without seeing him, frowning. Then his eyes seemed to focus and the frown lifted. 'Changing the subject to something more hopeful, any news on the job front?

'I've got an interview next week, 11th October. It's working for a surveyor as an assistant. I think that means I hold a pole whilst he looks through his theodolite and takes all the measurements. '

'Why didn't you tell us before? How long have you known about it?'

'Sorry, Mum, I had a phone call yesterday. This is the third interview I've had, none of them wanted me, so I decided not to shout about this one. I was going to tell you if I got it. I'm getting seriously fed up. Pete's moved into his digs in Wakefield, Sam's been working for over a month, Mark's now in Exeter. I'm the only one going nowhere.' Dad came over and gave him a hug. 'Please don't say it'll all work out or something'll come up. I don't need platitudes I need a job.'

Donjeta could see his son was close to crying, so he backed away, grinned and said, 'The English always find comfort in a cup of tea. I'll put the kettle on.'

'I'll make it,' said Rita, who wanted to escape from the atmosphere of gloom. 'Anyone want a biscuit?'

'I'll eat the whole packet,' said Alek.

On Wednesday Alek dressed as smartly as he could, without a suit. He remembered Dad's panic to buy a suit for his interview. Should he have got one? Was that why he was not getting the jobs? It was too late now.

He left the house with his ears ringing with 'good luck', 'thinking of you', 'fingers crossed' and 'Don't forget to smile and shake hands.' If family support could get him the job he would have no trouble. He was meeting Mr Sawyer, the surveyor, at a building site. He thought he would be going to an office but he had a phone call Tuesday night changing the plan. 'They've got a problem at the site, down Eastham Road, so can you meet me there, same time, 10am?' Alek had agreed and then panicked. He rushed to find the Leeds map and look for the street.

Now he was nearly there. He got off the bus and soon saw the site, a huge gap between old buildings, fenced from the public eye, but with pictures and explanations of what was going to be built; a supermarket. Alek walked the length of the fence until he came to a door in it and stepped through. The space seemed vast but there were several portable huts so he went towards them, wondering which one Mr Sawyer was in. As he approached a large man with a hard hat on emerged, stopped and beamed at Alek. Even before he spoke Alek knew he would like him. He was thick set, middle aged with a beer belly and oozed confidence and authority. 'You must be Alek Dhomi. Welcome. Come in. I'll make us a mug of tea and then we can have a chat. Do you want sugar?'

Alek refused sugar and watched as Mr Sawyer put three spoonfuls into his own mug. They sat with a very untidy desk between them and he shuffled papers until he found Alek's application. He glanced at it, took a big gulp of tea, sat back and said, 'So, why do you want to work with a Quantity Surveyor?'

The questions were searching but Alek answered them all truthfully. Finally Mr Sawyer summed up the interview. 'To clarify this, Alek, I understand you were disappointed not to get to university and I'm surprised because your grades are good. You'd hoped to work at a degree to become an architect. As this has not worked out you would like to travel so you need to work to save towards it. So you applied for this.'

Alek looked rueful. 'I'm sorry, sir. I certainly don't want you to think I'm just passing the time until I have enough money to travel. I've done some research and wondered if being a quantity surveyor may be the job for me. If I could work with you it would enable me to decide my future whether I travel or not.'

Mr Sawyer smiled and all the lines around his mouth and eyes, crinkled. 'Now that was a good answer and, as you've taken pains to be honest throughout this chat, I assume you're being honest now. I'm impressed. I'd like to be able to say you've got the job but I have another applicant coming this afternoon, so I must keep an open mind. I'll ring you tonight to let you know, one way or another.' He stood up and held out his hand. Alek shook it and left.

Walking to the bus stop he wondered if he should have been less open about his plans but it was too late now. It was going to be a long day, waiting for that call. It was lunchtime when he got home and there was only Mum there so he told her about the interview and she said it was better to tell the truth than to lie and be caught out.

He repeated an edited version for his father and was playing his guitar in his bedroom when he heard the phone ring. He ran down the stairs but Dad had picked it up. He handed it straight to Alek and stood, watching and waiting. He was relieved when he saw a smile on his son's face.

'Thank you Mr Sawyer, Monday morning, 8.30 in your office. Yes sir I've got the address. I'll be there, thank you. Bye.' He clicked off, punched the air and whooped. 'I've got it!'

It was six months later when a letter arrived from Kosovo. Fadil read it to the family.

March 1999

Dear Fadil, Marigana, Alek and Rita,

Forgive me for leaving it so long but there was no significant news. Now there is.

I am sorry to tell you that Ajeshe's mother died and was buried, very quietly, yesterday. My poor wife is totally exhausted, having nursed her day and night for such a long time. Vjolica and I helped when we could but she has borne the greatest burden. You would hardly recognise her. The buxom woman you remember is now thin, almost emaciated. Her distress has made it hard for her to eat and we are all worried about her health now.

I am sure you know that NATO has been bombing Belgrade but so far Milosevic seems to be immovable. Things here are even worse, particularly the food situation. Vjolica has a stall in the market but many traders have already left and fresh food is harder to come by. There has been some talk of shutting down the market altogether and this would mean Vjolica's income, which we all share, will cease.

I know it is time for us to leave but I must allow Ajeshe to get some rest, and regain some energy. She also needs some time to grieve.

On a happier note I am thinking now of your Alek and hope he has a place at university. I wish my children could have had such an opportunity.

Perhaps it will not be so long now before we meet again. Please send Allah some prayers for our safe journey.

Your very good friend,

Donjeta

Chapter 21

Vjolica

Feb 30th 1999

It seems a long time since I wrote in my diary but I need to record Grandma's death. After expecting it for so long, I was surprised how shocked we all were. Mum has been in bed ever since but I'm glad to say she's both eating and sleeping really well. When I took her lunch in today she was sitting up and had some colour in her cheeks. She says she's going to get up for the evening meal. Having said that, I went in to collect her tray an hour later, and she was sound asleep again!

You might wonder how I can write in the middle of the day when I should be at work? Well the market closed yesterday. I couldn't write last night because I was so miserable I'd have dripped tears onto the page. It was going to close soon because the manager, Lule, said she was no longer making any money, with so few traders left, but none of us expected what actually happened.

I was bending down packing my stock into boxes, which I did at the end of every day, when I heard shouting somewhere near the entrance. I bobbed my head up and saw policemen bullying traders to leave and, making sure they got the message, by tipping stalls over. Above the crash of falling tables and breaking glass there was a loud hailer.

'This market is closed. This market is closed for all time. You will leave now. Anyone resisting will be arrested. This market is...........'

It went on and on like a mantra. I grabbed my cash out of the tin box, shoved the notes into my underwear and the coins into my shopping bag. I'd bought some veg and some eggs. I prayed they'd let me through without searching my bag. Someone grabbed my arm and I nearly screamed but it was the Lule. She whispered urgently. 'Vjolica, quick. Come this way. Keep down. If they see us, they'll rape us!'

We crouched and ran between the stalls into her office and out the back door. She gave me a hug and I could see tears glistening in her eyes.

'Allah protect us all,' she said.

I ran home, shaking with the horror of what might have been. I'm so grateful for her help and will probably never see her again. Can't write any more, – exhausted.

Davud

Everything seems to happen to my sister. It's just one drama after another but I'm glad she escaped the police. No man, even a kind one like Erind, would ever want to marry a Muslim woman who'd been raped.

I don't know what's going to happen to us now. I'm still going to school with Mr Dushku and Mum is talking about helping out at the clinic again when she's fit. When Dad and I are out today they're going through Grandma's things and clearing her bedroom. I expect Vjolica will have the bed. She's always moaned about sleeping on a mattress on the floor and making her bed every night. I'm not sure I'd want to sleep in a bed where someone had died; a pathetic, childish thought I suppose.

March 1999

Greg came home with Dad last night. We were all pleased to see him and he asked about Grandma as soon as he arrived. Dad told him.

'I'm sorry for your loss,' he said. Mum's face reddened. It is much harder when someone is sympathetic.

'Will you be able to eat with us?' asked Dad.

'Have you enough food? I understand they're making it very difficult by shutting markets. Is your's still open?'

Vjolica shook her head. 'No it was horrible. They were really violent. Not many women worked there and I was lucky not to be....hurt.'

He nodded. 'I thought that might be the case so I bought some things to help out. He undid his rucksack and produced cheese, a chicken, potatoes and carrots and finally a large bar of chocolate. My mouth was watering just looking at it.

'Now don't ask where I got it, just enjoy.' He smiled broadly at our incredulous faces.

'Thank you. What a wonderful gift. I'll start on that chicken right now.' Mum collected everything, Vjolica helped and they disappeared into the kitchen. I could hear their voices excitedly discussing what they were going to make for dinner.

'I suspect it'll take a while, so maybe, we could have a sneaky preview of that chocolate. I saw your face Davud when I got it out. So here's a smaller bar just for you.' I took it, saying thank you, ripped off the paper and was about to cram it into my mouth when I remembered my manners and broke it into pieces, offering it to Greg and Dad. Dad took a piece but Greg refused.

'Should I offer Mum and Vjolica some?' I asked looking at the little bar, wistfully.

'Why don't you just be a kid and eat it?' I did and it was wonderful, melting as I sucked, so sweet as it clung to the roof of my mouth. I concentrated on the sensation and nearly missed what the men were discussing.

'It was yesterday and I think they were trying to bomb a Serbian position by a bridge. It wasn't far away. Didn't you hear it?'

'Oh. Was that bombing? I thought it was thunder.' I said.

'It was a total mess. They took out a civilian bus. Annihilated everyone on board. This is really why I've come to see you and your family, Donjeta. My information is that the Russians don't approve of the NATO bombing and they're leaving their base in Bosnia to come here, to Pristina. They're making their way to the airport. It's strategically important and the next target for NATO bombs.'

I looked at Dad. His face was pale and he was frowning but he said nothing.

'Even if the town itself is not a target, you are too close to the airport to be safe. Mistakes, like the civilian bus, happen too frequently. You're now in real danger. You should leave. Tomorrow isn't too soon.' His expression was grim but it softened into a smile when Vjolica came in to lay the table.

Nothing more was said about leaving or the bombing. We just sat and enjoyed the meal together. The chicken was soft and moist, the vegetables perfect and, apart from appreciative comments, we were silent. When we were full, pushing back our chairs to be more relaxed, Vjolica cleared the table and made some tea. She brought the chocolate in with it and we all had a couple of pieces as a pudding. I felt slightly guilty about having had some earlier but kept quiet.

'There's something wrong isn't there?' said Vjolica. 'We would normally be talking all through the meal and you'd be telling us where you've been, Greg, and the latest news. You've been talking while we were cooking.'

'Vjolica. If the men discuss something perhaps it is not for our ears.'

'No Ajeshe. She's right. Greg says we should prepare to leave very soon because NATO is going to bomb the airport.'

Mum's face was suddenly ashen. 'No, not yet. I'm still mourning and I'm not strong enough. Please, Donjeta, just a little longer.'

'We'll discuss this tomorrow. I know it's been a shock. I need to plan a route. I had hoped to fly out of here but that is obviously out of the question now. Have you any ideas Greg? I've heard Albania is inundated with refugees already.'

'The first thing coming to mind is to ask at the clinic. Wherever there are large numbers of refugees there is usually some support from the Red Cross. I'll also contact my office and see if they have any suggestions. Where do you want to travel to?'

'England. We've got friends there, in a town called Leeds and they're having a great life,' I blurted out.

'Ok. I'll go now and do some research. I'll be back as soon as I've got useful information. Meanwhile take care of yourselves and thanks for the lovely dinner.'

Greg left, Mum burst into tears and Vjolica and I looked at each other bleakly.

'What shall I tell Mr Dushku? Shall I stop going to school after tomorrow?' I hoped the answer would be yes.

'Mum needs a little time to get used to the idea. We need to make plans and pack. Tell him you will finish school at the end of the week. You can help pack after that if we're still not ready.'

It was getting late so we sorted out the beds but once in it sleep would not come. I was frightened of the bombs, the dangerous journey, starting a new life. Did I know enough English? Would they understand me? Eventually I slept. We all did.

I said goodbye to Mr Dushku on my last day and he seemed upset. 'You have worked hard for me, Davud, and I'll miss teaching you and our music sessions. Your father is right to leave and I know you'll cope well in England. Just promise me one thing.'

'What is it?'

'When you get settled in England you will write and tell me all about it.'

'I will,' I said.

Everything was chaotic when I got home and in amongst the packed rucksacks, sat Greg. He had a large envelope in his hand.

'Ah, Davud, I've been waiting for you to come home because I wanted all of you to hear my offer. My editor has enjoyed the articles I've sent him about you. He's published them under the title, 'A Family in Crisis'. The readers would love a happy ending so he wants to help you leave, in return for the story of your journey.'

'What exactly does that mean? Are you coming with us?'

Greg laughed. 'I wish, Donjeta. No he wants me to help you with some train tickets, and some cash and in return you all write a journal.'

That set everybody buzzing. Mum and Vjolica were worried about writing in English but Greg said we could write in Albanian because they could translate it. The babble stopped briefly, so I said the journals would all be the same so why didn't just one of us do it? I was thinking of Vjolica who wrote in her diary all the time.

'That's true, Davud, but you'll all do it from your own point of view. Your parents will be worried about you and your sister. You'll see everything differently because you're younger. When you get safely to England you can mail the writing to my editor and, if he likes it, there may be some more cash, but I can't promise. So wha' d'you think?'

Dad looked around at each of us and we nodded. 'We've nothing to lose and everything to gain. So train tickets to where?'

Greg shuffled in his seat. It was obvious we were not going to like what he said next.

'Skopje, Macedonia and then South to Greece, Thessaloniki.'

'Why should we go south, when we want to go north east?' asked Dad.

'Albania is inundated with refugees and it's possible they'll close their borders.'

'Won't Macedonia be the same?'

'Yes but if you have tickets to take you all the way to Greece you can just change trains without lingering and, hopefully, you can get to Greece quite quickly. From there you will have to find your own way but by then you will be safe and can take your time.'

He stood up. 'I'll leave you now and will look forward to seeing your story in print.'

He shook hands with all of us and Dad went with him to the door. When he came back he was holding the large envelope and opened it. There was a lot of money, at least it seemed a lot to me, and tickets.

'The tickets to Skopje must be used tomorrow, late afternoon. We must go early and hope the station and the lines are undamaged.'

We went to bed and the bombing started. We'd heard it before but it was close, too close.

'Quick, grab your clothes, rucksacks, water. We must go to the basement,' shouted Dad.

My heart was pounding with fear. We ran down the stairs, opened the door to the basement and hurried down the stone steps. An elderly couple, the only residents left in the building apart from us, were huddled together. They smiled bleakly at us. With every boom the building shook and dust and debris fell from the basement roof. The single light bulb swung with every explosion making crazy shadows of the piles of old furniture and the cold boiler. It went on for hours and I sat, curled in a ball, head down rigid with fear. My eyes were shut but I opened them wide with the last bomb that must have been right above us. The light went out, complete darkness. The noise stopped. We waited and waited.

'I think it's finished.' Dad flicked on his torch. 'I'll go up and have a look. It must be daylight now.' He went up the stairs to open the door. It should open outwards but it was stuck.

'I can't open it. Can you give me a hand?'

The old man went up and Vjolica joined them. I stood at the bottom watching, wishing I was bigger and stronger. They shoved and kicked until it opened just a little letting in clouds of dust, brick shards and a welcome breath of air. Through the crack, where the corridor should be, was piles of rubble and dusty daylight.

'I think our building's collapsed,' shouted Vjolica. 'Davud, you're the smallest can you squeeze through this gap?' She came down the stairs to make a space for me. I tried but I was too big.

'We're trapped, we're trapped. We'll die down here!'

The wail came from the old woman and her husband, at the door, hushed her kindly. 'We'll get out. We must push with our backs.' They strained and pushed, their legs shaking with the effort and as the door inched a little wider I wriggled through. Vjolica was right but I tried not to think about the wires, festooned and crackling above me, or the thick timbers snapped like matchsticks; I needed to move the rubble away from the door. The rough bricks scraped my hands and they soon felt sore but I kept on and on throwing the pieces behind me until I reached a huge slab of concrete. I called out. 'I've moved a lot but there's a big piece of concrete. Could you push again as I pull?' I hauled on the edge of the door and felt it move. With another great effort we had moved it enough for everyone to get out. The old man helped his wife and she cried even louder when she saw the mess. 'We've lost everything, ohh.....'

She sobbed and sobbed but there was nothing her husband could do, except hold her in his arms. Mum, Vjolica and Dad came out dragging coats and rucksacks with them. We put them on and struggled over the rubble out to the road. The sun was shining weakly. It was very early and cold.

Across the road the buildings looked almost untouched, just a few windows smashed but when we looked behind us the scene of devastation made it unrecognisable. Some apartments still stood but all their fronts had fallen making them look like a doll's house. I could see tables and chairs, in dining rooms, beds and wardrobes with doors swung open showing clothes still on the rails. Further along the street a petrol station was burning fiercely with black smoke hanging above in the still air.

Our throats were dry with the dust. We needed water but we'd drunk what was in our bottles during the night. Dad said we had to move and begin the long walk to the station. We picked our way around the heaps of bricks, glass and concrete, Dad stopping when he saw a body. He checked each one for signs of life before he moved us all on.

'We've been so lucky to survive last night,' he said. 'I'm glad so many people have already left or there would be hundreds more dead and injured.'

The road led us past the cemetery. We had all been gathered there just a few weeks ago but now it was full of craters. The neat rows between graves and flowers beds were a mess of broken marble, earth and bones. Mum stopped when she saw it and swayed as if she was about to faint. Dad put his arm around her waist to support her. She was horrified and would not turn away. I was scared to look closely in case I saw a partly decomposed corpse that might have been grandma.

'Mum and Dad are there. I must go to them.'

'No Ajeshe they are dead and the desecration of their graves will not hurt them. It's you who are full of pain. We will stand here and say some prayers for them.' We stood, heads bowed, as Dad said a prayer but our quiet vigil was blasted by a piercing scream. Someone was hurt. We all looked towards the sound but could see no one. Dad and I clambered over the devastation. A middle-aged woman was inside the shell of her house, crouched, cradling the upper half of an old man, probably her father. The rest of him was still held fast by masonry. Her hands were cut where she'd dragged bricks and concrete away only to find him, lifeless. Dad crouched beside her and as she rocked and wept he said another prayer. It seemed to help because she became calmer. He gently explained that she was in danger. The walls might collapse and bury her. 'Come with us, please. He has gone. There is nothing left. My wife is across the street. She will look after you.' She refused to leave so we returned to the others.

Dad looked really concerned for her. 'If I could find a strong man I could take the body to the cemetery, place it in a crater then she might feel she had buried him.'

Vjolica offered to help but Mum suddenly recovered from her state of shock. 'No. It's dangerous to go back in there.'

'We can't just leave her.'

'Donjeta, we have only walked half a mile. We can't help every person we meet. We must try, if they're injured but she's not physically hurt. She's grieving and she's refused to move. You said we had to get a train today so we should go on, now.'

Dad's head went down onto his chest for a moment. He took a deep breath, let it out and said, 'You're right. Let's move.'

Chapter 22

Diary Entries

Vjolica

We struggled to free ourselves from the basement of our apartment block, now reduced to rubble and were making our way to the station, when Serbian soldiers stopped us. We had already discussed what to do if this happened. They demanded our papers but we knew if we showed them we would not get them back.

'Last night when the bombs came we rushed down into the basement. I never thought to take papers and there's nothing left.' Dad's voice rose higher, as if he was crying, 'I don't know what we're going to do.' (Dad's a great actor)

'You come with me.'

We followed. He took us to an open backed truck and there were other people in it, many in a wretched state. We climbed up into it, sat and held on tight, saying nothing until the truck lurched forward.

'Do you know where they're taking us?'

At first there was no answer to Dad's question and then a man with a bandage around his head, encrusted with dried blood, shuffled to a more comfortable position. 'They treat us like cattle so they'll take us to special trains, cattle trucks and send us to Albania or Macedonia. That or they'll shoot us.'

That caused a wail from a woman cradling a toddler.

'Enough talking!' shouted a soldier and then there was silence only broken by the whimpering of the child.

The journey took a long time because some of the smaller roads were completely blocked and the driver had to find another way. The metal floor was cold and hard. I took my coat off and sat on it. In the distance there was a black pall of smoke and a smell like burning tyres. Davud whispered he felt sick. I think it was the lurching and fumes. I told him we were nearly there, but I really had no idea.

We arrived at a goods siding and joined what seemed like hundreds of others, all distressed and fearful. There was nowhere to sit, no food or water. I don't know when I've ever felt so thirsty.

Then we waited and waited. A man asked a guard for water. The guard shook his head. When the man pleaded for his wife and family the guard shoved him so hard he fell, then unslung his rifle and threatened to shoot him. No one else asked.

Mum was exhausted, very pale and looked ill. Dad had sat her on his coat and she leant against him. 'What's going to happen?' she whispered.

'I don't know. I suppose we'll get on a train at some point, but if they keep us without water much longer we'll be ill with dehydration.'

'I know water is more essential than food but all I can think of is that bar of chocolate Greg gave us.'

Davud 's words brought a smile but before anyone commented the train arrived. I had expected it to be literally a cattle truck but was pleased to see it was a proper train with seats. We stood and moved towards the doors suffering some pushing and panic but eventually we were all aboard.

There were not enough seats. Dad managed to find two and Mum and I sat quickly, grateful for the comfort. Dad and Davud stood in the aisle and were constantly buffeted by people moving along the carriages, trying to find a vacant seat, or people they'd lost.

The journey from Pristina to Skopje in Macedonia should take three hours, but it took all day just to get to the border. In between there were stations and we stopped to pick up other refugees until I wondered if the engine had enough power to pull all the weight.

At lunch time the train stopped, where there was no platform, and guards lined up ordering everyone out of one carriage at a time. Everyone thought they were going to be shot but then some buckets of water were placed beside the track and metal mugs dipped in. We were allowed one mugful each and I have never tasted anything so good.

Watering took an hour and after that two more hours saw us at the border. Once again Serbian soldiers demanded our papers and Dad said he had none. There were so many refugees they had no time to search him and so we left Kosovo and began a new life in a tented refugee compound.

Davud

I know that Vjolica has written the story of our journey so I'm writing about our arrival at the camp.

It had been built by NATO and was well organised. When we were shown our tent we were each given some food and bottles of water. I threw my rucksack on the camp bed and tore open my packet. It had bread, cheese, a nutty biscuit and an apple. I tried to eke it out, stopping after the bread and cheese but I was famished and in minutes it had all gone. The tent held four beds and there were sleeping bags and pillows on each. There was space under each bed to put the rucksacks but nothing else.

'How do we cook? Where can we wash ourselves and our clothes?'

'Never mind that, Mum; where do we go to the toilet?'

'Well,' said Dad. 'If we want to be able to answer those questions we'd better explore.'

He made it sound like an adventure and I bounced up ready. Vjolica felt the same but Mum said she'd rest and we could show her when we returned.

The tents were in regimented rows and seemed to stretch forever in each direction but there was a prefabricated building to our left so we headed for that. It was a block of toilets with sinks for washing inside and taps to collect your own drinking water on the outside. Vjolica used the ones for women and came out with a smile.

'They're clean. I didn't expect that. Mum will be pleased.'

A much longer walk took us to another hut for washing clothes. There were deep sinks and washing powder but no obvious way of drying the clothes. Later we discovered a rotary washing line fairly close to our tent that we could use.

'So far so good,' said Dad. 'But we still haven't found how to cook or any shops. That little snack won't last long.

A NATO flag was flying, in the distance, so we made for that and found it was a really large building. It held a small clinic with notices of opening times on the door, a grocery shop and a reception desk. At first we couldn't see that because of the number of people crowding around it. They were shouting and some were crying. We entered the shop and Dad asked what currency they would take. We then walked around all the shelves tempted to buy everything. In the end we came out with four mugs some tea, milk and biscuits.

'How do we get hot water for the tea? We still haven't found out how we cook?' Vjolica was whining, which was not like her. She was tired. We all were.

'Perhaps there's a communal kitchen. Can you find your way back to our tent?' We nodded. 'Right, go back to Mum and I'll see if the crowds have got any less around the reception desk.'

An hour later, when we had eaten nearly all the biscuits and drunk half of the milk, he arrived back, a smile on his face. He was carrying a box and on top was a cardboard folder.

'There is a communal kitchen and hot water for tea is on the boil all the time. They have given me a starter pack and said I must buy anything else we need. I haven't looked at the paper work yet, but I understand, talking to people, we have to do our share of work. Mum, Vjolica and I must register tomorrow and we'll be given our duties.' He turned to look at me, 'Whilst we're doing that you have to attend school.'

My face must have registered total disbelief and disgust because they all laughed. Suddenly things seemed to be better. We had somewhere to live, where we felt safe from Serbian cruelty and bombs. I curled up on my bed and went to sleep.

Ajeshe

I keep thinking of my mother, not as she was at the end but when I was young and she was strong, hard working and cheerful. I remember the songs we used to sing as we kneaded dough or turned the churn to make butter. When these memories come I usually cry but mostly it's for the happiness we shared then, and the carefree childhood I was so fortunate to have.

Then my mind jumps to my own children and I worry constantly how they will be affected by the horrors they have seen and the hardship we may still have to endure. Perhaps this is not what readers want to hear, but surely all mothers will understand my fears. We are homeless, stateless and our future is unknown.

I am too tired to write more now.

Donjeta

I needed to know if the authorities here would let us leave. Our train tickets were valid for a month, so if we could get to Skopje, we could continue our journey.

We found the school and Davud went in, reluctantly, then we went to register. There was a long queue but eventually we were at the counter. The clerk did not look up at us, just reached for a fresh form and said, wearily,

'Name?'

He wrote our names, ages, sex, religion, ethnicity, and it seemed to go on forever. The only time he looked at me was when we got to previous occupation and I said surgeon, for me, and nurse for Ajeshe.

'Excellent, you two can help at the clinic.'

'Can I help there, too?' asked Vjolica but he said no and asked her if she had ever worked.

'I worked for a while on a hardware stall in the market.'

'Then you can clean and help in the shop.'

When registration was complete I asked my questions.

'Skopje is about twenty miles from here,' He said. 'There are buses several times a day and, providing you let me know when you intend to leave, it is not a problem. Refugees are still arriving and we need more tents.'

Before I could thank him he gave me a warning. 'Our country is tired of refugees. The people are less than welcoming now. It has been going on so long and we are not rich. All these extra mouths to feed.........' He sighed. 'They may bar you from buses or refuse to serve you in shops. Please take food with you and try to forgive any lack of warmth you may meet. Remember, don't just leave; let me know.'

I said I would and then we all went to our workstations. The time passed very quickly and Ajeshe was allowed to finish earlier than me because she needed to collect Davud from school. When Vjolica and I arrived back at the tent we all had things to share but Ajeshe said we should cook a meal first and talk after it. Communal cooking was chaotic with women having to wait to get a hot plate and a saucepan so we had pasta and vegetables sprinkled with grated hard cheese. It tasted good and, after years of frugal living, we were soon full.

After the meal we sat on our beds and shared our day.

Davud began. 'The teacher spent most of the day trying to get my level right. He said I was well in advance of my years in everything.'

'Perhaps he sets his standards low,' said Vjolica.

'That's mean,' said Ajeshe. 'Let him have his moment of glory. So did he manage to find some work to make you think?'

'Yes. He gave me a maths test for older boys and I did struggle. Have I got to keep going there Dad?'

'Just for a little while, I said. 'What about you Vjolica?'

'Well, I ache from mopping, dusting and scrubbing. I had to clean the shop and the toilets in reception, which was no fun. The only good bit was when the shop got busy and I served customers. The woman in charge kept watching me, to make sure I gave the correct change and didn't pocket anything but, by the end of the day, she relaxed. She even said I'd been a great help.'

'Well done, I can see my teaching you how to clean has been of some use.'

It was lovely to see Ajeshe smile, her whole face brighter than I'd seen for a long time. There had been so many months when she was too stressed and sad to be able to see anything beyond her own misery.

'Dad and I enjoyed our day sorting out cuts, a broken arm and some more serious problems. I think we both felt we'd been useful and I was pleased to find I had the strength to keep going, although I'm very tired now.'

At that point I mentioned moving on. 'Perhaps we should stay here for three or four days, to give Mum time to get even fitter, and to buy the things we'll need for the journey.'

Ajeshe looked at me, shaking her head. 'No let's not delay. We can only take what we can carry so we can't buy much. We'll get packed tonight, buy what we need as soon as the shop's open and then set off. We can be on our way by nine thirty.'

There was a flurry of activity, checking space in rucksacks and writing lists of what was required and we all went to bed.

Chapter 23

Alek loved his new job. Mr Sawyer had missed his vocation, being a born teacher. He gave him experiences of all aspects and was rewarded by Alek's enthusiasm. After two months he said they needed to talk things over. Alek was nervous; afraid he'd not done well enough. He made two mugs of coffee and they sat in the office.

'Now, Alek, you've had your second wage packet and I think it's time we discussed your future. I've invested time and energy on you and you've done well, but I need to know what your plans are. At your interview you said you'd like to travel, but you might also consider becoming a chartered surveyor. Have you made a decision of any kind?'

'I'm really enjoying this job. It's varied and interesting. I worry about the responsibility and am really glad you check everything I do. You're a good teacher but I'd need qualifications. I've decided I'd like to study to make it my career.'

'Excellent. I hoped you'd say that. So, what about the travelling you wanted to do?'

'We never really discussed holidays.' Alek shifted with embarrassment. 'I wondered if I could have two weeks in the summer and tour Europe. We saw places so briefly when we came from Kosovo I'd like to see some of them as a tourist.'

'Right.'

Mr Sawyer's face gave nothing away and Alek hoped he hadn't asked for too much.

'Let's look in the diary and plan some holiday dates.'

He unearthed it, from the piles of paper on his desk, filing not being his strong point, and opened it. 'This job will be finished by the middle of July so what about a break at the end of that month? You could finish on Friday 23rd and come back Monday 2nd August?'

He looked up eyebrows raised.

'That would be brill. Thank you.' Alek stood up, a smile lighting his young face.

'No don't get up yet, Alek. I think we need to discuss how you can study for the exams. I'll find out but I'm fairly sure you can do it on a day release scheme. This means you work most of the week and also attend college for one day. Or it may be possible to continue to work full time and study in your spare time using The Open University. Decide what system you'd like to do and let me know.'

They went back to work but Alek was finding it hard to concentrate. The future was opening up with exciting possibilities and he wanted to tell his family and friends.

Rita was thirteen and full of pubescent problems. Her skin had erupted with spots and blackheads, she was coping with periods that were awful, she'd suddenly got breasts and boys were embarrassing but interesting. It was a confusing time for her and she struggled to be pleased for Alek when he came home from work, full of his news. What was she going to do when she left school? She knew she was not a brilliant scholar but if she worked she'd probably get some O levels, perhaps even stay on for 'A' levels. But right now she had to choose what subjects to take next year. Most of her friends said they would go for arts but she favoured sciences.

'Rita, will you stop sitting there moping. I could do with a hand in the kitchen.'

She made a face but got off the settee reluctantly. Why was she always so weary these days? In the kitchen Mum was bustling getting out vegetables, knives and chopping boards.

'We're having a creamed vegetable curry. I saw them making it on television but it takes a lot of preparation.'

'How small?'

'Well bite sized. Not too small or they'll go all mushy.'

They worked in silence until Mum could stand the atmosphere no longer, put down her knife and looked at her daughter.

'Rita, please tell me what's wrong. You were less than pleased for Alek and you've been miserable for days. All women have to put up with periods. You just have to cope.'

'It's not just that, Mum. I'm really tired all the time. Everything is such an effort and I don't know what subjects to choose for next year.'

Mum frowned. 'How long have you been feeling tired?'

'Weeks and weeks.'

'Why have you only just mentioned it? There could be something wrong with you.'

'I thought it was what happened, you know, hormones and things.'

'Well it might be but we should tell Dad. He'll have some ideas. You might need a blood test. And what is the problem with choosing subjects? Surely you know what you like doing.'

'Yes, but I actually like most things, well not History. I don't like that much.'

'Let's finish getting this meal on to cook and then you can write a list of subjects that you're able to choose and we'll talk about them.'

'OK'

By the time the curry was ready the decision had been made. Rita was going to go for science subjects, dropping geography, history and art but keeping music. It was a brighter girl that sat down to try Mum's new recipe. But, after the meal, she felt a wave of exhaustion and begged to be excused the washing up. Alek helped dry the dishes and Dad talked to Rita about her symptoms. 'I'll organise a blood test for you tomorrow, after school. Could you get to the surgery by half past four?'

'Yes. I hate injections, but I'll be there.'

But, Rita was too unwell to go to school the next morning so her father did the blood test himself and sent it off to the lab as soon as he got to work. She stayed off school for the rest of the week, fretting about not giving in her options.

On Friday she was told the results proved, what he had suspected, that she had glandular fever. 'I seem to remember you were off colour a few weeks ago with a sore throat and your glands were a little swollen. Well I'm afraid that was the beginning of it.'

'Can I have some medicine to give me energy so I can go back to school?'

'No, there's nothing I can do to hurry up the process and for a while you'll be contagious, so you can't go to school.'

'How long will it take?'

He shrugged. 'Some people take months but others just a few weeks. I'll write to your school and explain. I'll also tell them your options and ask if there's any work you can do at home when you feel up to it.'

Rita relaxed back into her pillow and shut her eyes. 'Thanks Dad.'

For a while Rita slept all morning, dressed and came downstairs for lunch, then rested in the afternoon. She watched some television, tried to read books, but often fell asleep during both. Then after two weeks she woke up feeling better and came down for breakfast.

'Wow. Who's this? Do you realise it's only half past seven?'

Rita smiled at Alek's ribbing and sat down at the table. She suddenly felt ravenous and filled her bowl with cereal.

'I'm glad you've got your appetite back but you'll still have times when you're exhausted so, it will be another week before I'll be able to pronounce you fit to go back to school.' Dad looked at her pale face and added. 'If the sun comes out today go and sit in the garden or even try a short walk.'

Mum cleared away breakfast and Rita got dressed. Later they walked to the local shop and her spirits rose as she achieved this and felt she could have walked further.

When Alek came home that evening she finally apologised to him. 'Alek I want you to know that I'm really pleased you've been offered a career in Chartered Surveying. When you told us Mum and Dad were all over you but I was a mean cow and I'm sorry.'

'It's okay, you were ill.'

'Yes and I've had lots of time to think. Have you decided how you're going to study for your qualifications?' She saw his eyes light up with enthusiasm and was glad she'd asked.

'Yes. I'm going to do day release. I have to go to college one day a week and also one evening and the rest of the work I do at home. That way I can still work, get paid and gain experience. It will take longer than going to Uni but then I would come out with a lot of debt. I'm sure it's the best option for me.'

'Then you were talking about holidays. Have you decided where you're going?'

'Not completely, but Peter's on board. He's really keen and we're getting together to make plans next weekend.'

'That's great. Somehow travelling on your own didn't sound much fun. I think while you're away we should have a holiday too. All my friends are talking about Florida and going to Disney Land. It sounds very expensive so it's probably out of the question.'

'Well you won't know if you don't ask, will you?'

He smiled and the conversation ceased as Mum called that dinner was ready. During the meal Alek mentioned his holiday and said he would like to go to Rome and Athens.

'That's a lot of kilometres in just two weeks. How will you get from place to place?' asked Dad.

'I don't know, train probably. Peter and I thought we'd go to a travel agent and see if they'll help us organise it.'

'What makes you want to go there when you could go to France, Switzerland, Holland or Germany?' asked Rita.

'The history really. I know it's not your favourite subject but I'd get a real kick out of standing in the Acropolis or the Coliseum. Just to see where the gladiators fought and died all those centuries ago.'

'The Romans conquered Britain too. It'd be cheaper to go to Bath,' said Dad.

'Yes but not so warm and sunny.'

'Whilst we're talking about holidays,' said Rita. 'Can we go away somewhere in the summer?'

Dad looked at Mum with his eyebrows raised and Mum nodded. Rita was watching them. 'What? Have you planned something already?'

They both smiled. 'A little bird told us you wanted to go to Disney Land in Florida so that's where we're going.'

'Oh cool!' Rita got up and hugged Mum then Dad. 'I can't believe it. Can't wait to go back to school and tell everyone.'

'The only thing we couldn't do was time it to coincide with Alek's holiday. I can only take time off work when there are enough doctors to cover and the school summer holiday is very popular. But I was given the last two weeks in August so that's when we're going.'

'That means Alek will be here on his own.'

'Don't worry about me Rita. I'll be fine. I'm sure I can heat up a pizza or make scrambled egg.'

Rita returned to school, several weeks went by and then a letter came from Donjeta Kahshoven.

Dad read it out,

Skopje, Macedonia

April 20th 1999

Dear Fadil, Marigana, Alek and Rita,

As you can see we have had to leave Pristina. I am sure you will know how bad the bombing has been and will not be surprised. We were in a refugee camp at the border, for a short while, but then set off to make our way to Skopje. We had rail tickets to take us from there to Greece but nothing is straightforward and we had several set backs.

We left the camp and tried to get a bus but were repelled by locals. There was a lot of resentment of refugees that had been coming to their country for so long. They saw our rucksacks and immediately blocked us. We were forced to walk about 20 miles and Ajeshe is not strong, so she quickly tired. On our first day we managed about ten miles and then we looked for somewhere to stay.

All the lodging places said they were full and we felt ourselves fortunate when one woman took pity on us and let us sleep in her barn with the animals. It was a very uncomfortable and smelly night, but it did rain, so sleeping outside would have been far worse. During the second day we needed water- there is a limit to what you can carry – and people did, grudging, fill our bottles.

Finally, we entered the city and decided to go straight to the station. We would all have preferred to go to a hotel and have a bath but thought we might meet more hostility.

At the ticket office we were told, although our tickets were still in date, the train was full for the whole of the week and it was likely to be the same story the week after. At that point Ajeshe collapsed and that night found us sitting on hard plastic chairs in the hospital!

The doctor said they thought it was just exhaustion and she was discharged the next day, even though I protested we had no place to stay. They just shrugged. I took the family to a cafe that did agree to serve us. We all had a good hot lunch and I left them cradling their second cups of tea and went to do battle at the station.

I was relieved to find a different person in the ticket office and he booked us seats on the train this evening. There was no mention of the train being too full!

So I will have to stop this letter now to post it before we leave the town. I will write again when I can to let you know our progress,

Your good friend

Donjeta

PS All the family send their love.

Chapter 24

Journal entries

Davud

I felt really excited when we got on the train at Skopje. The ordinary people in Macedonia had not been very kind to us and I was sure the Greeks would be better.

The journey took us along a valley flanked by hills and mountains on either side. I watched goats and sheep, chewing contentedly and thought of Granddad and Grandma. My eyes began to prick with tears and I realised I had not just lost them. I had lost my young life. Everything, and everyone I had known, left behind. I looked at Mum, who had fallen asleep, immediately the train set off. She looked peaceful and my heart gave a lurch. I prayed to Allah to help her get strong for we all needed each other more than ever.

Dad must have been watching my emotional struggle and he said, 'It will be ok, Davud. We are together. That's the main thing.'

I nodded, not trusting myself to speak, knowing tears would fall. Vjolica was looking out of the window too. Was she feeling sad, like me?

Vjolica

I feel I can breathe at last! Every clatter of the wheels going over the sleepers means we are moving further away from the misery of these last years. This is my chance to have a new life, free from fear. The memories will never leave but I'm sure they'll fade.

In England I might be able to go to school or college. I'm not too old. The world seems to beckon me, full of promises.

This journey should take about five hours and then we will be at Thessaloniki, by the sea. Now I must confess I've never seen the sea. I hope we can stay there for a week or two, like other people do, having a holiday. It's unlikely Dad will agree because he's intent on getting to England but I think a rest would do all of us good.

My eyes are tired so I'll shut them, just for a moment. I wonder what sand feels like between your toes?

Donjeta

Both the women in my life asleep and poor Davud frightened and upset at leaving Kosovo behind. I can't wait for this train journey to end so we can feel less like refugees and more like ordinary people.

Thessaloniki is on the Eastern side of Greece and we really need to get to Athens so we can get a flight to England, if I have enough money. Going by sea would probably be cheaper but will take much longer. I'm so glad we were prepared and have our documents. I must follow the protocol and make sure I do nothing wrong so we'll be accepted. I've really set my heart on seeing Fadil and family again, living and working in Leeds. I'm even trying to write this in English and hoping it makes sense.

When we get off the train I will ask at the station for directions to a cheap hotel so we can have the luxury of a shower or bath. It's difficult to plan much more than that. Davud has fallen asleep now and his head is resting on Vjolica's shoulder. I love them so much and hope with all my heart that they will settle happily into their new life. My eyes are tired now so I think I'll join them in sleep.

Ajeshe

I must have slept for over an hour and when I woke I saw all my family asleep, exhausted by the trauma of our departure. I am looking forward to seeing Greece with all its ancient history but it would be better if we already had somewhere to stay. It is a strange, bleak feeling to be homeless.

It is hard to look back and remember when Donjeta was a highly respected surgeon and we had a large, beautiful apartment. Then we both lost our jobs, had to sell the car, move into a pokey little apartment in a poor part of town. Now our descent is complete, no home, no country, no work, refugees. I suppose the only way now is for things to get better again and I think I will hang onto that thought.

Donjeta is stirring so I'll stop writing and talk about our plans.

Davud

The train slowed and juddered to a stop with a squeal of brakes. We had arrived. I felt stiff as I stood, shouldered my rucksack and made for the door. Dad alighted first, helped everyone else get off and we walked down the platform towards the sunshine. At the entrance to the station Dad asked us to sit on a bench in the shade whilst he went to find an official who could speak English. About ten minutes went by and it was uncomfortably hot. Summers in Kosovo rarely reached these temperatures. Vjolica fanned herself with her notebook. 'Here he comes,' she said.

'Sorry, I was having difficulty making myself understood. Apparently there is a small hotel just around the corner. The ticket collector thought it would have room because it's not in the tourist holiday area. Do you want to come with me or shall I find it and come back for you?'

'Let's all go. It might help if Davud is with you because he can speak some English and, if there are rooms, I can't wait to have a shower.' Mum stood up as she spoke and we walked to the hotel.

It looked drab on the outside but, when we went into the foyer, it was cool and clean. Vjolica and Mum sat quietly on a settee, leaving Dad and I to organise the rooms. The receptionist said she spoke some English and looked at Dad so he did his best to explain. After some errors and laughing at our mistakes we had booked two rooms and took the keys to Mum.

'Dad did really well and then he couldn't remember the word for breakfast but I could.'

'Well done, both of you. Let's go and find the rooms and hope they have lots of hot water.'

'I'd settle for cold water,' said Vjolica and we laughed as we went up the stairs. There was some discussion about who should share with whom but in the end Muslim propriety won and Mum and Vjolica had one, Dad and I the other.

An hour later we emerged into the cooler dusk, refreshed and ravenous. The hotel would serve breakfast in the morning but did not do any other meals. We had been advised to go to a taverna that was cheap, but served good food. The walk took about fifteen minutes but before we got there I heard something odd and stopped. 'Listen everyone. Can you hear that strange sort of swooshing noise? It's not traffic or a train. '

We all stood, listening and then Dad laughed. 'I know what it is. It's the sea. Come on let's find it before the sun goes down.'

There was a feeling of freedom and excitement when we arrived at the promenade to see a large harbour full of boats. A brightly lit ferry was manoeuvring and its reflection rippled and danced.

'It looks magical,' I said. 'Where do you think it's going?'

'I don't know but Greece has lots of islands so it could be going to one of those.'

'I love this place Dad. Can we stay for a bit before going on to England? I want to explore and see some of the really old places. They might have a beach and I could paddle in the sea'

'One step at a time, Davud. I do think Mum could do with a rest and I need to organise the next stage of our journey. Let's agree to stay at least two nights. That will have to do for now.'

In the restaurant we chose safe things to eat like cheese salads or vegetarian dishes, assuming any meat would not have been butchered the Muslim way. It was all delicious and not expensive, by European standards, but when Dad paid the bill it seemed a lot for just one meal.

'Perhaps we could find a market, or a grocers shop, tomorrow,' said Mum. 'We could buy bread, cheese and fruit for a picnic lunch.'

'We could eat it on a beach, if we could find one, and then we could swim in the sea.'

'Calm down, Davud, you need swimming trunks and we don't have any.' Dad laughed to see my crestfallen face. 'Let's get a night's sleep and explore tomorrow.'

During breakfast it was lovely to see Mum smiling and some colour back in her cheeks.

'We need a plan for today. I want to find a travel agent and find out about flights and I'd like Davud with me because he has better English.' This really pleased me and I think my cheeks went red. 'Perhaps you two would like to find a supermarket and buy some food for this picnic. We could meet back here about half past eleven. That should give us all time.'

'I'm happy with that. But I'm a bit worried about not being able to speak Greek and my English is almost non existent,' said Mum.

'Don't worry Mum we can muddle through and just think of the freedom of two women being able to walk about without fear. I can't wait.'

Vjolica's excitement was infectious and everyone left the hotel with a lighter step.

The receptionist had given directions to a travel agents and a supermarket so we knew where we were going and could now enjoy just being in Thessaloniki. The previous day, at the station, Dad had changed some money into drachma so he gave most of it to Mum and kept just a little for himself. Any flight was going to cost serious money and might mean changing all the rest of his deutschmarks.

Vjolica

I'm writing this in my diary, not the one for the American public. Mum and I went out in Thessaloniki this morning

The supermarket was small, so not scary. We easily found bread rolls, butter, cheese and fruit. There was also bottled water and other fizzy drinks. I picked up a bottle of cola but Mum shook her head. Money was not to be wasted on whims, big sigh. We got all we needed for lunch but lingered looking at all the tins, trying to decide what was in them. The Greek words were indecipherable but most had a picture of the contents.

'Perhaps we should buy some salad and make an evening meal of it. I know Dad was worried about the money it cost eating in the taverna last night.'

'Good thinking, Mum, but we don't have any plates. I can see us managing a picnic but not a salad meal in the hotel room. Let's see if there are any paper or plastic ones.' I walked quickly back to where the shop had some hardware and returned moments later with a pack of paper plates and some plastic cutlery.

A few minutes later we emerged into the hot sun with a bag each to carry and not many drachma left in the purse.

'We'd better go back to the hotel and wait for the others. It's too hot and the butter and cheese will melt if we stay long out here,' said Mum.

I could see she was wilting as we walked back. Her pace slowed until I was quite concerned and took the bag from her.

When we got into our room I wet a flannel and bathed her forehead as she lay on the bed.

'Oh that's lovely, thank you. I'm not ill so please don't worry. Just not used to the heat.'

'We've got half an hour before Dad and Davud get back so shut your eyes. I'm going to write in my diary,' I said.

Davud

The Travel Agents was quite a long way from the hotel and walking was not fun. Dad looked exhausted when we arrived and he sank thankfully into a chair.

'I must be getting old. I'm so hot and really tired.' Beads of sweat ran down his face and I wondered if he was ill.

A woman behind the desk spoke but Dad looked completely blank so I asked if she could speak English.

'Yes, but not good. Would you like water?'

''Yes, thank you. My father is not feeling well, too hot I think.'

The water arrived and Dad looked better when he had drunk it. He was able to say what we wanted to do. She sat at the computer and discussed different routes and prices. Dad said he wanted the cheapest routes she could find. Thessaloniki had an airport but there were no direct flights to London so it seemed it would be necessary to go to Athens. It was taking a long time. Dad seemed to be struggling to breathe and concentrate. I was shocked to hear him say, 'I would like to go back to our hotel because I'm not feeling well. Would you work on this for us and we'll return tomorrow?'

'Yes. Tomorrow would be good.'

We stood up to go. Dad took one step and collapsed, unconscious, on the floor.

'Dad, Dad.' I shouted, kneeling beside him, tears gushing. The travel agent rang for an ambulance and then turned Dad onto his side. She felt for a pulse and smiled to reassure me. Another lady got cold water and bathed his forehead. He came round and tried to sit up but she pushed him down again. She had lost all her ability to speak English but he understood.

The ambulance arrived and two men came in with bags of equipment. They took his temperature, blood pressure and spoke but I could not understand.

'Can you speak English?' I asked.

'Ah, tourist, yes?' I nodded. 'We take to Hospital.'

'What shall I do?'

'You come with father.'

'I need to tell Mum. She's in the hotel. She'll be worried. I don't know where the hospital is. I don't know what to do.' The tears flowed again.

'Davud, come here.' When I was close Dad held my hand. 'Can you find the way back to the hotel?'

'Yes, but what about you?'

'I'll be looked after in the hospital. I think I've got some kind of infection.' He closed his eyes, exhausted by the effort to think and talk. As the ambulance crew brought in a stretcher to take Dad out, the travel agent gave me a map.

'Name of Hospital is AHEPA. I write in Greek and also English.'

'Thank you.' I followed everyone outside and stood bleakly watching as they shut the back doors of the ambulance and drove away. I've never felt so alone.

Chapter 25

Leeds

Alek whistled, breathily, as he laid piles of clothes on the bed. Finally, he looked at the array, then at his rucksack and frowned. It would be impossible to get it all in. He knocked on Rita's door and went in when he heard her shout. She was reading and looked up with eyebrows raised. 'What?'

'Fancy a trip into town I need to buy a suitcase?'

She bounced off the bed with a smile. 'On one condition. You let me look at make up.'

'Yes, but if you buy any you'll have to hide it. You know Mum thinks you're too young.'

'Brill, let's go.'

When they got off the bus they walked up the Headrow. It was crowded and buses made crossing the road difficult. It was quite a contrast to enter the relative quiet of the department store. In the luggage department Alek looked at medium suitcases, picking each one up before moving on to the next one.

'What are you doing?

'They've got weight restrictions on luggage so I want a light case.' He found one, eventually, and paid for it. 'Ok I don't want to lug this around all morning so let's go to the make up department here and we're not going on to any other shops.'

'That's fine there's plenty to look at.' Rita picked up lipsticks, eyeliners and foundation and was then approached by an assistant. Her make-up was so heavy her face looked like a mask. 'Would you like to see the effect of that foundation? I'd be happy to do a short makeover and it won't cost you anything.'

Alek shook his head but Rita nodded. 'Yes please.' She sat on a high chair and Alek stood watching with disapproval. He wondered how women could spend so much time and money trying to look beautiful. He walked away and tested some of the male perfumes, then came back. Rita slipped off the stool and smiled shyly at him.

'Wow, Rita you look stunning.'

His little sister had become a woman with just a few skilful dabs of makeup. She looked fresh and beautiful; nothing like the masked woman who had applied it. Rita bought the foundation and lipstick but that was all she could afford. She almost danced out of the shop but Alek realised he would have to burst her bubble of joy. 'You do realise, if you go home looking like that, Mum and Dad will have a fit. You'll be on bread and water for a week.'

She giggled. 'Who cares? I've loved every minute of it. I feel like a princess and I'm ready to face whatever punishment they give me.'

'We could find a public toilet and you could wash it off.'

'No way. I'm keeping it on.'

Alek sighed. He envisaged the scene and decided he would go and see Peter, who would also be packing today.

When they got home the row Alek had envisaged, happened and he slipped away. Peter had finished his packing and explained the final arrangements for their trip. 'Dad will pick you up tomorrow at eight. That should give us enough time to get to Manchester Airport, check in and then hang around for the flight to Rome. I don't know why you have to be so early for flights. I'm sure it's so you'll spend money in the restaurants and duty free.'

'Is your Mum coming to see us off?'

'No way. Mum doesn't miss church for anything. She probably thinks she'll go to hell if she misses one service.'

'My family go to the mosque, occasionally but we make an effort when it's a special festival.'

'Yes, even I go at Christmas.' They chatted for a while longer and then Alek went home, hoping the friction would be over. It was but started again on his arrival. Rita had been banished to her room after having to clean her face but he was in trouble for allowing her to do it.

'I've a good mind to send you to your room too,' said Mum. She was even angrier when he laughed at that but he offered to make them a cup of tea and she calmed down. Rita was allowed to join them for the evening meal and Alek was glad because he really wanted harmony at home before he left.

The next morning, he was ready in plenty of time and as soon as the car pulled up he dashed out dragging his case and shouting goodbyes to everyone. He felt excited and nervous. Peter had been on holidays to Europe with his parents several times but this was his first time without them. He said he felt the same way.

Rome was everything they could have wished for. First they visited the Trevi Fountain, so lavish with statuary, waterspouts and the glitter of coins in the bottom, enclosed in such a small square. Then the Roman Forum followed by the Pantheon that seemed to instil a sense of peace, like a cathedral. They queued for the Colosseum for forty minutes but declared it was well worth the wait. Alek gazed down at the arena and could almost hear the roar of the lions, the crowd shouting and victims screaming.

'It's really impressive,' said Peter, 'I'm glad we came.'

Their last day in the city was excessively hot. The evening before they had gone to a bar where the music got their feet tapping and soon they were dancing. Peter drank too much. They were both exhausted so they had a slow start the next day. When they did emerge, Peter groaned, as the sunshine hit his eyes. 'I've got a hell of a headache, hangover I suppose.'

Alek grinned, 'I don't know what a hangover's like but I gather you feel rough. Come on, I need some food. It'll probably help you too.'

They looked for a small cafe and found one with tables outside, in the shade. They ordered cheese omelettes with salad. It was delicious, melting in their mouths, contrasting with the fresh crunchy salad and warm ciabatta. When they had finished Alek sighed. 'I could sit here all day, just people watching. It's been pretty full on since we got here and I'm enjoying this breather. Anyway, I'll have to move 'cause I need a toilet.'

He returned, grinning. 'It's a cyber cafe. Let's go inside, pick up our e-mails and write home.'

They both paid for half an hour and were relieved to see the familiar, QWERTY keyboard.

Alek scanned the list and opened the one from home.

Dear Alek,

I do hope you find a way to read this because I've had a very worrying letter from Vjolica Kahshoven. They are still in Thessaloniki but Donjeta has been taken seriously ill and the rest of the family are frightened. They have had to leave their hotel and have taken a cheap apartment close to the hospital, at 25 Evaggelistra.

I wondered if you could visit them when you're in Greece? I know you were going to Athens, and Thessaloniki is a long way from there, but hope you may be able to spare a few days to help them. I am really sorry to have to ask you.

Love Dad

Alek stood up and asked if he could print out the e-mail. Then he took it to Peter and explained. 'It's your holiday too and I don't know what to do?' Peter shrugged. 'It's a no brainer. We must try to help them. I don't mind a change in our plans and it's obvious your dad's really worried.'

'Thanks, Pete, That's what I hoped you say.' Alek wrote back saying they would do their best to find them and give whatever help they could.

On the way back to their hotel, Alek told Peter about the Kahshoven family and how they had decided to stay when his family had left.

'We've been in touch by letter fairly regularly all these years and Dad always said they should join us in England. He even sent them some cash to help them with their journey.'

'So how old is the daughter who wrote the letter?'

'Vjolica must be seventeen now.'

'Interesting. Is she pretty?'

'I don't know really. We haven't met for years. She was ok as a child. Anyway she had to leave school early so I don't suppose her English will be very good. You won't be able to talk to her.'

'There are other ways of communicating,' said Peter, his eyes dancing with mischief.

'You needn't think she'll be interested in you. She's a Muslim and we have very strict rules where women are concerned. Everything is so lax in England it's not surprising there are so many illegitimate births. It's different for us.'

'Yes but when in Rome......... as we are...' and they both laughed.

The next morning they flew to Athens and checked into the hotel, as planned. As soon as they found their rooms they dumped their cases and returned to reception to see if they could change their booking.

'You are lucky. There is one of our hotels in Thessaloniki and we can transfer your booking so it will cost you nothing more. When do you want to leave?'

'I'm not sure how long we'll need in Thessaloniki. What do you think Peter?'

'I think the sooner we see your friends the better. Athens will still be here and perhaps we can see some of the sights before we go to the airport to fly home.'

Alek turned back to the receptionist. 'We'd like to move on tomorrow, please and then come back the day before we fly out.' They worked out the dates, hotel arrangements were made and then they asked the cheapest form of transport to get them there.

The cheapest was a slow train that stopped very frequently and took six hours. The bus also took six hours and even driving, if they hired a car, would take, six hours.

'Looks like the slow train then. I don't suppose you have a time table?'

'Even if I had, I must tell you, our train service is, well, unreliable. It is best that you go to the station early in the morning and be prepared to wait.'

Alek thanked him for his help and was about to go when he turned back? 'Sorry, just one more question. How much would a taxi charge to get us to the Acropolis? We must see something before we leave tomorrow.'

They could see the Acropolis, a citadel built on a high rocky hill and its most famous and elegant building, the Parthenon, long before they got there. The taxi dropped them and they agreed to be collected two hours later, hoping that would give them time to see everything. The climb to the top was a lot of steps and some older people had to stand to one side to take a rest whilst others went past them. For all their youth, both Alek and Peter were out of breath when they reached the top.

'Oh, wow, just look at that.'

They stood in awe gazing at the collection of ancient buildings their eyes roaming but always returning to rest on the magnificent Parthenon. With one accord they went there first. They were not alone but everyone was amazed by what they saw so their appreciation was enhanced by the similar reactions of others. They listened to a guide from a cruise ship and discovered the temple was dedicated to the goddess Athena.

'I suppose we could've guessed that,' whispered Peter.

They left the guide and moved to the other buildings and spent a long time enjoying the view of the modern city, sprinkled with ancient ruins, below them. Finally their time was up and they descended the steps to their waiting taxi.

'You like?' asked the taxi driver.

'Fantastic', said Peter. 'I'm just amazed at the skill people had so long ago to build such a beautiful building.'

'Only the best for the Gods. You want go some other place?'

'No thanks.' They both spoke as one and then laughed.

That evening they ate outside in the little courtyard of their hotel. Peter had a beer and Alek sparkling water.

'Have you ever cheated and tried an alcoholic drink?'

Alek smiled. 'No. The evils of alcohol are drummed into us at an early age and it doesn't bother me. No doubt you've been drunk a few times.'

Peter nodded. 'It's not a nice feeling. You're not really in control, the room seems to revolve and, ultimately, you're sick as a parrot.'

'Yet people continue to do it. I don't understand why.'

'Well......,' Peter paused to think. 'If you have just one or two drinks there is a merry stage that makes you bolder, funnier, and you feel you are enjoying yourself. Want to try a sip?'

He held his beer out to Alek.

'No thanks. The guilt isn't worth it.'

They went to bed early that night, anticipating the need to be at the station the next morning.

It was going to be another scorcher but at seven, when they set off to walk to the station, they enjoyed the relative cool.

'I'm looking forward to being by the sea, warm breeze, a cool swim,' said Peter.

225

'The problem is, we don't know if we'll be able to enjoy Thessaloniki. What state will they be in? What kind of help will they need?'

'Perhaps we'll be asked to entertain the children. Then we could all go to the beach. After all that sight seeing a few lazy days sunbathing and swimming would suit me down to the ground.'

'You know, Peter, we're not tied together. If you'd like to do something different to me you're welcome. These are friends of my family, not yours so you owe them nothing.'

'True, Alek, but one of them is a seventeen year old girl so, if it's ok by you I'll stick around.' They grinned at each other and Peter knew Alek was glad of his support.

At the station they bought single tickets and found out the time of the next slow train. It was 8.30 so they went to the cafe and had breakfast.

'This Koulouri bread is delicious but I'm not sure about Graviera cheese. I think I'll have honey with mine.'

Alek sipped his coffee. 'You should try it, mild and sweet. I could definitely have this again.'

Breakfast finished they dragged their cases to the platform and stood, clock watching, hoping it would be on time. It was only ten minutes late and when they got on board they could see the train was showing its age. The seats were going threadbare but it was clean, it was taking them to Thessaloniki, so they settled down to enjoy the ride. It clattered along leaning dangerously around bends, even though it was not going fast. It stopped frequently but by half past four they arrived, on time.

They followed the other people off the platform and then out into the glaring sun. Taxies were shuffling up as the one before was filled so they joined the queue. Alek had the name of their hotel written down and when they got into the taxi he showed it and then asked, in English, how much it would cost. He was not sure if the price was fair. It sounded a lot but there were 546 drachmas to a pound. There was really no choice, so he nodded and they drove to the hotel. On the way the driver became a guide pointing out places of interest on the way.

'See, Our famous White Tower. You must visit, very good museum.' Here, Great statue of Alexander the Great, good for photo, Yes.? We have many, many places you can see and I can drive you.' He waved a card above his head and Alek took it and thanked him.

The hotel was modest but the receptionist, a pretty woman, was all smiles as she handed them a key and explained about the breakfast times. They walked up the stairs to their room and Peter looked at Alek.

'I'd like to take her out for a walk on the beach wouldn't you?'

'No, too old for me I think.'

'Older women have experience, so you can learn how to please.'

'So you know all about it do you? Have you actually, you know, done it?'

Peter smirked, 'Well there's lots of opportunities at Uni.......'

Alek opened the door to their room, stood his case on the floor and looked at Peter. 'You didn't answer the question so I assume you're still a virgin.'

'Ok, you're right. Not a bad room is it.'

They both laughed at the obvious change of subject, lay on the beds and discussed what they should do next. The decision was they should see if the delightful receptionist had a street map. If Evaggelistra Street was nearby, they would go there and take the family out for a meal.

The map showed the University Hospital was quite close and the street they wanted even closer so they set off.

The walk took just ten minutes and they soon found the building. Inside it was cool but they felt hot again as they climbed two flights of stone steps to their front door. Alek knocked feeling very nervous.

Chapter 26

Davud

Thessaloniki

I walked down the street watching the road shimmering like water, in the heat. Perhaps Dad had heat stroke, whatever that was. I stopped at a junction, looking first one way then the other, feeling panic rising. The map; that would help. I tugged it from my pocket and opened it out. Where was the hotel? The words danced, the white paper glaring in the sunshine and, just when I felt like crying again, I saw the symbol for the station. The words steadied. I looked around, saw the name of the road and found it on the map. It was a left turn then a right turn at the next junction. I set off with some confidence now that I could find my way.

When I got into the hotel, hoping Mum and Vjolica were back, I burst into their room, without knocking. They looked anxiously at me as I blurted out my news, weeping again. Mum hugged me, whispering soothing noises, like she had when I was little. Vjolica fetched a glass of water. I drank it quickly and the tears stopped, replaced by a sniff or two.

Mum released me, took a deep breath, and said, 'We must go and see him but we should have something to eat first to give Davud some energy.'

'I'll make sandwiches and Davud can show you where the hospital is on the map,' said Vjolica.

It was a very quick lunch, Mum having very little and me gobbling mine. Vjolica made us all drink water because it was easy to get dehydrated in such heat and off we went. It was too hot to talk and I think we all felt frightened. It was shocking to realise how much we all relied on Dad.

The hospital entrance was large and the reception desk obvious. Mum and Vjolica held back leaving the talking to me but I struggled to find the English words I needed.

'Excuse me can you speak English?'

'A little.'

'My father, Donjeta Kahshoven is here, this morning, in......er....ambulance.' I looked at her anxiously to see if she understood.

She tapped into her computer and smiled at me. 'He is in ward sixteen,' she gestured upwards, 'floor two'.

When we found him he was asleep and a nurse suggested we come back later in the afternoon when a doctor could explain his condition. Davud asked if we could just sit with him but she shook her head.

'Too many peoples. One only permitted. Yes?'

'We will leave Mum here. My sister and I will come back, at what time?'

'Four. Doctor will be here then. Also visiting permitted.'

Mum looked at me anxiously but relaxed when I translated. 'What will you do?'

'Don't worry we can spend a couple of hours exploring the town and we'll see you later.' Mum nodded and turned back to look at Dad. We went quietly out of the ward and left the hospital.

'This would be fun if I wasn't so worried about Dad,' said Vjolica. 'I love the freedom to walk about and not be forever looking for Serbian police. Mum and I really enjoyed going to the supermarket together this morning. We browsed for ages looking at everything. Anyway where shall we go now?'

'I want to go to the harbour again and watch the ships. Perhaps if we walked along we could find a beach.'

The map, still in my pocket, proved useful. When we arrived we leant against a railing watching the ferries manoeuvring, docking and unloading. Vjolica smiled at me and then frowned.

'Davud, you're burning. Your face and neck are really red. I have my headscarf but you need a hat. We must see if we can find a place that sells them.'

'Do you have any money?'

'Yes. Mum asked me to look after the purse so I paid at the checkout. I still have it. Look I think there's a beach up ahead and if the tourists go there we should find a shop.'

The shop had sun hats, buckets and spades and post cards. I tried several caps on and eventually chose a red one. The sea sparkled; the waves tumbled in, splashed down leaving a foamy trail on the beach as they went back. We couldn't resist it and soon we were both paddling.

'When we were on the train I wondered what sand would feel like. It's soft and squidgy when it's wet. This is wonderful isn't it Davud?'

Eventually we had to return to the hospital. As I brushed the sand off my feet, pulling my socks and shoes back on I said, 'I feel a bit guilty with Dad ill and Mum worried.'

'Me too but I'm sure they'd be happy for us.'

We walked on using the shady side of the street and arrived just a few minutes after four. When we entered the ward it was great to see Dad sitting up in bed. Mum and he were talking to a doctor. Mum quickly told us that Dad had pneumonia, with minor complications.

'The doctor says he'll have to stay for several days to see how he responds to treatment and it could take two to three weeks before he'll be fit enough for travelling.'

Dad beckoned us closer when the doctor left. His voice was breathy and speaking seemed a great effort. 'I'm sorry about this. I'm really worried about money, now, because my treatment will cost a great deal. I'm so tired I can't think straight. We need help.' He closed his eyes and was instantly asleep.

'Do you know how much money we have left?'

Mum looked at Vjolica bleakly and shook her head. 'Let's go back to the hotel and gather it all together, but before that we need to find out the cost of his treatment.'

I asked at the front desk and was told we had to see the almoner but we needed to make an appointment. She made it for the following morning.

In my room we searched bags and pockets for cash in various currencies and found two small gold bars. Mum and Vjolica brought what they had but counting it and understanding the value proved beyond us.

'Tomorrow we'll take it all to a bank and get it converted into drachma then we'll know what we have. Let's do this before meeting the almoner. Now, Vjolica, do you think there's enough left of our picnic to make a meal? We must save the salad until tomorrow.'

Mum looked exhausted and as soon as the food was eaten she went to bed. I helped Vjolica tidy up and went to bed too.

It felt strange having the room to myself. Before trying to sleep I wrote what had happened in my diary. I thought it unlikely anyone else would think of it and a money crisis on top of Dad's illness would surely make good reading for the rich Americans. Finally, I put the light out but my mind was in a kind of panic. I turned over, threw out a pillow then put it back. I would never sleep in this state so I sat up and put the light on. It seemed a light went on in my head too because, at that moment, I realised what we should do. We must write to Mr Dhomi. With that thought I was able to relax and sleep.

In my dream bombs were falling and there was a crashing of timber and bricks. I jerked awake, relieved to see where I was. Vjolica was knocking on my door. 'Hurry up Davud or you'll miss breakfast.'

We'd agreed to eat as much as possible, at breakfast, so we could miss lunch and save money. On my third piece of toast I remembered my idea to write to the Dhomi family. 'They are the only people we know who have enough money to help us and I'm sure they would. What do you think?'

Mum's face grimaced. 'I feel I've really reached rock bottom when I have to beg. I know it's a sensible idea but let's wait and see what the bank says. I had a thought too. We could rent just one room and ask if they have a mattress we could put on the floor. That would halve the cost of living here.'

Feeling a little more in control, we all went to the bank, before going to the hospital. It took longer than we thought, so Mum left Vjolica in there, whilst we went to see the almoner.

Her English was much better than mine and she understood our problem. 'I'll make it as little as possible but you really should have insurance.'

'We are refugees from Kosovo, not tourists,' I said.

She nodded and worked on her computer for a few minutes, then looked up, 'I'll print this estimate based on three nights in hospital, antibiotics both oral and intravenous, food, staffing costs, and ambulance.'

She handed the sheet to Mum. I looked at it after her and, even knowing there were a lot of drachma to the deutsche mark, it looked a huge amount. We thanked the almoner, left her office and met Vjolica outside Dad's ward. She deducted the cost from our funds and went white. 'How much does it cost per night in the hotel?'

Armed with that information she did some more calculations and whispered. 'We have enough to stay here for two weeks, eating very little, and then there is nothing left for travel, or anything.'

'You may go in and see Mr Kahshoven now, just one at a time and for only ten minutes because it is not the proper visiting time.' The nurse led Mum to his bedside, checked her watch, and left. He was awake and smiled weakly at her. I could just hear what they were saying from the doorway.

'I'm getting better. They let me walk to the bathroom and I made it, after sitting down to rest on the way. The distance to the bathroom was only ten metres. Mum looked as if she was about to cry.

'I hoped you'd be able to leave here tomorrow. I could nurse you if they gave us the antibiotics.'

'They won't let me out until the course is finished and the doctor said at least three nights. I'm not sure I'd be capable of walking back to the hotel. I'd need an ambulance or a taxi because I'm so weak. It's frustrating to be stuck in here and far too expensive.'

'You mustn't worry, just relax and rest. We're fine at the moment. We've had a look in your room and found some gold, deutsche marks, and drachma. You haven't any other money anywhere have you?'

'Did you search all my pockets? I also hid some in the cover of my diary.'

'We'll find it.'

There was a swish of skirts as the nurse bustled up and Mum stood up to go. She kissed his cheek, said she would be back at visiting time in the afternoon, and managed not to weep until she was with us, and walking out of the hospital. Vjolica gave her a hug and suggested we go back to the hotel and see if any more money could be found and then look for cheap lodgings.

I found a wad of deutsch marks in Dad's diary and a few drachma notes in the pockets of the trousers he had worn when he collapsed. It was enough to make a difference but we still needed to be very frugal. In the afternoon Vjolica went to the hospital to see Dad whilst I helped Mum look for somewhere cheap to stay.

We met back at the hotel and Vjolica said Dad felt a little better. Mum told her we had found a small, furnished, two bedroomed flat and we could move in immediately.

Then came a flurry of packing. We checked out of the hotel and walked to 16 Evaggeslistra, not far from the university and the hospital. Mum had rented it for one week and the whole week cost less than the two rooms in the hotel for just one night.

That evening Vjolica wrote to the Dhomi family explaining our predicament and giving our new address. She posted it and returned to the flat with a worried expression.

'I've just sent that letter but it'll probably take a week to get there and we're only planning to be here for a week. How can they reply to us?'

'I think we'll leave that to Allah. Now we must live for each day and pray for your father's quick recovery.'

His recovery was not quick; the days dragged and even the seaside and sunshine lost their magic. Vjolica and I had explored all the free sites of antiquity, The White Tower, The Monument of Alexander the Great and the Arch of Galerius. The soles of our shoes were wearing thin with the walking but it took our minds off the dire situation we were in.

Dad's three nights in hospital turned into seven. He had responded initially to the antibiotics and then had a relapse.

It was our last day at the flat. The landlord said we could have it for another week but Mum was not sure what to do. There was a good chance Dad would be discharged tomorrow but he would need to gain strength before he could travel. She decided to agree to stay one more week.

We were all sitting, writing our diaries, a few days later, when there was a knock at the door.

'It's probably the landlord we don't know anyone else. Will you let him in Davud?'

I opened it and looked blankly at two, tall young men, both beaming at me. The dark haired one spoke in Albanian, 'Hello, you must be Davud. I'm Alek Dhomi and this is my friend Peter.'

'Alek? Mum, Vjolica, look who's here! Come in please.'

When they entered the small living room they seemed to fill it and for a moment it was a chaos of greetings and hugs. Peter watched it all, excluded from the reunion. Vjolica looked properly modest as she invited him, in English, to sit and asked if he would like some tea.

'Yes please, thank you.' She went to boil the kettle. I wondered how she would manage because there were only four cups but when she brought it in on a tray there was a glass of water. Peter was staring at her. She looked down with a little smile and busied herself with giving out the drinks.

'I don't understand how you can be here so quickly when Vjolica only sent the letter just over a week ago,' I said.

Alek explained about their holiday and it all made sense.

'So how long is it since you were all friends in Kosovo?' Peter asked.

There was a silence whilst everyone, but Mum, thought about it. I translated the question for her. Finally Vjolica said, 'It's about seven years. So much has happened it seems longer.'

'You certainly look different now, Vjolica. All grown up.'

'So do you Alek. Do you still play the guitar? In one of your dad's letters it said you were in a band?'

'We both do.' He turned to include Peter. "Peter plays bass and I play acoustic. We had a group and played several concerts for a while, but then Peter went to college and we broke up.'

I was translating this for Mum. 'Ask Peter what he studies at college, Davud.'

Peter explained he had three years before he would be qualified to teach.

'Mum says teaching is an honourable profession,' I said.

Alek changed the subject, bringing it back to the present. He asked if they would be able to visit Dad in hospital in the four days they had in Thessaloniki. I said I was sure Dad would be delighted and just as surprised as we were.

'We've had no time to explore the town yet,' said Alek. 'Would you like to come for a walk with us and then we could have lunch, our treat?'

I quickly translated and Mum shook her head. She asked us all to go whilst she did some washing and saw the landlord. She had enough food for lunch and would meet us at the hospital.

Vjolica and I led the way we knew so well, to the harbour.

Chapter 27

Davud

Thessaloniki

Dad was overwhelmed when he was introduced to Alek and Peter. I saw tears in his eyes.

He asked how they could have been told about Vjolica's letter, written just a week earlier, when they were in Rome. Alek explained the wonders of e-mail and he shook his head in amazement.

'So can you get a message to your father from here?'

'Yes. I could ring him or find a cyber cafe where they have computers and I can pay to use one.'

'Amazing. Such fast communicating shrinks the world. But Alek I would really like you to … It's so hard to beg. We are desperate, Alek, with not enough money to continue our journey because of the cost of my treatment here.'

'Please don't worry. I can write to him tomorrow and I may even get a reply immediately. I know he'll want to help. When will you be fit to leave?'

'The doctor says tomorrow morning. They'll give me one more course of antibiotics just to make sure there's not another relapse. Will I see you again before you leave?'

'Yes, don't worry we are here to help. We still have two days. I'll book a taxi to take you back to the flat tomorrow. If you are well enough I'd like to hear about your journey.

Dad will want to know all about it and will be cross if I only have half the story.'

That made him smile and when they left he held Mum's hand. 'I prayed you know, for help.'

She smiled, 'I did too and Allah has been merciful. We'll be forever indebted to Fadil. He has proved to be a true friend.'

The officious nurse bustled in, calling an end to visiting, and we left Dad in hospital for the last time. When we emerged into the hot sun Peter and Alek were waiting for us. We all walked together and Peter walked beside Vjolica.

'I think you must be very shy. Why do you always look away from me?'

'I do not understand. My English is not good.'

'Say something to me in English.'

She giggled, quietly, probably aware I was listening. 'My name is Vjolica. I am a refugee from Kosovo. Do you understand?'

'Yes, very good. How old are you?'

'You know I am eighteen. How old are you?

'Nineteen.'

By then we had reached the flat and although they were invited to have a cup of tea. Alek refused saying he wanted to find a cyber cafe. As they walked along he said, 'You were enjoying Vjolica's conversation, I noticed.'

Peter smiled and related it to him.

'Ah, not exactly riveting then.'

'No. Is she very shy? She never looks at me.'

'That's the Muslim way. It would be considered very forward for a woman to look directly at a man. She must always be, what's the word, looking down. It's very different from English girls. Look here's a travel agent. Let's see how much flights from Athens to London would cost for the four of them.'

They went in and explained the situation. The agent asked how Donjeta was, explaining that he had collapsed in their office and she'd called the ambulance.

'I will get as good a price as I can. I was very sorry for the young man who had to go home and tell his mother. Now there are two flights everyday at midday and at nine in the evening. August is not a good time because flights are more expensive but I will write down the prices, days and times. At the moment there is space on all these but I cannot guarantee until you book.'

They thanked her and walked out into the sunshine heading with just one thought to get a cold drink. As the cold beer slaked his thirst Peter asked about the English attitude to refugees. Alek shook his head, frowning.

'I don't know. It was easier for us because there were not many from Kosovo. Since then they have come in greater numbers. I'm just hoping they'll allow them to stay. Donjeta is a surgeon and was much respected so perhaps they'll see his value.'

Peter stood up. 'I'll ask if they know of a cyber cafe.'

He returned with a crude pencil drawn map and they left the bar. It took about ten minutes and there were several free computers so they paid for half an hour each. Peter wrote to his parents telling them about their changed plans, the plight of the Kahshoven family and their beautiful daughter.

Alek typed quickly,

'Hello, from Thessaloniki.

We have found the Kahshovens and Donjeta is recovering from a very severe bout of pneumonia. He will be discharged tomorrow and they cannot pay the bill. I have some drachma left and some traveller's cheques but that is not enough. Even if I use the emergency credit card there is not enough in my account. I hope you have some ideas.

Very worried,

Alek.

The letter had only taken five minutes to write and he had time left to check his e-mails. There was a long one from Sam, telling him about her latest conquest, and asking if there was a chance of the group meeting up for a session whilst Peter was home from Uni. He asked Peter, who said he'd like that, then wrote back to her. With just five minutes to go a new e-mail arrived and he saw it was from his Dad.

'Dear Alek,

Thank you for all your efforts to help the Kahshovens. I think the best, immediate solution is for you to use the emergency credit card. I will put the money into your bank as soon as you tell me how much you have actually spent. It can wait until you get home because you will not incur charges until the end of the month.

Please tell Donjeta that I will contact the charity that found us accommodation here and they may be able to help with his immigration.

I can't believe we are going to see them soon,

Thanks again,

Love Dad

Peter and Alek walked back towards their hotel with a sense of relief that their responsibility was nearly over.

'It's our last day tomorrow,' said Alek. 'Shall we take the family out for a farewell dinner tonight? They look like they could all do with a square meal.'

'I think Vjolica looks just perfect as she is but yes I think it's a good idea. This will be my treat. I have more cash left than you and we won't need drachmas much longer.'

They turned towards Evaggelistra and were welcomed warmly with the inevitable cup of tea.

'We've lots to tell you,' began Alek and Peter let the Albanian chatter waft over him as he watched Vjolica's face change from smiling to smiling with tears. She even looked lovely through all the gamut of emotions. Perhaps he should learn Albanian so he could talk to her. His reverie was broken by Vjolica, who spoke in English. 'Thank you, Peter, we will like dinner tonight.'

'Good. Shall we meet you at the Taverna at seven?' She nodded and they left the family in a much more relaxed state than when they arrived.

'Do you think we've time for a quick dip in the sea before we go out?'

'Sounds good but we'd better hurry.'

With those words Alek began to run and they were in their hotel room, changed with towels over their arms in fifteen minutes. Only a short walk from the sea they were soon wading, splashing and swimming, the late afternoon sunshine still beating down upon them. Peter swam away from the shore but Alek, not a confident swimmer, contented himself with floating and swimming a few strokes in the shallows.

Peter returned and they reluctantly came out of the sea. As they towelled themselves he said, 'I can now say I've swum in the Aegean Sea. It was brill but we'd better hurry now. They broke into a stumbling run over the soft sand, reached their hotel room, showered and changed with just enough time to get to the Taverna.

Peter looked at Vjolica. He could not stop looking at her, wondering what her hair was like under her scarf. Was it long, flowing over her shoulders or short? He wanted to hold her and run his fingers through it. Could he ask her about her hair? Would that be too personal a question? He needed to talk to Alek about protocol.

Davud

The dinner was long and lovely. We all managed to eat two courses, the last being baclava.

'In Albania we eat this as a pudding. My mother makes it. Her baclava is really good,' I said. Mum saw everyone looking at her and frowned. Alek quickly translated and she smiled at the compliment. She then surprised everyone saying, in English,

'Thank you Peter, dinner good. Thank you Alek.'

Everyone clapped. It was lovely to see her smiling and happy. The evening went quickly and I yawned, so Mum said we ought to leave. Peter and Alek escorted us home. Once again Peter walked beside Vjolica. I think he found her attractive.

The next morning promised to be another glorious, hot day. Peter had agreed to stay behind because there would be too many people in the taxi. When Alek arrived at the ward we were assembled. Dad had been given the bill and

Alek took it from him and went to the almoner's office to pay it.

'Please tell your father how grateful I am for paying my medical expenses. We escaped with some money but not enough for an emergency like this.'

'I'll tell him but, hopefully, you'll be able to tell him yourself soon.' The conversation was interrupted by a nurse who insisted Donjeta went to the taxi in a wheelchair. Alek pushed it, helped him into the taxi and the nurse wished him good luck.

'I'm sure I could've walked to the entrance but there was no point in arguing. But I could not have walked to the flat, wherever that is, so I'm grateful for the taxi, Alek.'

The journey was just a few moments and when they arrived Alex got out quickly, paid the fare and helped Mum and Dad to get out, saying,

'I won't come in with you. I need to pack. Peter and I are catching the train back to Athens tomorrow and fly out in the evening back to England. But we will both come after lunch to see how you are and to talk about your journey.'

'Thank you Alek, for everything,' said Mum, and he left.

Dad was suddenly exhausted so after a cup of tea and a look around the flat he fell asleep in the armchair. Vjolica and I went to buy some food, leaving Mum writing her diary.

Ajeshe

Donjeta's sudden illness was shocking but seeing our money disappearing, in medical costs, was terrifying. I have never felt so vulnerable and frightened. Then, unexpectedly, Alek appeared, with his English friend Peter, and solved our biggest problem. They go home tomorrow and I'm already feeling bereft. Donjeta, asleep just across the room, is not strong enough to travel and we still have to worry about funds. I'm not sure we have enough for our train fare and flights, more rent for this flat and so on. I know this diary entry is full of anxiety but that's my state of mind. I wish we could go home but there is no home now. We must make a new life in England, if they will let us.

I can hear the children returning from the shops so I need to get lunch. I hope my next entry will be more positive.

Davud

We crept in, not wanting to wake Dad but he opened his eyes and sat straighter in his chair. 'I haven't been asleep,' he said, his eyes twinkling.

'Don't believe a word he says,' said Mum, laughing. 'He's been asleep, snoring, all the time you've been out. Stay and chat to him whilst I unpack the groceries and get lunch.'

In just a few minutes Mum had laid out a plate of cheeses, tomatoes, sliced cucumber and a plate of buttered bread bringing it in on a tray.

'It's ready, sit up,' she said. When we were all sat at the table Dad said, 'I had no interest in food when I was in hospital but this looks so inviting I think I could eat it all.'

'You'd better not, I'm hungry too,' I said. We all laughed, ate, talked; everyone glad to be together as a family again.

Chapter 28

As the slow train lurched its way along the line, seeming reluctant to leave Thessaloniki, Alek and Peter relaxed into their seats.

'It was good wasn't it; being able to help them. I'm glad we did it,' said Peter. Alek smiled, remembering the incredulous delight when he pressed train and flight tickets into Donjeta's hand with a wad of Drachma. They had pooled what they had, kept just enough for something to eat as they travelled that day, and given the family the rest. 'Me too. But, even though we've helped them, they've got an uphill struggle once they get to London. They need to convince immigration that they fled in danger of their lives and that they really have no home left in Kosovo. Then they'll have to live on Social Security for six months before being allowed to look for work. I really don't understand why they can't apply for jobs immediately.'

Davud stopped talking as he glanced sideways at Peter and saw he was asleep. He shut his own eyes and the long train journey seemed much quicker than before when they both woke with only an hour to go before Athens.

Everything went to plan and they were back in England in the early hours of the following day. There was no one to meet them because of the unsociable hour. They caught a train to Leeds and finally a bus. Alek arrived home exhausted, just as the family were getting up. He took a cup of tea to his bedroom, got ready for bed and was asleep so quickly his tea was untouched.

It was Saturday, so all the family were around, when he surfaced just after lunch. Mum fussed over him getting a sandwich and tea, obviously pleased to see him. The others were waiting to hear about his travels and the Kahshoven family.

'Ok, where shall I start? Rome. It was amazing and we nearly wore our trainers out visiting all the sights. The highlight for me was the Colosseum. It was huge and such a lot still standing after all those years. You know they even had pulleys and a lift system. They could flood it and have fights with ships. Technologically amazing for so long ago.'

'It's a place I've always wanted to see and one day we'll go there. Now tell us about Greece,' asked Dad.

Alek related everything they had done answering questions about Donjeta's health, how tall Davud was, and so on.

'Thank you for being so kind to them, especially giving what drachma you had left. I'm proud of you, Alek. I hope they were grateful,' said Mum.

'They really were. Peter and I enjoyed helping them.'

'So when will they arrive in London?' asked Dad. 'I'm quite tempted to meet them at the airport.'

' Next weekend but is there much point? Won't they get whisked away by immigration? I think you would do better to wait until they ring you. It's a long way to go and be disappointed.'

'You're right, of course, but I wanted them to see a friendly face. It can all seem so bleak at first, although I don't suppose you remember.'

Alek snorted. 'I wasn't that young. It wasn't all bad either. I loved the beach at Clacton.'

'So did I,' said Rita. 'Hearing all about your holiday makes me want ours to hurry up. At least in Florida they speak English so we can speak to everyone.' The computer made a noise and everyone looked towards it.

'Well it can't be you this time. Let's see who's writing to us.'

Dad got up and moved the mouse. He was quiet for a moment and then looked around at them all.

'It's from Vjolica. I'll read it out.'

'Dear Mr and Mrs Dhomi, Alek and Rita,

I am new to using computers and e-mail but there was a kind tourist in the cyber cafe that helped me. Mum and Dad wanted me to tell you how grateful we are to you for all the money and to Alek and Peter for all their kindness to us. Dad is getting stronger every day and can now walk to the port and back but has to stop for a sit down. Alek will know how far that is and I hope he is impressed. We are now confidant that he will be well enough to travel and are looking forward to seeing England. It is very hot here in Greece so we will enjoy the cooler weather when we travel north.

Thank you again. We hope to repay you one day.

Vjolica Kahshoven.'

'Is that a long walk?' asked Rita.

'Yes, we did it often. There and back is probably two or even three kilometres. When Donjeta came out of hospital he could manage no more than a few steps so that's great progress. I'm going back to my room to unpack. There's a lot of washing, Mum. Shall I put a load into the machine?'

'Yes please. I've done all ours anticipating a suitcase-full.'

The weekend passed quickly and Dad and Alek returned to work. Alek was surprised at his enthusiasm. When he was at school he dreaded the idea of going back after a holiday. Now he wanted to share his holiday stories with Mr Sawyer and could hardly wait for his course to begin. He was so lucky to have all these opportunities and he wondered what might have happened if they had stayed in Kosovo like the Kahshovens.

Travelling

Donjeta

This record of our journey has been sadly neglected by me but I think the others have been writing.

Having pneumonia was a huge shock. I was totally helpless, just when my family needed me to be strong and looking after them. When I think of what might have happened if Alek had not rescued us; it frightens me. But he did come and now, thanks to him and his father, we are on a plane to London.

When we get there I will show our papers and say we are refugees. Then I'll have to hope the immigration officials believe our story and allow us to stay. Fadil has written to support my case so that may help.

All my life I have worked and been in control of my life. Now I am destitute and have no control over my/our future. It is a bleak prospect and I'm finding it hard to keep positive. I suspect I'm still weak from being ill.

A steward is approaching with trays of food so I'll put this away and hope my next entry is happier.

Davud

Seeing Dad writing in his diary made me get mine out. I want to say how excited I am about being on an aeroplane. I couldn't believe how big it was when we saw it land. Now I'm inside this great beast and it's lovely being waited on. We have had drinks, peanuts and I can smell hot food so it won't be long before that arrives.

I don't know what to expect in London or where we'll sleep tonight but I don't care. We will be in England, at last and I just know it's going to be good.

I must write to Mr Dushku when we get settled because I promised. It would be lovely to be able to tell him I'm going to an English school.

I'll write more next time but everything must be put away so there is room on my little table for food.

'Ladies and gentlemen welcome to London, Heathrow. The temperature is eighteen degrees, overcast but dry. Please keep your seat belts fastened until the plane has come to a complete stop and the seat belt light goes out. Thank you for flying with Aegean Airways.'

I translated this for Mum. She looked anxiously out of the window watching the plane turn and taxi until it stopped. Then she looked around as the plane erupted with activity. The little corridor was filled with people trundling small cases behind them and it seemed unending. Eventually Dad stood up and halted the traffic so we could move and we shuffled to the door. The draught that met us seemed both chill and welcoming. But there was no pausing to breathe in the fresh air. We had to follow everyone until they went through immigration where we were asked to accompany an officer to a small room. Chairs were found for all of us and we were asked to show our papers again.

'My name is John Robinson and my job is to assess if you are genuine refugees. It will be up to me, in the next few weeks, to decide if you can stay and live in this country.' I nodded but he had spoken quite quickly so I was not sure if the others had understood.

'You are Albanian Kosovars form Pristina?' He said, looking at the documents. "Do you speak English?"

'I am quite good but my mother speaks no English,' I said. Mr Robinson smiled. 'Please ask your family if they are happy to talk to me today or if they are too tired. Do you understand?' I nodded and asked them.

Dad answered, 'I would like to talk now but are you good with my son...... erm,' 'Translating?' I said. It was agreed that I could do it and the interview began. The questions were straightforward. I had to concentrate hard and was soon wilting with the effort. He seemed to be aware of this and offered a short break with a cup of tea.

When we were ready for the next session he summarised what had been established so far and asked us to confirm it was correct. 'There is not much more to do today. I have a letter of recommendation from a Mr Fadil Dhomi and I will be contacting him. I also have a letter from a charitable organisation in Leeds so I need to talk to them as well. You will be tired now and you will be escorted to a hostel for refugees. The accommodation is basic but meals are provided. You must report back to me next week.......' he flipped through his diary, 'Monday August the sixteenth, at

10am. I'll write that down for you on my card.' He stood up and we did the same. 'Have you any questions?'

'Are we free to...... leave the hostel, to go into the street? Also we have no English money.' Dad looked very tense and worried.

'There is a bank for changing money just outside this office and you can do that while you wait for your escort. I need to see some more people now so please wait in the chairs out here. Oh and you are free to go out. A hostel is not a prison.'

The hostel was bleak, grey and very unwelcoming. We were given two bedrooms and there was a tiny communal kitchen where we could make drinks. The ground floor had a larger kitchen where meals were prepared and tables and chairs to use at meal times. Everything was clean but cheerless.

'I hope we don't have to stay here a long time,' said Vjolica.

'It'll seem better in the morning after a night's sleep,' said Mum. We unpacked our few possessions and went to bed.

Breakfast was from seven until eight so we were ready in good time and I was surprised at the number of people queuing and the noise. There were no soft furnishings to deaden the sound and everything resonated. Everyone seemed to be shouting at each other to be heard and were speaking in many different languages. We didn't try to compete and ate quietly, listening for the familiar sound of Albanian. When we had finished eating we lingered in the dining room because we had not decided what to do with the day.

Suddenly the door burst open and a Muslim woman entered, trying to control her boisterous son. He was tugging at her hand and he was speaking our language.

'I'd like to talk to her,' said Mum. 'I'll let her get her breakfast and sit down before I do.'

We watched as Mum was invited to sit with them and they talked for a long time. Finally she stood, came back to us as we waited curiously but she just asked us to come and be introduced.

'This is Drita and her son Erion.'

We said hello, told her our names but cleaners had arrived and we had to leave the dining room. We promised to speak more at lunchtime. On the way back to our rooms Mum told us Drita's story.

'Her whole family were killed, husband, mother, father and brother when the bombs missed the airport and hit her village. Most of the houses were destroyed. Those left alive were given no help so they walked to Pristina and Serbian police took them to the station like they did with us. She had nothing, no extra clothes, no money and little Erion to look after.'

Tears were running down her cheeks as she spoke. 'It makes me realise how lucky we've been to be here, safe and to have friends we can rely on. She has nobody.'

'So how did she get here and why did she come to England?' asked Davud.

'I don't know but I expect we'll meet again. Listening to her story was emotional but it was good to speak Albanian again.'

'Let's go for a walk and see what's around here,' said Vjolica. 'We've done nothing but sit on trains and planes and I need to get some exercise.'

'I know you're right Vjolica but I'd much prefer to rest,' said Dad. 'I'm happy for all of you to explore but I need to sleep.'

I wanted to protest that we had only just finished breakfast so how could Dad be tired, but remembered how ill he'd been and held the words back.

In the street there was no sign of shops so we had no idea which way to go. Vjolica tossed a coin,

'Heads we go 'left.'

'Tails,' I called.

'Ok, you've won.' We turned right and walked briskly, revelling in the fresh English Summer, such a contrast to the stifling heat of Greece. We found a small parade of shops, several churches and a Mosque.

'"Dad will be pleased,' said Vjolica. 'He said he wanted to kiss the ground, like the Pope does when he arrives somewhere, but better still he'd like to give thanks in a mosque.'

'Davud can show him the way this afternoon,' said Mum. 'It's not that long a walk. Let's buy some tea and milk on the way back. I'm missing having a kitchen to work in already.'

Vjolica suddenly darted into a newsagent. I waited with Mum for a while and, as she seemed a long time, I went in after her. She was looking carefully at a thick book and when I got closer I saw it was a street map of London.

'It's too expensive to buy but I've found our street and was wondering how far it would be to walk to our meeting on Monday.' Before she could find it a sales assistant came up. 'Are yer buyin' that or what?'

'No, thank you,' said Vjolica.

'In that case don't dog ear the book.' Neither of us fully understood what she meant but the tone was enough. The book was returned to the shelf and we left. Mum said she thought we had walked far enough and she wanted to go back so we bought the tea, milk and some biscuits then returned to the hostel. In the half an hour left before lunch we wrote in our diaries.

In the dining room there was no sign of Drita so Mum was unable to find out more about her. As soon as lunch was over Dad and I went to the mosque.

Vjolica

When Dad and Davud left us this afternoon I looked at Mum who confessed she felt totally lost. 'There's nothing to do and I'm not enjoying it. I don't even remember what day of the week this is.' She looked so bleak I hugged her. Then I told her it was Friday and we had two more days to fill before our appointment on Monday. I suggested we explored the hostel a little more to see if there was a laundry room. We had so few clothes we needed to wash every other day. Mum cheered up with that suggestion and we soon found it. There were two washing machines and tumble dryers that needed lots of coins. There was also a soap powder dispenser but that needed coins too.

Our afternoon went quickly with another trip to the shops to buy washing powder and to accumulate a lot of fifty pence and pound coins. By the time we were putting clean, dry clothes into drawers, Dad and Davud had returned and we all went to the dining room for the evening meal.

Davud

Drita and Erion entered the dining room at the same time so Dad asked if they would like to join us. We pushed two tables together and once we were all seated, with food, Mum asked Drita what her plans were.

'I'm waiting to hear if I can stay in this country. If I can they will find me a house and give me money. Are you the same?' We all nodded and Dad said, 'We're lucky that we have friends in a town called Leeds and we hope we can go there to live too.'

The conversation flowed freely and we all enjoyed speaking Albanian but, inevitably, the subject of the bombing and cruelty of the Serbs came up making us feel sad. When we parted to go back to our rooms Vjolica said, 'I really hate going over all that has happened again and again. First we had to say it to Mr Robinson and then again tonight. I really want to put all of it behind us and start our new life.'

'I know,' said Dad. 'It's Saturday tomorrow, Fadil could be at home, so I'll phone him. I'm sure he'll want to know we've arrived. There's a phone box at the shops, if I can understand how to work it. But now I'm ready for bed.'

Vjolica

Everyone's asleep but my mind is racing so I hope, by writing in my diary, I can then settle and relax. I should probably be writing my official one but I'm always aware that other people are going to read it.

All the awful things that happened in Kosovo haunt me. First the attack on Granddad and then Erin's violent death and the bombing. Every time I close my eyes I relive the horror. Talking about it only makes it more vivid. The journey, Dad's illness, having no money was hard to cope with on top of all that. I hate the uncertainty of our future and the total inactivity we're all enduring now.

The only light so far has been Alek and Peter. He's really handsome, Peter, I mean. I love his floppy fair hair and twinkling blue eyes when he smiles. He's taller than Alek, not fat but, how can I put it, well built? Anyway he's not skinny. Nearly all the people in Kosovo were skinny but he seemed the picture of health. I can't stop thinking of him. Mum would say I'm mooning because I don't have enough to do and she's probably right.

I wonder if he thinks of me.

Chapter 29

Leeds

The phone rang and Fadil leant over and picked it up. He listened and then sat up with a broad smile. 'How are you? We've been so worried.' His face showed concern and then smiled again when he received good news. 'So where are you? I'd really like to come and see you but I suppose you can't be sure how long you'll be at the hostel.'

He listened. 'Yes, I see. Ok I'll wait to hear from you after Monday. It's been so good to talk to you again and to know you're well. I'll tell Alek and he'll pass it on to Peter. They'll be so pleased. Bye now, love to the family, bye.'

He wanted to tell everyone but they were all out. He felt excited, needed to do something, so he went up into the loft and brought down the cases. They were going to Florida soon and Marigana had already asked him, twice, to fetch them. That only took a few minutes and then he put the kettle on, anticipating the return of the family and looked at his diary. There was only one free weekend and then they were away so if he wanted to go to London to see Donjeta it had to be next Saturday. He would ask Marigana................. His thoughts were interrupted by the arrival of large shopping bags beneath which were his wife and daughter.

'We've had such a brill time Dad. I can't wait to show you all the things I've bought.'

Rita's face was glowing and he smiled indulgently. 'I'll make some tea and you can both give me a fashion parade. I assume you've indulged too,' he said, looking at Marigana.

'Of course. I can't have my daughter showing me up, can I?'

They all laughed and Fadil went into the kitchen whilst upstairs the bags were opened and he could hear the chatter of happy voices.

When they appeared, shyly sporting new summer trousers and T-shirts he was struck how much they had changed in seven years and how influenced by the English way of life. His wife used to wear more traditional clothes but now the only sign of her religion was a scarf that she wore outside. She was also more confident and he knew she enjoyed the greater equality of the sexes.

'You both look beautiful and ready for the Florida sunshine. Are you changing into another outfit now?'

'Yes, just one more each, for the evenings.' They hurried up the stairs and he hoped the eveningwear would be reasonably modest. He had no wish to spoil their pleasure. The door burst open.

'Ta-da!' said Rita, posing like a model.

'Oh that's really pretty. Do a twirl. Yes it swings and swirls around your ankles. Lovely. Where's Mum?'

As he spoke she appeared in a long skirt with a toning top, a hint of glitter at the neck and sleeve tops.

'That's superb. I shall be a proud man with two such lovely women to squire on holiday. Now when you're back in your normal clothes I want to tell you something. Hurry your tea's getting cold.'

When they returned he told them about the call from Donjeta and his idea to go to London to see them on Saturday.

'That's only a few days before we go away. It's a pity you can't have a longer holiday then we could all go, stay there and fly out to Florida.'

'That's a good idea. It would certainly save a lot of driving, although I had thought about using the train on Saturday.'

'I don't really want to go on Saturday, Dad. Peter and Alek are playing at the youth club and I said I'd go.'

'Ah, I'd forgotten. Let me think about it.'

In the basement of the surgery Pete's Pizzazz was rehearsing. They were all feeling rusty and not quite in sync with each other.

'We seem to have lost the plot. Perhaps we were never that good,' said Alek.

'Bollocks,' said Sam. 'We were brilliant. Let's try it again, a bit faster.' She set a beat going on the drums, added taps on the cymbal and suddenly she seemed to have lit a spark.

''Ok, er-one, two, three, four.....'

Their first chord was spot on time and the piece came alive with rhythm and bounce. When it came to an end, with a flourish, everyone was smiling.

'Wow what a difference! Well done Sam.'

Her face lit up with Alek's praise and he was glad he had said it. From that moment the practice went well and by lunchtime they all agreed they would be able to do the Youth Club gig the following week. As they packed up Sam asked Alek how his job was going.

'I love it. I've finally decided what I'm doing with my life and start college for some qualifications next month.'

'So will you be away too, like Peter?'

'No I'm doing it day release so it's local. Why?'

She shrugged, 'Dunno really. I've missed all this, you,...... and the others. Anyway got things to do yer know, must be off.'

Suddenly she seemed in a great hurry and Alek realised she felt embarrassed.

'Sam, wait.'

She paused and unslung her rucksack, 'What?'

'Do you fancy having a coffee, lunch or something?'

'Ok, cool.'

They went out leaving Peter and Mark looking at each other eyebrows raised.

As he walked home, later, Alek felt excited and ambivalent about his feelings. He had really enjoyed being with Sam. She was so easy to talk to and a lot of fun. He was impressed she had already been promoted at the supermarket, now a supervisor. She said she had also applied for a management course. They had not held hands or kissed but he had asked to see her again on Wednesday evening. What would his Mum and Dad think of her? He knew her currant rainbow streaked hair, Goth make up and multiple ear piercings would shock them. He felt himself getting aroused at the thought of discovering piercings elsewhere on her body. She was much shorter than him, slim, small breasted........

The musings ceased when he got through the front door to be met with Rita excitedly telling him about her new clothes and the possibility of them leaving early for their holiday. Dad smiled. 'We've been talking about it and if Donjeta and his family are still at the hostel next week we'll go down a day or two earlier to London. It'll break up their week and be lovely for us to meet them again. Is that ok with you? It means being here on your own even longer.'

It flashed through Alek's mind that he might not be totally alone, if Sam was interested in taking things further.

'That's no problem. I'll be busy at work during the day and Peter's still around until mid September so we'll meet up.'

He instantly knew he would not mention Sam and then felt guilty. Was he ashamed of her?

On Monday evening Donjeta phoned. Dad listened as he almost gabbled with excitement. The others were all there in the living room, the television turned off, as they waited to hear the news. Finally, he said goodbye and hung up.

"It's great news,' he said, smiling. "They're going to be allowed to stay and he said my letter had helped. They will be getting a house in Leeds through the same charity that helped us but it needs decorating so it won't be ready for two weeks. During the next few days they will get their social security documents and they can't wait to see us. I think we'll take them out for a celebration dinner.'

'Brill,' said Rita, caught up in Dad's excitement. 'I can wear my new outfit.'

When they had gone the house seemed too quiet. Alek was glad he was going out with Sam that night and dashed around in the early morning tidying in case she was prepared to come back to his house after the meal. The day at work seemed unusually long and he knew it was because he was wishing it away to see Sam again. He decided to take her to an Italian restaurant. Would she tuck into a huge pizza or nibble at a lettuce leaf? There was so much he didn't know about her and he wanted to know everything.

After work he showered, changed, combed his hair and posed in front of a long mirror hoping he looked smart enough for a proper date. Then he caught the bus, got off at the bus station and walked up to the junction of Briggate and The Headrow. She was not there yet so he stood for a while and then looked at his watch.

'Only five minutes late. Did you think I'd stood you up?'

She looked different. He smiled, 'you've changed your hairstyle. You look great.'

The multi-coloured mess had been cut in a short bob, now shiny dark brown. The Goth look had been replaced by subtler make up, her lips no longer a scary black, a nearly natural pink. He bent downwards and kissed them, instantly worried that he was doing something wrong. They parted and she whispered, 'Call that a kiss?' stood on tiptoe and kissed him long and passionately. When they broke free, breathless, she took his hand, 'Come on. I'm starving. Where are we going?'

'Da Mario's?'

'Brill, I love Pizza.'

In the restaurant, they ordered and sipped their drinks while they waited. Alek asked why she had changed her look.

'I'm really trying to move up in my job and the HR bitch-from-hell told me I looked like shit and if I ever wanted to get promotion I needed to do something about it.' She grinned, ' Sorry if you thought I'd done it just for you.'

Alek felt himself going red, for that was what he'd hoped, but he was saved from replying with the arrival of the food. They both ate with relish and he was pleased she wasn't a nibbler.

'You're a Muslim, right?'

'Yes. What are you? No let me guess, an atheist.'

She shook her head. 'Nope, Wanna guess again?'

'Roman Catholic?'

'Closer, C of E actually.'

'Really? I'd never put you down as religious. I suppose it was the Goth look. So, do you go to church every Sunday?'

'Well I do if I'm pushed. My Mum's very keen and I don't have a Dad. There's just us two and I want to please her.'

Alek paused, his last forkful not reaching his mouth. Was it prying to ask if her parents were divorced? He said nothing so she filled the silence explaining that her father had died fighting in the Gulf War.

'That must have been really hard.'

The conversation was saved from becoming maudlin by the waiter clearing their plates and asking if they would like a sweet. They both refused, so he offered coffee, more cold drinks but Sam shook her head. Alek asked for the bill and when it came she insisted on paying half.

'I'm earning and don't hold with this old fashioned thing about the bloke having to pay.'

'Ok, ok. I won't argue.'

When they got outside she thanked him and he offered to walk her home. She refused, saying she was going by bus, so he walked her to the bus stop. When it arrived she gave him a quick peck on the cheek and got on it. He waved as it drove off and was pleased to see her waving madly too. Feeling slightly forlorn he turned and walked home, thinking.

If she had been more forward and come back to his house he would have been so muddled about her. He wanted to respect his girlfriend, as a good Muslim boy, but he was also longing to hold her, touch her. Smiling as he remembered her passionate kiss he decided he would be content with that. It was not long before Saturday when they'd meet for another band practice.

The following evening he had a call from Dad. 'It's been great meeting them again, but they're so thin I wanted to buy them the whole menu! Is everything alright with you?'

'Yes I'm fine.'

'They're staying in an awful place, Alek, and have nothing to do. I've offered them to come and stay in our house whilst we're in Florida. It'll work well if their house is ready on time. What do you think?'

'Erm.......'

'I know it will be putting a lot on your shoulders; you'd have to change the beds so it's all nice and fresh for them. You see if they're in Leeds they can explore their new area, have a look at the house they've been allocated. Please Alek.'

He finally found his voice. 'I suppose so. When would they come?'

'Well they have to wait for all their documents so I should think it would be some time next week. They've got our number so they can let you know. Thank you for agreeing. I'll ring again before we leave. Bye'

Alek switched off the phone and said, 'Shit!'

Chapter 30

Vjolica,

Writing her diary

I really felt we were like the poor relations when we went out to dinner. It had been wonderful to meet them again. Mum and Marigana were crying and even the men's faces were red with emotion. Couldn't believe how tall and beautiful Rita has become (Hate her!)

No, getting back to the dinner, they all looked so smart and, of course we still have so few clothes, most of them in need of binning. Donjeta wanted to take us to this really expensive restaurant but we would have stood out like Cinderella in our rags. Very embarrassing!

The meal was superb. Actually almost any meal would have been great compared to the food at the hostel. Dad calls it brown sludge or red sludge depending on tomato input and we get rice or potatoes. Sometimes there are carrots, whoopee. We're all looking forward to having a home of our own and being able to buy food and cook it ourselves.

Just between these pages I felt insanely jealous of the Dhomi family. They're so wealthy they can afford to go on holiday to Florida! Rita was prattling on about two days in Disney and then Water World, or was it Sea life? I don't know it was one string of attractions most of which I've never even heard of.

When I mentioned a little of this to Mum she reminded me that they had once been as poor and needy as us and had turned their lives around. She said I needed to trust in Allah, that we could achieve the same. I'm trying. I really am.

We are going to go to Leeds sooner than we thought and stay at their house. That means I might see Peter next week! Can't wait!

Meanwhile we are sitting in this hostel waiting for letters enabling us to claim money. Dad has already written to the BMA asking about his qualifications and if he will be able to find work in the Leeds area, when he is allowed to work.

Now we've been accepted as refugees they've offered us English-speaking lessons, starting tomorrow morning. I'm looking forward to that as a break from the dull grey walls of this place. The Dhomi's fly off on their holiday tomorrow morning and we will be going out with them tonight. I wish I had a lovely flowing skirt to wear, a pretty blouse and strappy shoes with just a little heel.

I've written loads today. I suppose it's because something good has happened. It's hard to write when every day is the same boring day as the one before.

Davud has been writing his diary for the Americans but he's signalling to me so I'll stop.

Davud

'I've finished another entry and I think, as a family, we should decide when to send it off. Perhaps when we move into the house in Leeds.

'So, what do you want to do now? We've all the rest of the day to kill.'

Vjolica seemed to be challenging me as she stood with her hands on her hips. I had no chance to answer because Dad came in his face alive with excitement.

'Fadil and family are here. They want us to come with them and spend the day seeing the sights of London.

'Wow. Why didn't they mention this last night?' I asked.

'I don't know. It doesn't matter. He just said they haven't explored London so they're keen to make the most of the day and have us with them. Can you get ready to go now?'

We went to our rooms and emerged combed and spruced as well as we could in two minutes.

The street where the hostel is and the small area we have explored to the shops is quiet, mostly residential. Getting an underground into the tourist part of London was amazing. We used a lift to go down inside the station, found the line we needed and stood on the platform. As we waited for the next train, a flashing sign said it would come in one minute. There was a rush of warm, wind and the black tunnel was suddenly filled as the train burst through and stopped with a screech of brakes. Doors slid open, a few people got out then we entered and sat down. It lurched off and at each station more people got on than got off and soon people were standing, packed bodies pressed together.

'We'll have to push our way out when we get to Westminster Station,' said Vjolica. 'I never expected it to be so crowded.'

Dad leant towards us to say we needed to get off at the next stop. I knew that because I'd been following the map on the wall, but I didn't say so. We stood up as it slowed and followed people off so there was no need to push.

Our first destination was Westminster Palace, a massive impressive old building right beside the River Thames. Fadil thought this would be good for us to see because it's where the members of Parliament meet to make decisions about the country. You can have a tour round it but Dad said he was happy just to have seen the outside and Big Ben of course. I think he was worried about the cost of the day. The Dhomi family said they were happy to treat us but we have our pride and we had paid our underground tickets ourselves.

After that we walked across Westminster Bridge and stopped in the centre to look at the river. Sight seeing boats were going up and down and you could just hear the tour guide talking as one slid beneath us, competing with the rumble of traffic.

'It takes your breath away doesn't it,' said Rita. It's so busy, noisy and exciting.

'Is Leeds like this?' I asked.

'It's very busy with traffic and people, but much smaller than London and no underground trains. The bus service is good though.'

I tried to imagine myself there, nonchalantly getting on a bus to go to school, and failed. I just felt frightened. This was all so different from my life in Kosovo.

'What's that wheel thing over there?' asked Vjolica.

'It's called The London Eye and will be open to the public quite soon I think. Fadil led the way over the bridge and we came to the London Aquarium.

'We don't want to go in there because we have booked to do to something similar in Florida. I hope you don't mind.' said Fadil.

'No problem,' said Dad. 'To be honest I'm feeling weary and would be content to go back and have a rest before dinner tonight.'

There was a flurry of apologies that they had forgotten his recent illness and we found the nearest underground and returned to the hostel. The Dhomi family explored a bit further and we found out later they went to The Tower of London.

Dad laid down immediately, Mum settled to darning a pair of socks and Vjolica and I stood irresolute.

'I'm hungry.' We had missed lunch. 'Can I go to the shops and buy some sandwiches?'

Mum nodded and gave me some money saying we were not to buy anything for her and Dad. We went out, walking slowly.

'It's been good seeing some bits of London but it felt wrong to me. We've spent so long being careful, only spending what we had to. Then we go and waste money on sight seeing.'

Vjolica was frowning as she spoke.

I nodded, but said nothing.

'I think the Dhomi family are kind and lovely but I'll be glad when they've gone on holiday and we can begin our new life. Well, say something Davud.'

'Sorry. I feel the same. The new school year begins in about three weeks and I want to be settled in a house by then. Are you too old to go to school?'

'I think so. I will have to try to get a job but I've got to be better at speaking English first. I'm looking forward to our classes tomorrow.'

We reached the shops, bought some food and then Vjolica lingered outside a charity shop. She went in and looked at the clothes.

'Can I help you?'

It was a soft, kind voice coming from an old lady with glasses and white wispy hair.

'My sister needs a dress to go to dinner. We are refugees from Kosovo and have no clothes.'

'Oh you poor things. What a terrible time you must have had. Are you staying in the hostel along the road?'

'Yes, but we are moving soon, to Leeds.'

She eyed Vjolica. 'You are very slim, size eight or ten I would think. Let me see what we have.' There was a jangling of metal hangers, a flurry of clothes and they both disappeared somewhere at the back to try them on. I browsed around the toys, books and then the shirts. I was wondering what size I was when they emerged for my approval. Vjolica looked gorgeous in a patterned summer dress that hugged her waist. It had puffy sleeves and was long enough for Mum and Dad to accept.

'It's lovely,' I said, wishing I had money to buy it for her.

'Now, young man. Your sister looks so glamorous she makes you look drab. Let's see what there is.'

She pulled me to a rack and held some grey trousers against me. Armed with a couple of pairs she moved to smart shirts and then ushered me to the changing room. I wanted to protest we had no money but I stripped and was soon feeling quite glamorous myself. I stepped through the curtain and Vjolica smiled with delight.

'So that's one summer dress, one shirt and a pair of trousers. A total of twelve pounds. Oh dear. I see there is a little tear here and a button missing. These are not fit to be sold. They'll have to go to the rag man.'

Surely she wasn't going to throw away such lovely clothes. 'No, please, no rag man,' I said.

She laughed, placed the clothes in bags and said, 'It's just my way of saying you need these clothes and I'm giving them to you. No money to pay. Good luck when you move to Leeds.'

We thanked her and practically ran back to the hostel to show Mum and Dad. At least tonight the pair of us would not feel like the poor relations.

Vjolica

So much has happened since I last wrote I hardly know where to begin.

Fadil and family went on holiday whilst we languished in the hostel, the only highlight being the English lessons. Marigana said it was vital that Mum learns to speak English; she said it had been hard for her but now she could hold a conversation.

'Many Muslim women in Leeds coming from other countries have been here for twenty years and still dare not open their mouths. They are lonely, so lonely. Promise me you will try.'

Mum had agreed and I must say she did really well in our lessons. The course lasted for two weeks but we only went for one because all our documents arrived. We could now claim benefit money from a post office. Mum and Dad did this together and then they asked at the hostel the cheapest way to get to Leeds. The next day we used the underground to Victoria and got a bus all the way to Leeds. It took hours but when we got off, tired and stiff, Alek was there to meet us.

Suddenly everything became exciting. Alek looked after us but we did all the cooking, cleaning and washing so, in a way, we looked after him too.

And guess what? He's got a girl friend called Sam! I met her, Mark and Peter when they played at the youth club. Davud and I were allowed to go and it was brill. They played so well and everyone danced. I wore my new dress and felt I blended in, until Peter said all the boys were looking at me. Then Sam said it was his way of saying I looked nice. She is amazing. The way she plays the drums is fantastic and she's so cool. When I said to Alek I envied how confident and strong she was he said it was an act. Underneath she was anxious and insecure, like most young people. I found that hard to believe.

Peter goes back to college in two weeks but before that we move into our house. It's been great staying with Alek but his parents and Rita come back on the weekend and we want to move out before then.

This is the best bit. We've seen our house. After sharing rooms for so long I can't wait to have my own bedroom. Davud and I argued who should have the bigger room. He won because Mum said he'd need a desk to do his homework. I don't care. The little room will be all mine and I can shut the door and have privacy. Yeh!

Sorry, rambling.

There's a large living room and dining room downstairs, kitchen with a door to the garden. Now don't imagine a lawn, flowerbeds and so on because it's a total junk heap with grass as high as my waist!

The council have decorated the house for us so it's clean and ready to move in. There are carpets, curtains and furniture so tomorrow is the big day!!!

Chapter 31

Davud

They came back from Florida and we all met on Sunday. They were tanned and Rita prattled on and on about their holiday. Their hotel was huge and luxurious. Disney was exciting and they had gone on so many rides that took their breath away and she'd screamed as they hurtled down slopes. Eventually Ajeshe managed to change the subject to us. She asked if we liked the house.

'It's lovely. Everything is decorated and clean but we have been there so short a time we still forget where things are and have to search all the cupboards. They have equipped it well and we are grateful to have it, and to be near you,' Mum said.

We didn't stay long because it was school the next day and I was not looking forward to it.

My first day at school was exhausting. I thought my English was quite good but everyone spoke really fast and they have a strange accent that makes words I know sound completely different. And then there's the slang. All languages have those but they don't teach you them when you learn English at school. So I struggled.

Going by bus had been easy but I was shocked by the behaviour of some of the people on it. They shouted rudely out of the window at pedestrians and pushed and shoved each other. It did scare me a little but they all ignored me so I hoped that would continue. Luckily Mum had managed to find a second hand uniform for me so I didn't have that new boy scrubbed look.

It's my birthday on Thursday and I will be 14 so I need to choose certain subjects to take for a series of exams called GCSEs. The others in my class have chosen already and went off to different subjects after registration. I've brought the list home, as well as some homework. I feel really unsure what to do. I think I'll go and see Alek. He must have been about my age when he arrived in England.

Rita opened the door, a pen in her hand. 'Hi Davud, I'm just doing my homework. How was school?'

'Hard. Is Alek in yet?'

'Yes about five minutes ago. Mum will be dishing up dinner soon. Come in and I'll call him.'

I stood in the living room feeling uncomfortable because I was holding up their meal.

'Problem?' asked Alek when he came in, gesturing to a seat. I sat down. 'I've got to fill in this form about choosing subjects for GCSE. I don't know what to do.' My eyes began to prick. I was close to tears.

'That's tough on your first day. Let me see.' He read the sheet for a few moments. 'You can only choose one from each column and the list along the bottom are compulsory. When I did this I felt I was happier with more practical subjects. You might feel the same. Do you still play the violin?'

I nodded. 'I haven't got one and I haven't played for ages but I loved it.'

'Right, so I think you should make music one of them. Geography is probably less wordy than History. Are you interested in science?.................'

He was really helpful and my problem was solved in just fifteen minutes. I went home feeling lighter and really hungry. The smells coming from their kitchen had been mouth-watering.

Vjolica

Well we are in and organised, sort of. We've found a local supermarket and post office. Mum has started to smile again, despite the difficulties of not speaking the language. She has a home, a kitchen and just enough money to feed us. Now it's Dad and I who are feeling the time hanging heavy. But we have a project now. We are taking charge of the garden. Our very elderly neighbour has a beautiful lawn, flowers and at the bottom a vegetable patch.

As soon as we emerged and started to gather rubbish and put it into bags he was hanging over the fence talking to us. 'Well, hello to you. I'm George, George Sanderson.' His face crinkled into its deep lines as he smiled.

'My name is Donjeta Kahshoven and this is my daughter Vjolica.'

'Well those are not Yorkshire names. Where have you come from Donjeta?' The conversation continued and I thought we would never even start the garden but then he said, 'I can see you want to clear up your garden and I wondered if that old shed had any tools in it. If not I have loads and would be happy to give you some. I used to garden but not fit now so I have a gardener. He comes every week and makes a grand job.'

George looks like he'll become a friend. He gave us loads of tools and said he would lend us his mower when we needed it. That really spurred us on and soon we had moved all the rubbish, everything from plastic bottle crates to a broken child's scooter, and piled it into a corner. The shed is about three metres from the back fence so we hacked down the weeds and grass of that section and then started to dig. It took ages and an enormous heap of weedy clods of soil piled up.

Our plan was to begin with the vegetable patch because then we could grow some of our own food. OK, so the autumn is beginning and then winter but we had to start somewhere. As I dug I remembered Granddad and how proud he was of his onions and carrots. This was the first garden we have ever had and the work was really satisfying.

Dad wilted before I did and then we stood and surveyed our efforts. It still looked a mess. We needed to find out how to get rid of our rubbish. George said it could go to a public tip but we needed a car to do that. He also said the council would pick up filled sacks but only if we had a lot and then they charged. We decided to keep piling it up for now.

So my days are active and tiring. But let me tell you about the evenings. Alek and Peter have been round nearly every night! First they brought an English style sponge cake filled with jam and cream that Ajshe had baked. (Truly yummy so we asked for the recipe) Then they returned with the recipe and some heavy duty sacks for our garden rubbish. The following evening Peter, who always came with Alek, asked if Dad would like some help clearing the rubbish. He could borrow his dad's car. So that happened and he asked me, as we carried sacks from the car to the skip, if I would like to go out with him for a drink that evening!

Obviously I wanted to go out with him but I was in such a muddle. Muslim girls don't go out with men, unchaperoned. What should I do? I'm ashamed to say I thought of several lies but in the end I asked Dad if I could.

He looked as muddled as me. He owed Peter a debt, for all his help in Greece and now the lift in the car to the tip, but was it right? In the end he said he needed to discuss it with Mum.

I explained as best I could to Peter and he said he really wanted to see me on my own because he only had a few more days before he returned to college. So no pressure!

Davud

I didn't need to listen at the door to hear the argument. I think the whole neighbourhood could.

'I don't know why you're even asking me this Donjeta. You know she can't go to a pub on her own with Peter.'

'Well, this is England. They do things differently here.'

'A Muslim is still a Muslim wherever they are and I say she must have a chaperone.'

'But...'

'Don't even try to argue the case any more. I've told you what I feel and you should respect that.'

I have never heard Mum so vehement. Dad had to cave in. He said he would go with Vjolica to the pub to meet Peter. 'I can then see what sort of place this pub is and the type of people there.'

When he told Vjolica she held back her disappointment but went red in the face with the effort. Dad then gave her a hug and whispered something into her hair. She smiled then and nodded.

Vjolica

Hello diary. I did go to the pub to see Peter and had to have Dad to hold my hand. Honestly they can't trust me at all. Anyway, after shaking hands with Peter and offering to buy him a drink, which he refused, Dad moved well out of earshot with his half a pint of orange juice and sat by the window.

Peter bought me a coke and we stood near the bar. My English is really awful and I wondered how we were going to talk without Alek as interpreter. Then Peter had a go. 'Why is Donjeta here?'

I got that because he said it slowly and clearly. So I laboriously searched for words to explain and gestured as eloquently as I could.

'Woman and man, not......... possible. Muslim, forbid.'

I think he understood it was a religious problem and not that Dad didn't trust him. I liked what he said next.

'You are very pretty.' I had no idea what to say next so I just smiled, looked directly at him and then lowered my eyes again. That was quite bold.

'You have brown eyes.'

'You have blue eyes.'

Ok so it was not scintillating, as conversations go, but at least it was clear he liked me. I think he's gorgeous but I couldn't really say that. We stumbled on and I found out he had no brothers or sisters. When we had run out of possible topics with my, oh-so-awful English, we joined Dad.

Peter explained our communication difficulties and Dad helped as best he could. By the end of the evening he had got Dad to agree to him giving me English lessons.

I am to go to his house, (Meet his mother......scary!) where his mother will chaperone me. He will teach me tomorrow, the next day and then he has to go back to college.

Can't wait for tomorrow.

Really, really, don't want him to go.

Davud

We all wrote in our diaries for America for the last time and Vjolica said she would take the parcel to the post office the next day.

This is my entry.

1st October 1999

We are now living in a house in Leeds, quite close to our friends. I have started school and found it really hard at first finding my way round, understanding the language and having girls in the same classroom.

The girls wear short skirts, which makes all the boys look at them, and talk about them with great disrespect. There are other Muslim boys and I talked to them about it. They say I must understand that this is a permissive society and accept it. One very good thing about school is the music. I have joined a choir. My voice is breaking, which is tricky, so I sing quietly but it seems I will be a tenor.

Our family still have very little money and Dad has to wait for permission to work. Vjolica has also asked permission to work but her English is not good so that may not be possible. There are classes to learn English, every Wednesday evening. I'm not sure if I will go because I have homework every night, but the others are going.

In Kosovo there was no government help if you were poor, especially if you were Albanian. People just starved.

The government here care for everyone. We can even go to the doctor or hospital and it will cost us nothing. They call it The National Health Service and it is wonderful. I remember Mum and Dad being paid with food for the work they did at the Red Cross clinic. No patient expected to get treatment for free.

You might ask if I am happy to be here and the answer is yes. We now feel safe from persecution and the real threat of being killed by bombs or by Serbian police. We can now walk down the street, our heads held high, without fear.

I hope you have found our experiences interesting.

Davud Kahshoven

Vjolica

2nd October 1999

This morning I took our diaries to the post office and sent them to the newspaper in America. I hope Greg has a chance to read them. He was so helpful to us when our lives were so awful I really want him to know we're safe and making a new life.

When it's not raining I work in the garden. We have finished the vegetable patch, a border for flowers and a lawn in the middle. Dad helped me scrape between the paving stones and they look so much better we can claim we have a patio too. We don't have any outside chairs or a table, no flowers, vegetable seeds or plants. All of that costs too much, but when we look out of the window it looks really tidy. Very satisfying but now I feel at a loose end again. This is really bad because it gives me too much time to miss Peter.

He will be back for the Christmas break so I'll just have to be patient. He does write to me; quite a challenge. I sit there with the English dictionary trying to translate it. I can't ask Davud or Dad to help because they might disapprove of some things he says. It is also hard to write back but my English is improving with the effort.

The lessons we're having are really good. Mum is doing better than I thought and sometimes we have an English only mealtime.

Ok diary I've nothing more to add. Roll on Christmas!

Davud

I understand that England has loads of history but Bonfire Night was a strange event. Our school organised a bonfire and fireworks, so all our family went. The note from the school said our tickets entitled us to hot pork pies and mushy peas but we couldn't eat that so we waited and had a late meal at home.

When we arrived it was dark, but a clear evening and lights were on in the school, so we could see a huge pile of wood with an effigy of a man stuck on top. I asked a friend from school who the figure was and why were they burning him. He quickly told me about Guy Fawkes who was caught trying to blow up the Houses of Parliament. I assumed his punishment was death by burning but that was wrong too.

We all loved the warmth of the crackling fire and were stunned by the fireworks, huge bangs followed by beautiful coloured circles in the sky. Some of them whizzed about whistling or shrieking and swirling smoke hung in the still air. I think it was the most amazing spectacle I've ever seen. Everyone clapped and cheered when it was over and then we set off for the bus stop.

'That was quite a show,' said Dad. 'Just think if Guy Fawkes had succeeded that beautiful building we saw in London would not have been there.'

That night I had a nightmare. Bombs were screaming as they fell and exploded so close, shaking our building as we cowered in the basement.

I expect the thwump of rockets shooting up into the sky triggered it.

Chapter 32

Ramadan

It would be Christmas in ten days time. All the shops were twinkling with decorations, tempting gifts, racks of cards depicting snow scenes, reindeer and Father Christmas. Carols playing everywhere, brass bands in the streets, carol singers knocking on doors and The Lions' Santa Sledge lighting up the streets, blaring its presence. It was impossible to ignore and particularly hard for Muslims who were enduring Ramadan.

The good thing was that the days were very short making the daylight fasting time easier than in the summer. Rita and Davud had to have permission from school to be excused from the lunchtime meal. They went to the same school but had not met often, being in different year groups. During Ramadan they provided a classroom, supervised by a Muslim teacher, to spend the lunch hour. It was, mercifully, a long way from the dining hall so there were no distracting smells to cope with. The students did not have to pray all the time but quiet was expected for those that wanted to.

Rita sat close to Davud and they exchanged notes.

'I'm starving. What about you?'

'I'm dreaming of fish and chips'

'Bread and jam would be fine by me.'

'I'd even settle for a school dinner!'

The last one made them both giggle and they looked anxiously at the teacher. She seemed to be ignoring them reading a book, so they had got away with it. The lunch hour passed slowly but it was warmer than being out in the playground.

Alek was also finding it difficult this year. He was working outside a good part of the day, getting very cold, using a lot of energy and suffering hunger, thirst and headaches. He looked forward to four o'clock when it was dark and he could go into the site hut and indulge in a cup of tea, and a large slab of fruitcake.

Sam was also putting pressure on him, expecting him to go with her to the staff Christmas dinner dance and wanting him to come to her Mum's house for Christmas lunch. He agreed to the dinner dance but obviously lunch was out of the question.

'So you don't do Christmas at all, even though you're in our country?'

'No we don't do Christmas but after Ramadan we have our own celebration, called Eid-al-Fitr and that will be on the 8th of January. It lasts three days; we don't go to work and we eat lots, visit friends and have a great time.

'Well that's something. Before that, of course it's the Millennium; can we celebrate that together?'

Alek sighed. He really wanted to please her. 'Yes but I'll have to pass on the Champagne.' Sam was cool about him not drinking and generally respected his religious views, finding them interesting. It was just the coincidence of Christmas, which she always enjoyed, clashing with Ramadan. He explained that the ninth month of the Muslim calendar was linked to the moon and moved every year.

'So when does it not coincide with Christmas?'

'Erm, 2001 I think.'

She pouted, 'So this is going to happen next Christmas too. It's not fair.'

They had been dating once or twice a week for two months now and Sam said she would like to introduce him to her mum. 'I told her I'm going out with you and she keeps saying she'd like to meet you. What about it? Just a cup of tea. No big deal.'

Alek agreed to go the next Saturday afternoon but his anxiety was tinged with guilt. She had been telling her mum all about him and he still hadn't even mentioned her name to his parents.

It was Saturday and he felt nervous entering their front garden but noticed how lovely it looked even though it was winter. The borders had lavender, cut back neatly and winter pansies nodded their heads in the breeze beside a small patch of grass.

Sam's mum opened the door and he was surprised because he thought he'd seen her before but couldn't remember where. Her short hair was neat but greying, laughter lines around the eyes and mouth. She was of a medium height and build. Her smile was Sam's. It filled her face, lit up her eyes and showed the intelligent, vibrant person she was. He warmed to her immediately, especially when she showed an interest in his religion. Knowing she was a devout Christian he'd been worried.

'I used to be a teacher and we had to teach comparative religions. The idea was to highlight the similarities. They all have special times of the year, feast days, places of worship and so on.'

'That sounds really good,' said Alek. 'I'm sure people are prejudiced because they're ignorant.'

'Yes, but the media make it worse. They use the word 'radical' to show they are fanatics but it can make life more difficult for people like yourself.'

'We've not had any problems here, but Leeds is such a cosmopolitan city.'

They chatted about general things, his holiday with Peter and the music they played.

Suddenly, Sam said, 'It's dark enough now to have tea and cake isn't it?' She looked at Alek.

He nodded, 'Yes please. I'm starving.'

'I'll do it,' said her mum and she went into the kitchen.

'Do you think I'm passing the test?' asked Alek.

Sam grinned, 'Yep but if you really want to please her, rave about the cake.' Mum came in before he could comment and he jumped up to take the heavy tray from her. She poured the tea and then offered the sponge cake oozing with strawberry jam and fresh cream. Alek took a piece, bit into it, sighing with delight. 'This is scrummy. My mum makes this type of cake but it's not as light as this.'

'Mum's a great cake maker and the jam's home-made too,' said Sam.

'I've been thinking about you no longer being a teacher but you seem too young to be retired.'

'Thank you kind sir; no I made a career change. I expect Sam told you her dad was a soldier so I taught at army schools. When he died we moved here, our first proper home. Somehow the whole idea of teaching lost it's appeal and I trained to be a librarian.'

'I thought you looked familiar. That's where I've seen you.' She dazzled him with another smile. The conversation turned to books and what type they preferred and moved on to films and theatre. It was enjoyable, but having finished his second cup of tea and another slice of cake, he thought he ought to go. Sam came with him to the door and whispered, 'I can tell she likes you. See you Wednesday and we can talk about me meeting your parents.'

Wednesday came, they met in the pub but he had still not told his parents about her.

'What's the problem Alek? It doesn't mean we're serious or anything. Are you ashamed of me?'

'No, no I think you're great, you know I do.'

'So...?'

'It's difficult to explain. Your mum was lovely and very understanding about me being a Muslim. My problem is I'm not sure how they'll feel about me dating a Christian.'

'Are you saying they don't even know I exist? You haven't told them about me at all?'

Alek looked down at his toes, hunched his shoulders and then made himself look at her. 'No, you're right and I'm really sorry. When you were a Goth I thought you'd scare them and then I, somehow, never got around to it.'

She stood up, nearly knocking the table over. 'I'm going home. You'd better think about whether you want to go out with me or not and let me know.'

He reached for her hand, 'Sam,' but she whipped it away and stormed off. He wanted to run after her but knew she had every right to be angry with him. How could he put this right?

Vjolica

I've got a problem and no one to share it with. So, diary you'll have to do. It's Ramadan and Peter's home from college. He wanted me to go round to his parents for lunch. His mum would be there, because she doesn't work, but I'm fasting. I really wanted to see him so I said I'd come after lunch.

When I got there she offered me a cup of tea, but I refused. Then alternatives were offered, coffee, an infusion or a glass of water! In the end I told her straight, nil by mouth until sunset because I'm a Muslim. She looked really shocked and I think she heard the irritation in my voice. It was my fault. She was just trying to make me welcome and I should have explained more gently. How was she to know it was Ramadan? She stood up and said, 'Well if I can't get you anything I'll go and do some baking.'

So she left us! Peter grinned wickedly at me, 'Alone at last,' he said and then pounced on me smothering me with kisses. His hands roamed everywhere. They were touching my bare skin, my breasts. I could scarcely breathe. I wanted to touch him too, kiss him back. It was exciting, shocking and very wrong. Finally I found the strength to push him off me. He looked hurt and asked me why. Didn't I like him?

My English has improved with all the lessons so I said I did like him but I had a headache.

He laughed and laughed as if having a headache was funny. Perhaps he should try fasting all day. Anyway I got cross, stood up, straightened my clothes, re-wound my scarf around my head, drew myself up tall and said, 'You laugh at my headache. Not funny. I don't understand. I go home now.'

He was contrite, said he was sorry and then tried to explain what had made him laugh. It seems English married women say it, even if it is a lie, to not have sex with their husband. This was shocking. I thought a woman obeyed her husband. I wonder if Muslim women do this too? Not easy to ask that. Mum would want to know why I was asking!

I did go home but we had a kiss and made up before I went.

As I walked along I giggled at the thought of Mum asking what I had learned in my English lesson with Peter this afternoon!!

Pete's Pizzazz had a gig at a pub. This was a step up from the youth club and they were going to get paid. It seems there were not enough bands around at Christmas to meet the demand. The manager had asked for jazz but they had to have some Christmas carols ready in case there was a request for them.

Alek was worried. When Peter had rung he'd felt excited and immediately agreed then remembered that Sam was cross with him. Would she come to a practise session on Saturday? Would she let them down altogether? They were nothing without her. He needed to make peace. He telephoned.

'Hi Sam. I'm really sorry. We need to meet to talk about us.'

'Have you asked your parents if they could cope with you dating a Christian?'

'No, not yet but there's a practise on Saturday.'

'I see. You want to make it up because you think I'll let the group down. You sure make a girl feel good.'

She slammed the phone down. He'd really blown it. She would probably never speak to him again. His heart gave a lurch at that thought and suddenly he found the courage to talk to Mum. She was clearing the kitchen after the evening meal and he helped her.

'This is nice but you've done a day's work and should be resting. We all feel tired during Ramadan.'

'Thanks Mum but I need to ask you something that's worrying me.'

She put down her tea towel and leant against the worktop. 'You'd better tell me then.'

'You know I've been going out a lot and said I was meeting friends from work?'

She nodded, smiled and said, 'You were really meeting a girl.'

'Yes.'

'So why the secrecy?'

'Mum she's a Christian and I thought you would be angry.'

She sighed, 'Not angry but disappointed. It will make life very hard for you if you continue this relationship Alek.'

'It's hard already. I've been to her house and met her mother, now she expects to meet you and Dad.'

There was a short pause whilst she thought. Alek held his breath. 'We are living in a different country now and we are in the minority. We will make...... what's her name?'

'Sam.'

'We'll make Sam welcome. When do you want to invite her?'

Mum said she would check with Dad that he felt the same. If he did she could come on Friday evening. She could join them for a meal or, as it would be quite early, she could come after it. Dad agreed and Alek phoned Sam again.

Her Mum answered. 'I'm sorry Alek but you seem to have upset Sam and she refuses to talk to you.'

He hadn't anticipated that. 'Please would you tell her I want to make amends and she is invited for a meal to meet my parents on Friday.'

There was a pause and he knew she was relaying this to Sam.

'Alek?'

He felt a fluttering of fear. Was she going to refuse to come? 'Yes. Did your mum tell you?'

'Yes. What time shall I come?'

She was coming! His grin must have been heard down the phone as he arranged the time and told her how relieved and pleased he felt. He rushed in to the living room to tell everyone and then Mum asked if she had any food allergies or things she hated.

'No Mum she seems to like everything. She eats really well. I don't know how she stays so slim.'

'We're looking forward to meeting her, said Dad.'

'Is she the same Sam that plays the drums in your group?' asked Rita. 'She's a Goth.'

'What's a Goth?' asked Dad.

'No she's not. I mean it's the same Sam but she's changed, Rita. She looks completely different now.'

It was all getting a bit complicated and he was glad when Dad did not pursue the whole Goth thing. He would never have understood. Alek was not really sure he did; something to do with expressing yourself as an individual, Sam had said, but what did that mean? He was not sure if he was looking forward to Friday or not.

Chapter 33

Davud

24 Dales Street
Leeds
19/ 12/ 99

Dear Mr Dushku,

I promised to write to you when we got to England but I waited until we had a permanent place to stay so I could give you my address.

We had a lot of difficulties and adventures before we got here and then the immigration people had to decide if we were genuine refugees and if we could stay. For a few weeks we had to live in a special hostel where we met a woman from Kosovo with her son and a very sad tale to tell. She was allowed to stay and is now in a house in Clacton.

Eventually we were given good news, they believed our story and we could rent a three-bedroom house in Leeds, near our friends. Dad and Vjolica have not been given a permit to work yet. As you can imagine they are finding this very frustrating. We are not starving because the government give us something called social security money and they pay our rent. It's a small amount to spend on food each week but after those last few years in Kosovo we know how to eke out what we have.

I'm getting used to being in a school again but schools in England are not so strict and sometimes children's behaviour can be bad, boys rude to the teachers and too much talking during the lesson. It is also peculiar to have girls and boys together and I find that distracting.

I know you will want me to keep up my music so you will be pleased that I now sing in the choir. As soon as Dad is earning I hope to be able to buy a violin and pay for lessons. Our music sessions were fun and I would like to continue to play.

Thank you for giving me an excellent start in speaking English; I also want to thank you for the help with maths. I am good at it and it is pleasing because other subjects, like English Literature and History are very difficult for me.

Now you know that we are all safe and well but I need to know how you are. Please write back to me and let me know if the bombing damaged your house and if living is any easier now.

I think of you a lot, look forward to hearing from you,

Davud Kahshoven

I had to take my letter to the post office to buy a special stamp for Kosovo but Dad was happy to give me the money.

'It's important to keep promises and I would be glad to hear from him too. When I think of all the people we knew and left behind. We've no idea what happened to any of them. So go and post your letter Davud. I'm sure Mr Dushku will be pleased to get it.'

There were just three days more at school and then the Christmas holiday. I was looking forward to being at home, lazing in bed in the mornings and no homework.

Christmas at school had been fun. I had a small part in a play, called 'A Christmas Carol' and we performed it last week. One of the sixth form boys played Scrooge and he had makeup, a grey messy wig and he walked all bent as if he was really old. I was just a street urchin so I had ragged clothes and bare feet even though it was supposed to be winter. Scrooge gave me money to buy a huge turkey after the ghosts had taught him to be kind.

Rita was in the play too. She was a poor girl wearing a skirt patched and torn. She had no lines to say but we were both in a street scene. I played hopscotch and she played with a hoop and we all sang a song.

Tonight Vjolica, Rita and I are all going to a pub to watch Pete's Pizzazz perform. Alek, Peter, Mark and Sam will sit with us until they have to play and we're going to drink cola and eat peanuts.

Vjolica

Today I'm writing about something good. When I look back there's a lot of whining and whingeing in my entries.

So....... I went to Pete's again on Friday morning and he was a complete gentleman! (Have to confess I was ready for another battle) We sat primly on opposite side of the table and he taught me useful vocabulary for food. I don't mean the ordinary things like apples, butter or bread. I learned aubergine, turnip, swede, celeriac and the differences between types of flour. His mum was happy for us to bake and we made some cakes but I had to ask for everything in English. It was quite testing but fun. We laughed a lot when I got things muddled and of course we had the pleasure of seeing our cakes risen and perfect on the cooling tray. It was just hard luck that I couldn't taste one!

I also felt his Mum was warming to me. She came into the kitchen and explained that mixing up the butter and sugar was called 'creaming'. It pleased me to see her smiling. I'm really muddled about my feelings for Peter. When I see him my tummy seems to flutter and I know he really likes me but is it sensible to get so keen on a non-Muslim. Why can't I feel the same about Alek?

Thinking about Alek dating Sam makes me wonder if he's having similar problems? English girls have different standards. Sex before marriage seems permissible. Perhaps Alek is having a really good time!! I'll find out more tomorrow night, maybe, when we all go to the King's Arms to see them perform.

Friday Evening at the Dhomi Household

Sam looked lovely when Alek opened the door. Her hair was shining. She was wearing just a little make-up and the black of her trousers matched the black and white print of her blouse. She shrugged off her coat and made a grimace of anxiety at him before donning her gorgeous smile to greet his parents.

Dad was sitting in the living room, with Rita and he stood up, shook her hand and asked her to sit. Rita just smiled and said hello. Then Mum came in from the kitchen and Sam stood to shake hands. It was all very formal and polite. Alek thought his family were being very starchy compared to the friendliness of Sam's mum.

'There's a lovely smell of cooking. What are we having?'

Mum smiled. 'I though I'd make a traditional dish that we would have in our country. It's called, 'Tavë Kosi', lamb with rice in a yogurt and egg sauce. It's ready now. I hope it's not too early for you to eat but in Ramadan.......'

Sam stood up. 'Yes I understand you're all very hungry and it's not too early for me.'

They went to the table and Sam noticed the formal settings; even a small floral table decoration. They were treating her as an honoured guest but she would have felt more comfortable with a tray on her knee. When they were sat, Mum brought in some warm herb bread and chunks were broken off and dipped in oil or there was butter. Alek and his Dad tucked into it with gusto but Sam had just a little piece knowing there was a rich dish to come.

'So what made you take up the drums?' Dad asked.

'It was offered at school and I've always loved drum solos, probably something primitive in me,' said Sam.

'I think enjoying rhythm is built into everyone so we all have that primitive side, said Dad.'

'Yes,' joined in Mum, 'I remember when Rita was just a toddler she would dance to music, bouncing about on her little legs, even though she'd never seen anyone dance.'

'Oh, Mum,' said Rita. 'I'm trying to be all grown up and you're making me feel three again.' Everyone laughed and suddenly Sam felt less alien. She relaxed, enjoyed the meal and the company.

At the end of the evening Alek walked her to the bus stop.

'It's been a great evening; yummy dinner and your family are lovely. Why were you so worried?'

Alek shrugged. 'I suppose I didn't expect them to have such an open mind. When we were in Kosovo we avoided the Serbs, who were Orthodox Christians. We viewed them with the same fear as people here view radical Islamists. Does that help?'

'Yes, yes I get it now. I'm sorry I was such a bitch. Do you think they liked me?'

He wrapped her in his arms, kissed her gently then hugged her to him. 'Course they did.'

The bus arrived; she jumped aboard, 'See you tomorrow.'

Alek waved and walked home with a spring in his step.

Saturday at The Kings Arms

The four musicians had arrived early to set up their equipment. Peter had collected Sam and her drum kit and they unpacked it in the corner. The pub was open for business and they provided a focus of interest for everyone. When it was set up they needed to test the volume so Peter used the microphone.

'Afternoon everyone. Our group is called Pete's Pizzazz and we're playing here tonight at seven o'clock. I'd like you to help us now to get the sound level right.'

'Sounds ok at the moment,' said a man leaning against the bar.

'Thank you. Well we'll try out a number and you can let us know if you've been deafened.'

They played, 'I got Rhythm' and they were pleased to see toes tapping and people smiling. When they finished there was some applause and a request for a bit less bass. The amplifier adjusted they played a few bars again and were given a thumbs up. There were no more preparations to do so they went home to change for the evening.

Rita was really excited at the thought of being in a pub, forbidden territory. It was only allowed because all the others were there. Davud sat on one side of her and Vjolica the other. It was quiet at first and they could chat quite easily.

'I really envy you all the different clothes you have, said Vjolica. 'We're still using charity shops for essentials and there's no money for pretty things.'

'It was like that for us when we first came to England but now it's great. Things will improve fast when your dad gets a job.'

'I'd like to get a job myself but I'm still waiting for a permit and I've no qualifications. The only experience I've got is selling hardware.'

'Rich people are always looking for cleaners and will often pay you cash so the government don't know. Why don't you look in the paper shop window?'

The music started to play and the pub soon filled until there were no seats available and people just stood. Talking was impossible but they got caught up in the festive atmosphere and even joined in when 'Jingle Bells' was requested. At the end of the evening the three of them helped carry the drum kit to Peter's dad's car and they all stood outside.

'It's been a really good night and you all play very well,' said Vjolica.

Rita noticed Peter had his arm around her and Alek was holding Sam's hand.

She looked at Davud. 'I don't know about you Davud but I think we're not really wanted now.'

They all laughed and then there was a flurry of hugs as they regrouped into family members and went home. Peter took Sam home and when they parked outside her house he said, 'Are you finding it tricky dating a Muslim?'

'Yes. We nearly split up because Alek was too scared to tell his parents about me. I suppose you two have a language problem.'

'That's getting better but Muslim girls are not allowed to date. Everywhere we go there has to be a chaperone. So I hardly ever get time alone with her. My Mum left us alone at my house and we had a cuddle but she pushed me away. I think she wanted to kiss more but her religion forbids it.'

'That's tough Peter.' She looked at him with a cheeky smile. 'Perhaps we should swap!'

She laughed and got out of the car. He helped her with her gear, still thinking about Vjolica. 'There's this Ramadan fasting thing too. It'd be hard to be eating lunch in front of your girlfriend who's starving.'

'I know. It's bothered me too. In the end, Peter, we have to love someone a lot to cope with those differences. I've only been going out with Alek for a few months and it's really too soon to be agonising about the future. Probably won't see you for a bit, Christmas next, so have a good one.'

He returned to the car, thoughtful. Vjolica. He couldn't imagine life without her. She haunted his thoughts all the time.

Chapter 34

Christmas was over and everyone was looking forward to the Millennium. There was great speculation, and some anxiety, that computers would crash sending the world into chaos. What would happen to the banking system, to all the electronic records, all the company data?

In the Dhomi household they were not thinking of computers. They were planning a millennium party. The Kahshovens were at the top of the list and then Alek wanted Peter, Mark and Sam to come. Rita wanted her friend Ellen. Should they invite Sam's mum because she would be on her own? If they did that perhaps they should invite Peter's parents too. Was there room if all of them came? What sort of food was normal at a New Year party?

Fadil made the decision. 'Let's invite everyone on the list, and their parents. If they all come we'll have to borrow chairs and move the furniture about but I don't suppose they will. After all, this is a dry house, and most English people would not see the fun in toasting a new millennium with fruit juice!'

Mum nodded and smiled. 'Now that's decided I feel we shouldn't try to do English food. In Kosovo we would have a hot supper, buffet style, with different savoury dishes, rice and breads to accompany them. We can make some of it in advance and freeze it.'

'I know,' said Rita, 'we could make some non-alcoholic mulled wine. I had some at Ellen's on Christmas Eve. It's really yummy.'

'That can be your job then, to borrow the recipe and make it. So what are you going to do Alek?'

Alek frowned, 'Not sure. The English put up Christmas decorations and they stay up until after New Year. We haven't done that so it will look drab to them. Shall I decorate the living room? I can also be waiter taking drinks around and so on.'

Everyone thought decorations would make it more festive and he was charged with buying some.

Davud

Three letters arrived this morning, a small one in a decorated envelope, a thick, A4 white one from America and one for me.

'It must be from the newspaper,' said Dad, tearing open the large one. 'There's some articles and a cheque.........$500 dollars!'

There were whoops and smiles from everyone, then quiet as he read the letter.

'Dear Donjeta, Marigana, Vjolica and Davud,

Please forgive the informality but I feel, having read all your stories, that I know you. My name is John and I am the editor. I have published the enclosed articles for several weeks, based on your diaries. I hope you feel I have captured the essence of what happened to you and I enclose a small cheque as a thank you.

Glen sends his best wishes to you all and we hope you will be happy and successful in your new life,

John Barton'

The articles were passed around and I translated where necessary.

'They're good. An excellent record of all that happened to us. We must put them into a folder and keep them. Then if life becomes difficult we can read them and remember what true hardship means.'

Mum gathered them up, as she spoke, and put them safely in a drawer. 'What about your letter Davud?'

'It'll be from Mr Dushku. I opened it and read aloud.

Dear Davud,

I can't tell you how delighted I was to get your letter. It seems a long time since you were my pupil and obviously much has happened to you and your family in that time. It gave me particular pleasure to hear that my English lessons have been appreciated!

I'm sure you would like to know what has happened here since you left so I will do my best but be prepared because it is not all good news. You will remember my friend that fought in the KLA and was wounded. I never told you his name because I felt it was better if he remained anonymous. That way you could never have told his whereabouts if the Serbs should hunt him down. I'll tell you now, he was called Fisnik and he died in the bombing. I felt his death keenly because, as you know, he cared for me and was a great help.

For a while after that I was very lonely and quite desperate, finding it hard to cope with the everyday chores from my wheelchair. There were also no children left for me to teach; one was killed, the other two, like you, left.

I paused when I saw Mum fumbling for a handkerchief to dab her tears. She waved at me to carry on.

When the bombing stopped and the war was over all the Serbian thugs left, fearful of reprisals, and so we were without a police force, without any administration and it was total chaos. Then the KLA waded in to keep law and order so it became a lot safer to go out. The schools were struggling without teachers so I managed to get a job, despite my disability, so now I have a regular income. It is enjoyable to be back doing a job I've always loved.

Please tell your sister that the market has started up again and is still being run by the manager that she knows, Lule. She told me about the day the market was closed, and how Vjolica had escaped, with her, through the office.

Lule has become a good friend and comes to my house to clean and cook. This is a secret, Davud, but I'm thinking of asking her to marry me. I just need to find the courage because I'm not much of a catch.

'Oh, Isn't that wonderful. She was so kind to me. I really hope he asks her and she says yes.' Vjolica smiled and then nodded at Davud to continue.

Please also tell your parents that the Red Cross clinic is still open and very busy because so many Serbian doctors and nurses left the main hospitals and surgeries.

I expect you are fasting at this moment and looking forward to Eid. But before that is the Millennium and everyone is talking about it. A good time for a fresh start. I feel optimistic about my future and the future of Kosovo.

Please write to me again from time to time and if you ever decide to visit or even return as a family, I would love to see you.

Your teacher and friend,

B. Dushku.

'Such a mixture of emotions,' said Mum. 'I cried at his loneliness and then felt happy for his friendship with Lule. I think I'll go and do some cooking to calm down.'

'Don't go for a minute because there's this other, local letter.' Dad opened it and scanned it quickly. 'It's an invitation from Fadil and family for us all to go to a Millennium party at their house.'

That created a hubbub of excited noise silenced by a wail from Vjolica. 'I've nothing to wear to a party. I can't go. How can I let Peter see me again in the same things I always wear.'

'Vjolica you should not be trying to entice a man with finery.'

'Oh Dad. You don't understand.' She got up and ran upstairs to her room. Everyone could hear her sobs. They all looked at each other and Donjeta appealed to his wife.

'Am I wrong? Have I missed something about Vjolica and Peter?'

Mum sighed, 'Yes and Yes. All women, even good Muslim ones, like to look their best on special occasions. As to the second point, Peter seems to like Vjolica and I think she feels the same.'

Dad blew out his cheeks, 'What shall we do?'

'Perhaps some of those dollars could be spent on new clothing for everyone. Vjolica is not the only one who feels dowdy. You also need to be smarter if you want to start going for interviews.'

'No, I mean yes we can spend the dollars on clothes but what about this thing with Peter? Should we try and put a stop to it? He's a Christian.'

'Alek is going out with Sam and his Dad hasn't tried to stop them.' My voice came out a little louder and harsher than I'd intended. Had I been rude?

Dad looked over his glasses at me. 'There's no need to shout Davud. I can see you think we should just let it proceed. Have you any idea of the difficulties of mixed marriages?'

'No, I'm sorry, but I think it would be easier for a mixed marriage in this country than in Kosovo.'

Dad continued to stare which made me anxious but then he looked away, picked up the telephone and phoned Fadil. He thanked him for the invitation and said we would be delighted to come. He then asked about Sam and Alek. He listened for a long time, then thanked him and put the phone down.

'Fadil says they've decided to adopt the English assumption that a man chooses his own wife. They like Sam, even though she's not a Muslim, and have discussed the possibility of them wanting to marry in the future. If it happens they will not stand in their way.'

I punched the air with delight, 'Yes! Will you take that attitude with me? I hope so.'

Dad put his head in his hands, 'I don't know, I really don't know.' He looked at Mum. 'We need to talk about this.'

307

I took that opportunity to slip out of the room and find Vjolica. She needed to know what had just happened. I found her lying on her bed flipping through a very old magazine.

'Have you come to tell me I'm in trouble for my outburst?'

'No I've got some good news and some not so good.' She didn't speak so I went on. 'Mum and Dad have agreed for us all to have some smarter clothes, using the dollars.'

She sat up, swung her legs off the bed and smiled. 'Now that's what I call good news. When are we going shopping?'

'Well, I wouldn't rush to go downstairs. I don't think you realise that you just told them you and Peter were, what's the phrase?'

'An item; so what's happened? What did they say?'

'Dad's just rung Fadil to see how he's coping with Alek and Sam.'

'And?'

'Fadil seems quite cool about it but Dad said he and Mum needed to have a discussion, so I came up here.'

Vjolica sat back on the bed and I sat beside her. 'Do you think they'll forbid me seeing him? I couldn't bear that. I think I love him.'

I put my arms around her. 'They love you and we'll have to trust they allow you to keep seeing him.'

Dad shouted to us to come down so we went, anxiously, into the living room. He motioned us to sit but he remained standing.

'We live in England now but it's hard for us to adopt English ways so soon. I understand, Vjolica, you are seeing Peter in a romantic light and he is interested in you.'

She nodded, too scared to speak. I noticed the colour had left her cheeks.

'We cannot allow you to see Peter unchaperoned, as Alek is seeing Sam. You are a Muslim woman and I expect you to behave in the modest way we've taught you. If Peter wishes to marry you he must approach me first. Do you think I should ask him what he intends?'

Now she went very red! 'I've done nothing to make you ashamed. Whenever I've gone to Peter's house his mother's been there too. He's not mentioned marriage and I would be embarrassed if you asked him. He still has three years before he becomes a qualified teacher. I'm sure he wouldn't think about offering marriage until he had a job.'

'Hm.......I'm really not sure how to proceed.'

'Would you like me to talk to him? It would be less...... heavy coming from her brother,' I said.

It seemed to be the best solution and everyone was relieved. Dad said I was to go tomorrow and explain the Muslim ways to Peter. The words had come out of my mouth but I was regretting them already. How was I, just a teenager, supposed to talk to a grown man?

The next morning I arrived at his house feeling very uncomfortable. I was relieved when Peter opened the door and I could mumble that I needed a private word with him.

'I'll just get my coat and we can walk,' he said. Moments later he returned, closed the front door, and we set off. 'Ok what's the problem?'

'My parents know that you and Vjolica like each other. Muslim women are not allowed to be in the company of a man, alone. She must have a chaperone.'

'She's come to my house alone for English lessons.'

He coloured slightly and I wondered if they'd been alone then. 'Vjolica said your mother was always there.'

'Yes, she was.' He stopped walking and looked at me. 'So explain to me, Davud, how I'm supposed to get to know Vjolica better if there's always someone else with us, listening?'

'In Kosovo, the parents pick a suitable man for their daughter and everything is arranged by the parents.'

'You're joking! They still do this in the, nearly 21st Century? What if the girl or boy doesn't like the choice?'

This was far too close to home. I thought of Vjolica, desperate not to marry Erind. I shrugged, 'It usually works out ok.'

We walked on in silence for a while. It was a crisp chilly morning; frost still laying on the pavement in the shadows. The low sun could just be felt on my face.

'I really like her. No it's more than that. I love her.'

'Are you going to ask her to marry you?'

'I'd like to but I can't offer her anything yet. I need to be qualified and have a job before I can marry. Could I see her alone if we were engaged?'

I shook my head. 'It might be a good idea to talk to my parents about how you feel.'

'Ok. It's scary but I'd better do that before the party, then there'll be no tension. Shall I come round this afternoon?'

When Vjolica heard Peter was coming to talk to our parents she was really panicking, walking up and down the bedroom as I perched on her bed. 'Do you think I should be there? Oh I don't know what to do. Is he going to ask them if he can marry me? What shall I do if they say no?'

I went downstairs and asked. Mum and Dad said it would be better if they saw Peter on his own first. So, when the doorbell rang after lunch, Vjolica and I sat in her bedroom, silent, trying to hear what was being said. There were no raised voices, a good sign, but it seemed a long time before we were called to come down. As we entered the living room my spirits rose because they were all smiling.

'Vjolica,' said Dad. 'Peter has asked to become engaged to you but he must finish college and get a job before he can marry. We are happy, even though your religious differences could make it more difficult. I must also warn you that his parents don't know how he feels and they may not approve.'

He looked at her with a slight frown on his face as if he was worried. Vjolica ran across the room and hugged him, then Mum saying, 'Thank you, thank you, thank you.'

She even hugged me before going over to sit beside Peter and holding his hand. Peter didn't stay long. He said he wanted to talk to his parents so that everything was in the open before the party tomorrow night.

Later that evening Peter's dad rang. Dad left the room to talk to him and we all waited. He came back looking strained.

'Well, that was a difficult conversation. It seems that he is happy but his wife is not. She is very religious and wants Peter to marry a good Christian girl. He said they would not come to the party because it could cause discord. He also said he felt his wife would come round to the idea, when she got to know Vjolica better.'

There was a general sigh of relief but Vjolica was still worried. 'I wish she could be more relaxed. I really don't want to be at odds with my prospective mother-in-law.'

'Don't worry,' said Mum. There's plenty of time and it seems you have charmed the son and his father so she will have to give in eventually.'

The party began at eight and everyone was welcomed with Rita's mulled wine and plates of crisps and nuts. The room glittered with purple decorations hanging everywhere and candles glowed. The Kahshoven family were all dressed in new clothes, though most were from charity shops, and there was a feeling of excitement in the air.

The meal was received with appreciative noises. People happily balanced plates on their knees or perched at a corner of a table or sideboard. It was relaxed, everyone talking, laughing and the time moved quickly towards twelve.

I was standing beside Vjolica and Peter when they spoke to Sam and Alek about their engagement.

'Where's your ring?' asked Sam.

'We haven't had time to buy that yet. This news is hot off the press,' said Peter.

They talked about Peter's Mum being unhappy with the idea of a mixed marriage. Sam said she had no idea how her mum would react.

'Are we getting engaged then?' asked Alek. ' If so, I hope you'll tell me before you talk to your Mum.'

They all laughed, Sam went red, but didn't give a retort because it was nearly twelve and Fadil had put the television on. Rita rushed around with more mulled wine and as the first deep chime of the Millennium boomed they all raised their glasses shouting, Happy New Year!' When the last chime died they watched the fireworks and then the television was turned off. Fadil spoke in the brief silence.

'I want to have a final toast to my closest friends, Donjeta, Marigana, Vjolica and Davud. Happy New Year and may this be a wonderful start to your new life in England.'

Sources

Kosovo: What Everyone Needs to Know by Tim Judah

Also the following articles on the internet:

Wikipedia

Ibrahim Rugova

Kosovo War

BBC News World Europe March 30th 1999

Refugees flee from Kosovo Horror

BBC News UK March 31st 1999

UK Prepares for more Kosovo refugees

FRONTLINE

A Kosovo Chronology

Islamawareness.net

Rules regarding wearing Hijab and Niqab

About the Author

I was born in London in 1946, the middle child of three. The family moved to Harlow in Essex when it was a very small new town with an enthusiastic, community spirit.

I went to S. Martin's College of education and became a primary school teacher, returning to Harlow for my first job. The following year I married John, we moved to Biggleswade in Bedfordshire and, during the next seven years, our two children were born. During this time I studied with the Open University and gained a BA.

John was offered a promotion if he would move to North Yorkshire. He accepted with pleasure, having had many camping holidays in the area. The gentler pace of life was good for growing children and for a writer.

Writing has always been something I enjoyed, poems, stories and holiday diaries but, when I took early retirement, I went to a creative writing class. Out of that a self help group was formed called The Next Chapter. We wrote stories and poems but were all excited when a local author suggested a course called, 'Write a book in a Year'.

The idea for this novel came from meeting a young boy, who came to my school, for a few weeks. He was a refugee from Kosovo and wanted to tell me about his horrific experience, running through the burning streets of Pristina. The picture he described haunted me and, although this is a novel, the character of Davud is based on him.